Dragon Knights

The Sea Captain's Daughter Trilogy

Dragon Fire

BIANCA D'ARC

Copyright © 2016 Bianca D'Arc

All rights reserved.

ISBN: 1539112853
ISBN-13: 978-1539112853

DEDICATION

To my friends and readers who wanted "more dragons!" Thanks for trying out this trilogy format with me. It's been fun trying something new within my dragon world and I appreciate your indulgence.

Just so you know, I plan to go back to the regular, single-book format after we finish up this trilogy with *Dragon Mates*, which will be released in January of 2017. We have just a few more stories left before we have the final confrontation, so stay tuned…

Thanks, as always, to my family, without whom I would be a much sadder person. Love you guys!

And special thanks to Peggy McChesney, my Canadian pal. She spotted some little niggles in this manuscript that had sailed right by both myself and my editor. (Or, more likely, they were put into the manuscript via the editing process! Grr.) You can thank Peggy's sharp eye for the lack of typos. You're welcome. ;-)

CHAPTER ONE

"Father!" Livia jumped to her feet, but the expression on her father's face wasn't welcoming. He looked absolutely livid, but willing to listen to whatever paltry explanations the three sitting at the breakfast table had to offer.

"Why are there dragons in my boathouse and knights at my dining table?" His cultured voice carried, though he wasn't thundering. Not yet, at least.

Seth cleared his throat, standing to face Captain O'Dare. "I'm not a knight, sir. We've met before. I'm Seth Nielsson, apprentice healer from the Lair."

"That only makes this worse, son. You'd better shut up before you dig yourself any deeper into the hole you're already in." The sea captain frowned at him.

Gowan had stood, too, and faced the older man with a bit more spine. Livia feared what might happen if they clashed.

"I am Sir Gowan. It is my dragon partner, Lady Genlitha, and her friend, the blind dragon, Sir Hrardorr, whom Seth tends, in your boathouse, sir. They are guarding the diamonds."

Now *that* got her father's attention. Livia hoped he'd cool down and listen, though talk of diamonds seemed to have sidetracked him from his initial anger. She'd always privately thought her father had just a bit of pirate in him, always on

1

the lookout for treasure.

"What diamonds?" he demanded, his voice going just a bit softer, though his eyes still gleamed with fury.

"Father, the weapons used against the dragons were tipped with diamond blades. Sir Hrardorr has been diving into the wreckage in the harbor to salvage them."

Her father hadn't been in port in time for the battle that had raged only hours ago, but he must have seen the aftermath as he sailed in. The harbor was clogged with sunken ships and the shore was littered with the dead and the prisoners, who were being kept under guard. The injured were also being treated under tents that had been set up down near the shore.

Things had quieted down considerably overnight, but the action would pick up as soon as everyone was awake. Yesterday had been an ordeal, to be sure, and there was much to do today to begin putting the town back to rights.

"I spent most of the night taking the big spears apart so the diamond blades could no longer be used against dragons," she went on. "We've got a basket full of huge, sharp crystals in the boathouse, and I've already lined up a few of our best, and most trusted, craftsmen to start cutting them today. We intend to finance the rebuilding and updating of the harbor defenses out of the proceeds, as well as pay our artisans, of course. The rest will go toward any damages to the town, but, Father…" She paused to let her words sink in. "There are *a lot* of diamonds."

Captain O'Dare looked closely at all three of them, and his eyes narrowed.

"I suppose you two stayed here last night to safeguard my daughter, as well as to be near the loot and the dragons." It wasn't quite a question, but both men nodded.

Livia saw their housekeeper, Rosie, scuttling up the stairs behind her father out of the corner of her eye. If the stars were aligned, Rosie was going up there to erase all evidence of the debauchery that had taken place in Livia's bedroom the night before. Stars bless Rosie!

"After the battle, there were many tasks," Sir Gowan said, his expression tight. "Your daughter offered us hospitality when it was clear the dragons would stay to guard the diamond weapons. Otherwise, we'd have had a long walk back to the Lair. Plus, we wanted to be near in case the dragons needed us."

Captain O'Dare made a scoffing sound. "I can't imagine what they might need you for."

"Sir." Seth's tone was both respectful and firm. "Despite his bravery and ability to navigate underwater, the male dragon, Hrardorr, is newly blind. He needs aid on land that another dragon cannot provide. It is my sworn duty to help him."

Finally, her father unbent a little. He came over to her and took her into a fierce hug that she wasn't expecting.

"I came home as soon as I heard there was danger. I ran into the scout ships you sent out, my clever girl," he told her, letting her go slowly.

"I'd wondered what happened to them. We never heard back from them. I feared they were lost to the enemy." Livia retook her seat as her father went around to the head of the table opposite her and sat down.

The captain gestured for the men to retake their seats as well, which they did.

"No. They were not lost," the captain replied. "I sent them on with my cargo while I came directly here. Alas, I find myself too late to help. Will you, Sir Gowan, tell me what occurred? I've heard garbled reports from those I encountered on my way here, but I was in haste and couldn't really stop to get details. What news of the enemy fleet?"

Gowan gave a concise report of the battle, including Seth's leadership of the pitiful harbor armament and Hrardorr's amazing underwater acrobatics, though he kept a bit in reserve. Some things were best kept secret—especially as related to Hrardorr's particular abilities—but otherwise, Gowan gave a very complete account of the battle.

Livia's father looked at Seth with new respect and even

went so far as to thank him for his work on behalf of the town. He then asked how the dragons had decided on his boathouse to stash the loot.

At this point, Livia decided to speak up. Better that her father hear about her surprising ability to speak to dragons from her than from someone else.

"I've been fishing, as I usually do, since you've been gone, Father," she began. "Sir Hrardorr and I first made acquaintance on the water. He has been instrumental in decreasing the shark population near the harbor and fishing grounds for the past months, and somehow…" She cleared her throat, trying to find the nerve to tell her father. "Well, it turns out, I can hear him. I can bespeak dragons, and we've become friends."

When her father made no comment, Livia went on, feeling a bit braver.

"There was a very bad storm a few days ago, and Hrardorr was caught out in it, unable to return to the Lair. I offered the boathouse to him as shelter, and he was able to pass the night in safety there. When it came time to store those dangerous weapons somewhere, he seemed to think our boathouse was a good place. He told me he wouldn't have to rise out of the water until he was in the shed, and nobody could see what he was doing. As far as we know, nobody knows about the diamonds yet but us. I only told the craftsmen to be ready in their workshops, but I didn't say who would bring the stones or where they were coming from. Of course, after today, the secret will likely be out."

"But it will be too late, because all the stones will be in the hands of the craftsmen under lock and key," Gowan put in helpfully. "And a knight from the Lair will be stationed with the craftsmen all day and all night, until the task is complete. We have a vested interest in making sure not one of those blades survives intact. They are *that* dangerous to dragonkind."

Rosie had come back at some point during Gowan's debriefing and laid out a place setting for the captain. All four of them were eating breakfast now, and the mood had gone from tense to something a bit less emphatic. The captain still wasn't happy to find his daughter entertaining two men at her breakfast table, but he was willing to listen to the extraordinary story of yesterday's events.

Captain O'Dare gazed from Livia to Gowan and back again before speaking.

"I respect the need for Lair presence down at the craft shop once the diamonds are moved there. That makes sense. And I can possibly understand why you two—" he glared at both men, "—saw the need to stay in my house last night. But I am here now, gentlemen, and there will be no further incursion into the sanctity of my home. Is that understood."

Gowan nodded once, as did Seth. Neither seemed to feel the need to speak, which Livia understood all too well. When Captain O'Dare gave orders, everyone hopped to it. He wasn't known as one of the most cunning captains on the high seas for nothing.

"I must say, Livia, your being able to speak with dragons is an unexpected thing. And I understand why there will, no doubt, now be a parade of young knights seeking your favor, but I will not have you cavorting with not just one, but *two* men, under my roof, without the benefit of marriage!"

His voice was thunderous by the end. Yes, the captain had not lost one bit of the fury that had claimed him when he walked into his home after a long voyage to find two men at breakfast with his only daughter.

"Father..." Livia tried to say something, but her father glared her into silence.

"Don't say another word, young lady. I have made my feelings on the matter perfectly clear. I am your father, and you will do as I say. You may have become used to doing as you like while I am away, but I'm here now, and by the stars, you will obey me in my own home."

She remembered this mood. He wouldn't hear a single word she said if she tried to argue now. He'd only grow colder and colder. She didn't relish that, so she wisely stopped

5

talking except to give him a meek, "Yes, Father."

"Now, if you gentlemen have no further business here, you should both go."

Everyone stood except Livia. Gowan looked coldly formal, as if he understood the captain's mood and knew he would get nowhere by arguing. Gowan was a man of strategy. Livia figured he knew when it was wise to retreat and live to fight another day. That thought almost made her smile, but she held it back.

Seth, on the other hand, looked as if he wanted to argue. She caught his eye and shook her head as vigorously as she could without drawing her father's attention. Seth, thankfully, caught on and said nothing further, though she knew he wanted to defend her...or himself...she wasn't sure which, but neither would gain any traction with her father in this mood.

Gowan paused by her chair and bowed respectfully to her.

"Thank you for your courage and bravery, Miss Livia. And thank you for putting us all up last night."

She was about to reply that it had been her pleasure, but that was skirting a little too close to the truth, and her father would probably blow up. She merely smiled and nodded at her lover. Her knight.

Gowan walked out without further comment to the captain, which was probably wise.

Seth, too, stopped by her chair. "Thank you, Livia. I'm sorry," was all he said, which made her want to cry, but she stopped herself.

Seth walked out, and she could hear them both leaving through the front door, Rosie closing it after them. That left her father to deal with. Livia didn't know how much more she could take without breaking down and sobbing. Her heart was fracturing. Her soul had just walked out the door, along with her two lovers.

Captain O'Dare paused by her chair, not looking at her, his voice frigid with anger.

"You are grounded, of course. You will limit your

movements to the house, the office, and I will allow you one visit per day to the craft shops to oversee the disposal of the diamonds. Other than that, you are not to spend any time in town, or anywhere else, until I say otherwise. Is that quite clear?"

"Yes, Father." She dared to ask a single question. "May I still go fishing? I fear Sir Hrardorr will miss me otherwise. He has few friends."

"I will not begrudge a blind dragon his fishing companion. Your soft heart does you credit, Livia, but it can also get you into trouble. You may fish with the dragon, but you are to have no further contact with those two young men. Do you understand?"

"Yes, Father." She was subdued, but already in her mind, she was thinking of ways around his edict.

She had always longed to have her father home when he went on his endless voyages, but for once, she wished he'd just leave. Go off on one of his adventures and leave her be. Couldn't he see he was breaking her heart?

At least she could still see Hrardorr. She loved that dragon almost as much as she loved her men.

Impossible as it all was...

Fishing was the only peace Hrardorr had since the battle in the harbor. The other dragons in the Lair treated him differently now. Where before they'd pitied him—which he couldn't stand—now they tried to curry favor with him, which was just as bad. They still didn't know how to act around a blind dragon, so awkward moments were more the norm than the exception when he managed to get caught talking to one of his winged brethren.

He preferred to avoid them, if at all possible, spending many hours at sea. Only there, would the majority of dragons leave him alone. Genlitha had found a fondness for paddling about on the surface of the water, and when she had free time, she often sought him out.

Genlitha was the only one he could talk to without

difficulties. But she was also hard to converse with for a whole other reason.

Stirrings of the attraction he had felt for her when they were both dragonets in training bothered him. What could he offer a beautiful dragon such as she? She was one of the greatest flyers in the land, tasked with teaching the best of the best youngsters. She was stealth personified with her sky blue coloring and ability to soar so high and creatively that nobody could spot her from the ground—even those who knew what to look for when she was aloft.

Hrardorr was miserable. He had nothing to offer the lovely dragoness. He would never pick another knight. He could not form the five-personed family that was the norm in the Lair—the two dragons, their two knights, and a human woman to complete the circle.

Genlitha was as miserable as Hrardorr, in her own way. She seethed quietly, doing her job with quiet dignity, teaching the younger flyers how to best utilize their wings on the tricky air currents in this area. She also flew reconnaissance missions with Gowan, who was as silent as stone lately.

He'd taken steely resolve to a whole new level since the battle. Genlitha still wasn't absolutely certain what had happened that night when she'd stayed in the snug boathouse with Hrardorr ostensibly *guarding* the cache of diamond blades that Livia's artisans had been turning into harmless baubles since the day after the battle. She and Hrardorr had talked long into the night, catching up on all the years they'd missed.

They'd known each other as dragonets, but their paths hadn't crossed again until now. Hrardorr had made quite a name for himself in the intervening decades. He'd been a ruthless fighter and leader of dragons and men in his own right. And then, he'd been blinded by skith venom.

And now, he was here. In the *retirement* Lair. Oh, nobody said it out loud where anyone who might be offended could hear, but everyone knew the Southern Lair was a cushy assignment in a lovely climate for old bones. Knights came here when they got old, and promising youngsters were sent to learn from their elders. Nothing ever happened here, it was said.

Until it had.

A foreign enemy had decided that, while the main part of Draconia's defenses were engaged on the Northern and Eastern borders, they'd hit the soft Southern coast at its heart. They'd raided a few smaller towns on their way to the small city of Dragonscove and the Lair above it, but it was becoming clear that their strategy had been to hit hard at the only place that could have given them real resistance.

They'd come armed with dragon-killing weapons. Costly diamond-bladed spears and giant crossbows mounted on a large percentage of their ships. If they'd succeeded in defeating the dragons, the entire southern coast of Draconia would have been theirs for the pillaging. Or invading. The lower half of the country could have been taken over before anyone preoccupied by the fierce fighting up north had a chance to do anything about it.

But the enemy hadn't bargained on Hrardorr.

Part sea dragon, he could swim like a fish—and somehow see underwater even though his eyes were blind—but he could also breathe fire, unlike a full-blood sea dragon. He'd been their secret weapon, and he'd turned the tide of the battle distinctly in the defenders' favor.

It wasn't going too far to say that he'd saved the town. Not that he'd let anyone give him the kudos he was due. Hrardorr spent more time out of the Lair than in it nowadays.

Genlitha suspected he was spending his nights in Livia's boathouse, but she wasn't certain. She couldn't swim gracefully underwater like Hrardorr. The only way she could get into the boathouse was if someone opened the door for her. Hrardorr, half sea dragon that he was, could just swim up under the doors and enter the structure from below.

He was back to avoiding her, and Genlitha didn't like it. Not one bit.

She'd thought they'd made such progress toward

understanding each other the night after the battle, but then, he'd closed himself off again and gone into hiding. Or as close as a giant blind dragon could come to actual hiding.

But Genlitha could be patient. She'd lived a long time already without Hrardorr. She'd survived the loss of knights and chosen new ones. In fact, her partnership with Gowan was still new. He'd been a fighting man—a soldier, leader and trainer of warriors—before he caught her eye and she'd decided he would be her next knight partner.

Gowan was still learning how to be a knight. Not having grown up among dragons, Gowan knew next to nothing about the life he had agreed to lead as her partner, but he was learning. Genlitha had hoped he and Seth were learning to share as paired knights do. She had great hopes that someday Hrardorr would wake up enough to see what was right in front of him.

Seth had been helping Hrardorr from the moment he'd arrived in the Southern Lair. Seth was the apprentice to the Lair's elderly healer, Bronwyn. As such, he'd helped Hrardorr with the tasks the blind dragon could not do for himself. Having no knight, Hrardorr needed human help from time to time, and Seth was the man to provide it.

Seth had also been studying sword work and other fighting arts with Gowan in his spare time. That had come in handy when the groups of enemy sailors had made it to shore. Seth had commanded the cannon fire from the top of the battlements at the mouth of the harbor. He'd also fought back to back with Gowan against large numbers of enemy sailors armed with cutlass and dagger when the aging cannons had not been enough and the enemy had made it to land.

The sword Gowan had commissioned as a gift for his student had come in handy that day. Seth had been blooded and proven. He'd shown all the doubters in the Lair where he'd grown up that he was much more than they thought. He was a capable warrior, like his fathers before him, even if he'd chosen to help the woman who'd been like a grandmother to him instead of carrying on his studies in warfare as a young man.

And then, Seth and Gowan had spent time with Livia, and Genlitha had gotten ideas. She hadn't shared her speculations with anyone yet, but she still thought it was awfully coincidental that the man Hrardorr liked most at the moment, Seth, was involved with Livia, who was also involved with Gowan. If Hrardorr and Genlitha got together, their knights would, of necessity, share a wife between them. With the attraction flaring bright between Gowan, Livia and Seth, it made sense that they would be the perfect human partners to a dragon mating between Genlitha and Hrardorr.

But Hrardorr refused to chose Seth as his knight. Unless and until that happened, Genlitha and Hrardorr could never be together.

If Genlitha were to give in to her attraction to Hrardorr and go so far as to join in a mating flight with him, the spillover of emotion and passion would fry Gowan's mind unless he had a mate of his own. Not just any woman would do either. It had to be a mate of the heart, bonded soul to soul. Only that kind of bond could handle the dragons' passion that would ultimately leak over to their knights.

It was a rule of being a fighting dragon and having a knight partner. Until your knights had a mate of their own, the dragons must never join.

Genlitha had always thought that a small price to pay to defend her land and people, but now that she was around Hrardorr again…

And so, Genlitha was miserable too, though she hid it better than most. She was a patient dragon. She could wait a little longer.

Gowan was angry. He silently seethed about the way Captain O'Dare had treated not only him and Seth, but Livia especially. She wasn't a child. She was a woman who had apparently grown up without benefit of having her father around much at all.

Now that he was here, though, he seemed intent on

treating her as the child he remembered rather than the woman who had evolved while he'd been gallivanting across the waves. The man shouldn't be allowed to have it both ways. He might be the wealthiest merchant in Dragonscove, and the most powerful, but he was just a man. Gowan could take him in single combat. At least, he thought he could.

But it would kill Livia if Gowan fought with the man. Despite everything—the neglect and the poor treatment— Captain O'Dare was her father, and she loved him.

But Gowan loved her too. Shocking as that thought was.

He'd realized, only after being summarily thrown out of her house, that somewhere along the line, he'd fallen for her. She was adventurous, intelligent beyond any other woman he'd ever known, and as gorgeous as a morning sunrise. She was perfect in every way, and he wanted to make her his wife.

Mate. That's what the dragons called it.

Now that he was a knight, it wasn't so simple. A mate would have to be shared between him and whoever the knight was that partnered Genlitha's eventual mate. Genlitha had shown no preference for any particular male dragon, though Gowan secretly thought she had a thing for Hrardorr—impossible as that was.

Hrardorr would never choose another knight. Everyone knew that. He had vowed it publicly and adamantly. It was a shame because, despite his disability, Hrardorr had proven himself to still be a formidable dragon. He had skills and abilities that no other dragon Gowan knew of could beat, or even match.

Those traits should be passed on, but what did Gowan know? He was only a simple warrior, plucked out of obscurity by Genlitha not all that long ago. She had made him a knight, and while he wouldn't change a thing about that, he also never forgot that he was just a soldier at heart.

Oh, he'd been born to a noble family, but as a younger son with no prospects and an older brother who wanted everything for himself, Gowan had had no expectations. He'd earned his own way since he was a young man, turned out on his ear by his older brother, with only the clothes on his back and his favorite horse, shortly after their father had died. Since then, Gowan had survived on his wits and brawn alone.

Until Genlitha. She'd changed everything in the blink of an eye. She was magic. And the best friend he'd ever had. He loved her as a sister, fighting partner and friend, but she'd changed what he could expect for the rest of his life. Because of her, everything had changed. Now, if he found a wife, he'd have to share her, and though Livia had been willing to be with Gowan and Seth at the same time on two incredibly memorable occasions, he didn't know if she'd be willing to accept that for life.

Or that she would be a mate for whichever knight turned out to be partner to Genlitha's ultimate mate. It was a chancy proposition, and Gowan had his doubts that so many variables would ever line up in his favor.

Frankly, just thinking about it all gave him a headache. And then, his thoughts turned back to Captain O'Dare, and Gowan wanted to growl in frustration. His thoughts went round and round in a vicious circle lately.

It was all he could do to keep his mind on his duties. Genlitha had laid into the leadership over their fear and near-inaction during the battle, which had earned him the far patrols for the past week. Suffice to say, he and Genlitha weren't the most popular pair in the Lair at the moment, but that was all right by Gowan.

He didn't need to be popular. He just needed all his people to be at their peak of performance, which, sadly, the leadership of the Southern Lair and many of its knights just weren't. The youngsters, he'd found, were eager and followed his instruction faithfully. It was the old timers who balked.

They'd embraced the usual tranquility of the *retirement Lair*, and when they'd been called upon to defend the city below their mountain Lair, they'd nearly failed. If not for Hrardorr, Gowan hated to think what would have happened.

CHAPTER TWO

The far patrols weren't that bad, really, Gowan decided after a while. He'd mostly gotten over the anger he'd felt at the way he and Genlitha were treated by the elders in the Lair after the battle. His respect level for those old men was at an all-time low, however. They would probably never regain his regard.

He wouldn't go so far as to call them cowards—the way Genlitha had done, which had earned them this form of semi-exile—but they certainly weren't what he expected of fighting men—especially knights of the realm. Gowan had fought beside and trained many warriors in his time. He knew the breed, and he had expected knights were a caliber higher than most soldiers.

However, if these men who ran the Southern Lair had ever been true warriors, they were far from it now. They'd spent too many years sitting on their backsides and letting others fight the battles in the country. They'd grown soft and scared.

Softness could be remedied with hard work. Fear, however, was another thing entirely.

"Heads up," came Genlitha's voice in his mind as they were flying yet another endless far patrol. *"Something comes on wings from the south."*

Gowan thought through what he knew of this region's geography. There was nothing to the south except ocean…and one island that had recently been rediscovered out of the mists of legend. Gryphon Isle.

"Is it a gryphon?" he asked his dragon partner. She had much keener eyesight than he did and would see anything approaching long before him.

"Can't tell yet. Too far." She veered southward to meet the potential threat. A few wingbeats later, she spoke again. *"Those wings are not like mine. They are feathered. It is a gryphon. I will try to bespeak it."*

Genlitha's wingbeats picked up speed as she glided toward the gryphon. She approached from above, Gowan noted. The gryphons had wicked claws and sharp beaks, but their feathered wings and furred bodies were vulnerable to dragon fire. In the unlikely event that this one was unfriendly, Genlitha took the high ground, using her coloration and the sun to hide her location for as long as possible.

"He says he's a messenger from Gryphon Isle sent to the Southern Lair with urgent information. His name sounds like…Flurrthith. I think that's it. Gryphons have funny names," Genlitha observed. *"I will fly out to meet him, then, if he is what he claims, we can guide him to the Lair."*

More a passenger than participant in this sort of mission, Gowan was eager to get his first close look at a gryphon. He'd heard about them, of course. There were a few making a bit of a splash in the capital at the moment, that were the talk of the town. But he'd never seen one up close or talked to any. He wondered if this one would talk to him. They were rumored to be somewhat aloof creatures that must be approached with what seemed like exaggerated respect.

He'd been taught the protocols, though he hadn't thought he'd ever have to use them. He remained silent, not trying to communicate with the spec in the distance that grew rapidly larger. If the gryphon wanted to talk to him, it would make first contact—or so he'd been told.

"Greetings, Sir Knight," came an unfamiliar voice in Gowan's

mind. *"I am Flurrthith, messenger from Gryphon Isle and the great wizard Gryffid."*

"Greetings to you as well, Sir Flurrthith. I am Gowan, partner to Lady Genlitha. My lady informs me we are to escort you to the Lair."

"Thank you, Sir Gowan. I have never been away from home before, but I am fastest of my age group, and they knew I had the best chance of evading the arrows."

"Arrows?" Both Gowan and Genlitha spoke at the same time, concerned.

"Oh, yes. The pirates came and have besieged the island. Gryffid is fighting them off with his magic for now. We tried first, but they have sharp arrows on giant catapults. Many of us were badly hurt before we realized." The gryphon's voice seemed awfully young to Gowan, though he was surely no judge of such things. Still, the tentativeness of the words and their delivery made Gowan think of a youngling.

"Flurrthith, if you don't mind my asking, how old are you?" Genlitha asked gently, including Gowan in the conversation.

"I have seen ten summers, milady," the gryphon answered. Gowan inwardly cursed. Things had to be really bad on Gryphon Isle if they sent a child out with their message. Gowan assumed it meant that all able-bodied fighters were otherwise occupied...or injured...or dead.

This news was grave, and Flurrthith hadn't even delivered his message yet. Gowan frowned, thinking what dire situations could have caused the wizard Gryffid to send out this child on such a dangerous mission, when he was purported to love his creations—the gryphons—so very much.

Genlitha began to curve her wings, tilting so she looped around and came up flying beside the small gryphon, both headed in the same direciton—toward the mainland. He really was small, but he had enormous wings for a youngster. No wonder he was the fastest of his age group. After watching Genlitha train the young dragons at the Southern Lair, he knew what to look for in wingspan and shape.

"All right, Flurrthith," Genlitha said softly, coming up

alongside the youngster. *"Just stay in my draft, and it should be a little easier for you. You've done marvelously well to get to us. We will help you get the rest of the way."*

"Thank you, milady. Land is a lot farther away than I imagined." His comment made Gowan want to both laugh and comfort the young creature.

Flurrthith was about half Genlitha's size. Gowan's instructors had claimed full-grown gryphons were as large as dragons, so judging by his size, Flurrthith was definitely a juvenile.

His wings were feathered, and the fur on the lower half of his body was mottled brown, tan and white. He had small spots in places, little stripes in others, as if the lower half of him couldn't figure out what kind of cat it wanted to be...tiger or leopard. Maybe he was a bit of both? It was said Gryffid was still experimenting with his creations on his island. Perhaps he was improving on the gryphons in some way and this remarkable youngster was the result?

Gowan would not ask. It seemed too personal a question and would probably be considered insulting. Even as a juvenile, a gryphon was not a creature to insult lightly. Flurrthith might look cute and fuzzy, but he was also deadly. Of that Gowan had no doubt.

"You have a very nice wingspan, Flurrthith." Genlitha conversed with the gryphon, probably trying to put him at ease and perhaps learn more before they reached the Lair.

"Thank you, milady." Flurrthith seemed tired, but they still had a long way to go. His aim had been a little off, but luckily, Gowan and Genlitha had been in the right place at the right time to intercept him.

"Genlitha was sent here to train the younger dragons," Gowan put in, hoping to help the cause of friendship. *"So she knows good wings when she sees them, even if yours are feathered and hers aren't."*

"I love to fly, but I have never been this far before," Flurrthith told them. *"The island has never come under attack before in my lifetime."*

"Can you tell us more about the attackers?" Genlitha asked gently. They could both hear the despair in the juvenile's

thoughts.

"They came in ships. Many ships with ragged sails. Some were burned on the edges. And they have dangerous weapons that can kill a gryphon outright. Then Gryffid came and did something magical to repel the ships, but he said there were too many, and that his protections wouldn't last for long. That's when they decided to send me to tell the dragons what was happening and ask if maybe some of them could come help us."

"We were also attacked not long ago by a fleet of ships," Gowan told the youngster. *"They tried to overrun the town of Dragonscove, which lies below the Lair."*

They were flying over land now, far up the shore from the town and Lair. Flurrthith had overshot to the west, in the scrubland where few people lived. He looked tired to Gowan, though he was no expert.

"Shall we land for a few minutes, to catch our breath?" Genlitha suggested just as Gowan thought it. She sent a private message to her rider. *"The child is at the limit of his endurance. He needs to set down before he falls out of the sky."*

Genlitha began a slow spiral toward a sandy stretch of beach. Gowan spotted a house and barn nearby, over the sand dune. Somebody lived out here, just in case they needed human help, but with any luck, they would be moving again once the youngster was rested.

"Have you eaten recently, Flurrthith?" Gowan asked, thinking ahead to how he might be able to help the gryphon.

Genlitha made her usual flawless glide to earth, not jarring Gowan much at all. By contrast, Flurrthith was a little less poetic with his weary wings. His hind feet landed hard, bending and skidding along the sand until his front feet caught up and his wingtips dragged a bit in the wet sand before he got them folded up properly. They were long for his small body, which probably had a lot to do with his awkward landing. When the rest of him grew into the wingspan, he'd be a lot more graceful.

"Not since I left the island, sir. It's not good to fly on a full stomach, so my teachers say."

"Are you hungry, child?" Genlitha asked in as motherly a tone as Gowan had ever heard from her. The juvenile responded to it, coming closer to her.

"Yess!" He spoke aloud, the *s* sounds reverberating through his beak. Gowan remembered then that unlike dragons, gryphons could actually speak aloud and be understood, though they were said to have a thick sort of accent.

Gowan thought through what was left of their supplies. He had brought along some snacks for himself as well as for Genlitha, but if the gryphon was very hungry, he'd have to either do some hunting or, perhaps, take a walk over the dunes to see if those at the farmhouse could provide something for them.

Gowan dismounted and took his bag of supplies with him, walking closer to the gryphon. He approached slowly, remembering the briefing he'd received on proper etiquette when meeting a gryphon for the first time. He stood several feet from the small gryphon, his gaze raised as he bowed his head slightly, in respect.

"And now I offer you proper greetings, Sir Flurrthith. Welcome to Draconia," Gowan said aloud, hoping he was doing this right. Even a half-size gryphon could slice him to ribbons with those claws and beak, and they were known to be extremely formal creatures.

But the youngster seemed friendly, returning the bowing gesture in his own way.

"Greetingss, Ssir Gowan. Thank you for the welcome." He seemed too tired to say much more, and Genlitha came closer, craning her neck over Gowan's shoulder.

"Stretch your muscles before you sit," she advised the youngster, comfortable in her teaching role. *"Gowan, it's a bit cold today. Can you let him sit on your cloak? His muscles will be overheated from the exertion and it's not good for them to cool too quickly against the damp earth."*

"Sure thing."

Gowan flipped his cloak off his shoulders. It was woven

of sturdy wool in a light color to match Genlitha's light hide. He placed it in front of the gryphon on a dry patch of sand. The creature was stretching in a cat-like manner, following Genlitha's instructions.

His paws were large, to go with the mighty wingspan, but his body was still small enough to fit onto Gowan's cloak. He stepped on daintily, holding his claws in so as not to damage the fabric. The gryphon had surprisingly good manners for a youngster.

"Thank you, ssir," Flurrthith said as he settled. "I will do my besst not to damage your belongingss."

"I am sending word ahead to the Lair that we are on our way, Flurrthith. They will be waiting to hear your message when you arrive, and then, you can rest your weary wings more fully," Genlitha told the gryphon.

"Thank you, milady. I'll be able to fly more, sshortly. It'ss jusst nice to ssit for a moment." Flurrthith's gaze went from Genlitha to Gowan and back. He seemed so very earnest. Gowan felt bad for the poor little creature. He'd been through a lot to get to them and would have to fly even farther before he could truly rest and recover his strength.

"Take what time you need, son," Gowan spoke from his heart. "I can give you the snacks I packed, but I will also go and check with the farmer who lives just over these dunes and see what kind of provisions I can secure."

Gowan placed a melon he'd brought along for Genlitha and a few apples he'd packed for himself on the cloak just in front of the youngster. Flurrthith's eyes lit up when he saw the fruit, and he only waited for Gowan to back off before attacking it with his beak.

"Oh, thank you, sir!" Flurrthith spoke in his mind. *"This is great!"*

Gowan smiled and backed off farther to speak privately with Genlitha while Flurrthith ate.

"I'm going over the dunes. I'll be back in an hour at the most. Is that enough time for him to regain some strength?"

Genlitha considered the gryphon. *"More food would help, I*

think. At that age, dragonets are growing fast and need lots to eat. I would think gryphons are the same. Get what you can from the farmer, and if you need me, just call. I'll be there in a trice."

Gowan's quest went reasonably well. The farmer only overcharged him a little for a slab of mutton, a bushel of pears and the sack to carry them. Gowan was back to the flyers in less than an hour, and the gryphon looked like he was napping. His head rested on his paws, and his body lay flat on Gowan's cloak.

"Is he asleep?" Gowan asked Genlitha as he approached.

"Yes. Poor thing. But we can't let him stay that way. His message needs to get through to the Lair. I've been in communication with the dragon council, and they will give him shelter, but the human leaders..."

"I take it they're not being reasonable. Again."

"They demand to see the child, unwilling to take my word that he is here and that he came to us for help. It is a snub of me, to be certain, and more idiotic behavior on their part. They delay organizing help for the gryphons because they're mad at me for telling them how foolish they are. And their dragons are siding with their knights, protecting the cowards." Genlitha's tone was scathing, and smoke wafted out of her nostrils. She was mad.

If Gowan's mind speech could reach back to the Lair, he'd have tried to intervene, but his gift wasn't as strong as the dragon's. All he could do was try his best to soothe her and fight on her behalf when they got back to the Lair. As far as he was concerned, this idiocy had gone on long enough.

Gowan roused the gryphon and gave him the food he'd procured. The youngster ate while they talked to him, learning about the island and his role there. He was just a child, really. A talented flyer who had been tapped to run the gauntlet of enemy ships with dangerous arrows because the larger and more experienced gryphons were all needed to repel the invaders. They also figured Flurrthith, with his compact body, would be a smaller target for the catapults.

The gamble had paid off, and the child had made it past the fleet of ships, but he wasn't completely unscathed. When asked, the youngster admitted that he thought a few of the smaller, man-sized arrows had probably hit his wings, but he'd had no way to really check. With a little coaxing, Flurrthith allowed Gowan to take a look.

Sure enough, Gowan found at least a half dozen shafts stuck in Flurrthith's feathers. Most hadn't penetrated the skin beneath the layer of fluff, but a few had and were still there, even though the majority of the shaft had been broken off. Gowan was no healer, but he had his sack of supplies, and every soldier and knight received basic wound care training.

Flurrthith let Gowan remove the arrows, stop the bleeding and apply a few small bandages that wouldn't impede his flight. Frankly, after he was done patching the gryphon up, Gowan was even more impressed with the youngster's heart and gryphons' overall sturdiness. The feathers might seem pretty, but Gowan had seen for himself that they were way more than merely decorative.

When he had done all he could and it was time to mount up again, Gowan silently asked Genlitha to send another message ahead to the Lair.

"Can you reach Seth and ask him to be waiting when we land? Bronwyn, too, if she's up to it. I did the best I could for him, but I want someone with real healing experience looking at Flurrthith's wounds."

"Already done, my friend," Genlitha assured him. *"This child has my utmost respect, and I will watch over him as if he were my own dragonet. That includes making sure he has the best care we can provide. Seth said he's happy to help and will stay with Flurrthith day and night if he must."*

"Good man."

Without further comment, Genlitha rose into the air, gaining ground gently and making sure Flurrthith could keep up with her.

"He really does have the most remarkable wings," she told Gowan as she watched Flurrthith gain altitude rapidly. *"I had no idea feather wings were so strong."*

"And nearly impervious to regular arrows. The ones I pulled out from between his feathers only had normal hunting tips on them. I don't

know how he'd stand up to those diamond-tipped monstrosities, but the regular ones seemed to have trouble penetrating the layers of feathers and shafts to get to the skin, muscle and bone beneath. He's got a few broken feather shafts, but I assume those will grow back in time, right? I wouldn't have believed it if I didn't see it myself."

"*Me either.*" Genlitha changed the subject after that exchange and began including the gryphon in her thoughts while they flew, commenting on his gliding technique and how it differed only slightly from those she taught the young dragons.

They passed the rest of the flight in easy conversation and a bit of instruction as Genlitha showed the youngster how to best conserve his energy and make every wingbeat count. Gowan learned a great deal just listening to her and seeing how both dragon and gryphon implemented her strategies. Gowan hadn't known there were so many nuances to flying, but he was gaining new respect for what the dragons did every day without fanfare or comment.

By the time they reached the Lair, night had fallen and the fires were lit on the landing ledge to guide them in. Flurrthith was afraid of the fire at first, and Gowan understood why he might be with wings made of oily feathers and flamable fluff. Genlitha had to coax the youngster to land, showing him the way and commanding the knights on the ledge douse all but one of the fires before Flurrthith would agree to come in.

Flurrthith wasn't quite as graceful as Genlitha when he landed, but he managed a decent presentation, skidding to a stop on all fours. Gowan leapt off Genlitha's back and immediately went to Flurrthith's side. The small gryphon had been flying hurt, and Gowan wanted his wings seen to first, before they did anything else.

Seth was already there, waiting to be introduced to the gryphon before approaching. Everyone on the ledge was holding back, having been briefed about the gryphon. Gowan signaled Seth to stand beside him.

"Flurrthith, this is my friend, Seth, who has knowledge of healing. I would like you to allow him to check the dressings I put on your wings. He is much more skilled than I, and I want to make sure you are as well cared for as possible. Will you allow it?" Gowan asked formally.

Flurrthith perched on his front paws, facing them. He looked from Gowan to Seth and bowed his head. Seth did the same, showing respect while not lowering his eyes.

"It iss an honor to meet you, Ssir Sseth," the gryphon said aloud.

"The honor is mine, Sir Flurrthith, but I am not a knight. I was raised here in the Lair. My fathers arc knights. I am the healer's apprentice. She would have come herself to tend you, but she is too old to climb to the ledge. She will see you when you descend but wanted me to make sure you had skilled attention at the earliest opportunity."

"Thank you, Sseth," Flurrthith said. "You do your people proud by treating a vissitor with ssuch courtessey."

Seth spent a few minutes looking over Gowan's handiwork with Gowan providing assistance and commentary. Gowan had kept each and every one of the arrows he'd taken out of Flurrthith's feathers and skin, and Seth examined each one, checking for signs of poison or barbs that might indicate further problems. Luckily, there were none, and only one of the arrows had a really sharp blade point. That was the one that had done the most damage, but it had cut through the flesh and struck bone, stopping there.

"You have quite a few broken feather shafts," Seth observed, talking directly to Flurrthith. "Is there something I can do for those? I have heard about the way hunting hawks sometimes have shed feathers blended back in with needle and thread until the new shafts have time to grow."

"We do ssomething ssimilar," Flurrthith agreed, "but I have no ssupliess with me for ssuch thingss. They'll jusst have to grow back on their own. I can sstill fly, sso it will be all right for now. Thank you."

Seth stood back, finished with the examination. "If you're ready, you can come with us to the great hall where the

24

leaders of our Lair are gathered to meet you and receive your message."

What followed went about as Gowan had expected. The young gryphon delivered a hastily scribbled message on a scroll he'd had secreted in a small satchel nestled around his neck and hidden among his chest feathers. The dragon council was eager to help the gryphons, but the human leaders were hesitant, and the key dragons backed up their human partners.

Gowan thought he understood the loyalty between dragon and knight, but this was bordering on the ridiculous as far as he was concerned. The dragons should be smart enough to see that the old men who were leading them had lost their taste for battle and risk. They seemed to want to hide their heads in the sand and just ignore all the problems that had cropped up on their doorstep. But that was naïve in the extreme, not to mention dangerous.

Something had to be done. And if the old timers weren't up to it, Gowan would by golly do the job himself.

CHAPTER THREE

Down in Dragonscove, talk was rife about the gryphon a few had seen flying over the town in company with the so-called air dragon. That's what they called Genlitha, due to her sky blue coloration. She blended into the sky so well on clear days that she almost couldn't be seen. The O'Dare's surly housekeeper, Rosie, bless her icy heart, had been keeping Livia apprised of the doings in town while she spent her days going from house to work and back again.

Livia was only allowed to fish with Hrardorr twice per week and was otherwise grounded now that her father was home. She was going a little crazy unable to see Seth or Gowan. The way they'd left things made her uncertain about her welcome should she try to contact them mind-to-mind, the way she spoke to Hrardorr.

Since Hrardorr spent as little time in the Lair as possible, he wasn't a very good source of information on the doings there, but at least she could talk to him whenever she wanted. Even if she could only meet up with him twice per week on the water. He'd taken to spending more time in the boathouse than her father realized.

The little structure had become Hrardorr's hideaway, where he could go and none of the other dragons could easily follow. Nobody except Livia knew he was there, except perhaps Genlitha, but she'd been sent on far patrols since the dust up with her elders. Hrardorr was as melancholy as Livia was about everything, and they talked silently about their misery from time to time, but it didn't really help to alleviate it.

The gryphon, though... That was something interesting and new.

It had been a full week since Livia's father had come home. Progress was being made on turning the diamond blades into cut stones, and buyers were lining up for them. Now that the captain was back in residence, he was handling a lot of the assignments for his fleet of ships and smaller vessels.

Livia felt superfluous in the office. The men her father had entrusted his ships to came in singly and in groups to share meals and closed-door meetings with her father to which she was never invited. It felt like everything she had done to keep the business running was for naught now that her father was home. It was like she'd only been a placeholder, keeping things moving, waiting for the *real* leader to return. At least, that's how the sea captains made her feel when they sauntered in to share glasses of port and loud guffaws with her father.

The fishing captains were a bit different. They were local men who had known her from childhood. They also knew she had befriended the blind dragon who had been so beneficial to their trade recently. With Hrardorr hunting most of the predators in the area, fish were more plentiful than ever, and nobody was going hungry in Dragonscove this year. The fishermen were also making a nice living, able to sell their fish far and wide with such big catches.

They made her feel marginally better when they came in for meetings with her father. They each paused by her office to say hello and share pleasantries with her, as well—as if she still mattered, even though the captain was back in residence. Frankly, that was the only thing that kept her going in to work each day.

Her father had sent word out to all his captains to return to Dragonscove as soon as possible, and each day, it seemed, another ship reported in. Most of these captains and crews weren't based out of Dragonscove. They were stationed far and wide along the coast, dispersed all over the trade routes their fleet traveled.

Many of the ship captains snubbed her in favor of her father, but Livia listened to their reports as best she could, piecing together the grim picture of where the enemy fleet had come from and where they'd gone. When the gryphon flew over the town on its way to the Lair with Genlitha and Gowan, Livia feared she already knew what the creature would tell them.

She went home at her regular time that night, giving nothing away of her concern. She ate dinner, as usual, with her father, speaking only of trivial matters, lest she betray her intentions. She excused herself early, claiming she was tired and wanted to go to sleep early. And then, she put her plan into action.

She wasn't sure exactly what she could do, but she wasn't going to sit meekly at home without at least trying to do something. She just had to move carefully and avoid letting her father know what she was doing at all costs.

"Hrardorr? Can you hear me?"

"Yes, Livia. Is something wrong?" He sounded closer than she'd expected.

"What do you know of the gryphon that was seen flying into the Lair yesterday?"

"It's all anyone can talk of, though you know I do my best to avoid speaking with anyone. Still, I've heard the news from Gryphon Isle is not good. The remainder of the fleet we faced turned toward the island, and they've been using those cursed diamond-bladed weapons on the gryphons. Many have fallen, and it is all the wizard can do to keep the enemy at bay."

The news was worse than she'd thought.

"Are you in the boathouse again?" she asked the dragon.

"As a matter of fact, I am. I hope you don't mind."

"Mind? Never. You are welcome anytime. You know that. If it were up to me and there was a way to manage it, I'd give you a bed in the house."

A dragonish chuckle sounded in her mind. *"I would like to see that, but I think it might require a major redesign of your father's home."*

"It would be worth it to make you more comfortable and have you near." She hadn't really realized how true her words were until they were spoken. She would do anything for Hrardorr.

"I am very comfortable here in the boathouse, Livia," Hrardorr said quietly. *"But thank you for the thought."*

While Livia spoke to the dragon, the house settled for the night. She'd heard her father's door open and close. His room was farther down the hallway, and she couldn't hear much once his door was shut. Likewise, he couldn't hear her tiptoeing around her room, packing a bag.

She was sick of being imprisoned in her room and was going on a little excursion. The only thing she had to be careful of was not to get caught.

If her father saw her climbing the trellis outside her window, either on the way out or the way back tomorrow morning before dawn, she would be in even bigger trouble than she already was. But it would be worth it for a few hours of freedom to spend as she wished. She'd decided to not go into the office tomorrow, and was prepared to claim illness. If she hinted at a female complaint, her father wouldn't ask too many questions.

She smiled to herself as she put on black clothing—a tight-fitting shirt, tapered pants and a jacket over it all. They were boy's clothing that she used from time to time when she wanted to walk about freely without gathering any unwanted attention.

Mostly, she used this outfit when her father was home. This wasn't the first time he'd grounded her and she'd snuck out. It had been a little easier when she was smaller, but she was still petite and agile enough to make her way down the trellis.

"Would you mind some company?" she asked Hrardorr, throwing her leg over the windowsill. *"I can't stay under house arrest one moment longer. I'm breaking out."*

Again, that dragonish chuckle sounded in her mind. Good. She had feared he might protest, but she should have known better. Hrardorr wasn't one for following the rules either.

"It's about time," was his only comment.

She was already climbing down the trellis, careful to not make any betraying sounds, but Hrardorr's words made her smile.

Seth heard light footsteps coming down the wooden stairs from above and tensed. Was someone approaching intent on doing harm? He scanned the area from his hiding place and waited, his sword by his side. He was hidden in the shadows between the steep stairs that went up to Livia's house, the jagged rock wall on which it was perched, and the wide wooden deck that started over land and spread out over the water. It branched into several docks, fingers of walkways leading out into the harbor.

Directly opposite the stairs, several yards away lay the door to the large wooden house that spanned two of the fingers of dock, enclosing them almost entirely. The open slip of water between them was enclosed by the boathouse, intended for Livia's sailboat. Only, right now, the sailboat bobbed out in the open at the end of one of the docks, while a very large, very blind dragon with sea dragon heritage occupied the boathouse.

Seth knew Hrardorr was in there. He checked on the dragon every night and knew every time the dragon wasn't in residence in his Lair chamber. Seth had decided to keep watch without Hrardorr's knowledge, spending more than one cold night huddled under the stairs, wrapped in his darkest cloak.

He was both surprised and pleased to learn on his first night on watch that Captain O'Dare had instituted a patrol on his dock. Every hour or so, at irregular intervals, two strong-looking seamen walked past, checking on things. They were deckhands from Captain O'Dare's own flagship, if Seth wasn't mistaken, and they took watch in turns. The same pair would work for a few hours, then a new pair would replace them.

The captain was taking no chances with safety while he was in port, it seemed. Seth watched the patrolmen walk up and down the docks belonging to Captain O'Dare's company, starting with his flagship, the *Olivia*, which was tied up at the deepest mooring, closer to the office, and ending with the boathouse below Captain O'Dare's home. The patrol would walk from one end of the large network of floating platforms to the other and back again, using different routes each time so as to be less predictable in their movements.

Seth wondered where the captain had learned to be so cautious. He also wondered why Livia's father believed such precautions were warranted in his home port. But Seth wasn't likely to get answers to those questions, so he kept them to himself.

As the black-clad figure scampered quietly down the stairs closer to Seth's hiding place, he realized it was either a boy or, more likely, a woman. Then he recognized the flash of her blue eyes, and his heart froze for a moment.

"Livia?" he whispered aloud.

She paused on the stairs, her black garb blending in well with the night, but not well enough to hide her from the approaching patrolmen. Seth's heart picked up its pace. She was about to get caught and dressed as she was, he was pretty certain she didn't have her father's permission to be skulking about the docks at this hour.

"Livia, it's me, Seth." He used their shared talent to talk silently with her. *"I'm below the stairs. Come down now, or you'll be seen. Your father has a patrol checking his dock, and they're about to arrive."*

"He does?" Even while she spoke silently into his mind, she was moving expertly down the stairs, ducking under and into his arms.

He opened his dark mottled cloak and wrapped her within, turning to face the rock, blending in with it as he had every other time the patrol had come past. So far, nobody had been able to see him in the dark. Seth prayed his luck would continue to hold.

"He does," Seth answered her hasty question. *"Quiet now. They're almost upon us."*

She pressed her face into his chest, and Seth almost forgot to breathe. He had missed her so much. Het simplest touch was heaven to him, but he couldn't let himself be distracted now.

"Why does my father have men patrolling the dock?" she asked in his mind as the men walked past. *"The last of the diamonds were moved to the workshop days ago."*

"He's a cautious man," was all Seth could come up with. *"Maybe he doesn't want his crew to grow lax sitting in their home port."*

"Most of his crew are not from here, actually," she said, surprising him. *"He picks them up from all over, along his route. Father is a stickler, in case you haven't noticed, and if someone doesn't measure up, he's put off the ship at the next port and summarily replaced. Or so I've heard."*

"Did you sneak out?" All the while he kept up the conversation with her, he also kept track of the movements of the patrol. They were turning at the end of the pier and would soon be heading back past them again. So far, so good.

"Of course I snuck out. I couldn't stand to be a prisoner one second longer." She paused, and he imagined she was inwardly fuming. *"I'll have to go back before dawn though. I don't want him to know I can get out whenever I want to, or he'll take the trellis down and put bars on my window."*

Seth had to stifle a chuckle as the patrol returned, walking right past them once again. It looked like they'd be in the clear in a few more moments, once the patrol passed out of sight.

"Were you going to visit Hrardorr?"

"Yes. But why are you hiding out here? Why aren't you in there with him?" She pulled her face away from his chest and looked up

at him in the darkness, her eyes gleaming in the uncertain light.

"He doesn't know I'm here," Seth admitted. *"I just wanted to be nearby in case he needs me."*

"Oh, Seth…" She patted his chest with one hand over his heart, her smile soft and filled with wonder. *"That's the sweetest thing I've ever heard."*

"Hrardorr won't think so. He doesn't like it when I mother him, as he calls it."

"Well, you can't stay out here all night. Come inside with me. We'll tell him I asked you to meet up with me. He knows we like each other."

Seth pulled her tight against his aroused body. *"I more than like you, Livia."*

She reached up and kissed him quickly. Just a peck on the lips that made his entire body stand up and take notice.

"Good. Because I more than like you too, Seth."

She smiled, ducking out from under the staircase, looking both ways and taking Seth by the hand. He had no choice but to follow her, straight to the boathouse door.

They entered without raising any alarms, and he closed and locked the door behind them. The interior of the boathouse was dark, but it was actually a little easier to see in here with Hrardorr sitting on the wide deck at the front of the house, and his gleaming scales reflecting off the water.

Hrardorr didn't seem at all surprised to see Seth.

"It's about time you came in from the cold," was the dragon's comment when Seth greeted him. *"I wouldn't have minded having someone to talk to the past few nights."*

"I wasn't sure of my welcome," Seth told the dragon quietly. "And I wasn't sure if you wanted company or not."

"Next time—if there is one—you should probably just ask," came Hrardorr's dry reply. *"Now, what's going on?"*

"We have to help the gryphons," Livia blurted out, taking Seth by surprise. Hrardorr, too, if Seth was any judge of the dragon's expression and head movements.

Seth turned to look at her. "You've been under virtual house arrest for days. How do you know about the gryphons?

And what in the world do you think the three of us can do about it that the rest of the Lair isn't already doing?"

But Livia didn't get a chance to answer. Hrardorr cut her off.

"The rest of the Lair isn't going to do diddly." Smoke rose from the dragon's nostrils toward the rafters of the boathouse.

"What have you heard?" Seth asked Hrardorr.

"Genlitha has been rather vocal in her disdain for the leadership of the Lair. That's why she and Gowan have been assigned all the far patrols recently. It was they who intercepted the gryphon, and she has told me all that the child told her."

"Child?" Livia prompted.

"The gryphon who escaped with the message was a juvenile," Seth told her. "He has massive wings for his age, but he's still quite young. Only about ten years old, I believe."

"Flurrthith is his name," Hrardorr added. *"If they had to send a child, they are in even worse straits than the message indicates. Genlitha wants to fly out at first light, but I've counseled her to patience. She cannot directly defy the leadership until they have made their decision. If, as she thinks, they're not going to do anything, then I've already promised her I will help."*

"Help how, exactly?" Seth asked, tilting his head toward the dragon, suspicious of what he was contemplating.

Hrardorr ducked his head in something like embarrassment. *"I thought I'd fly out, then duck under the waves before the enemy fleet could see me and surprise them from below, the way I did before, while Genlitha acts as high guard. She can tell me what she sees from above."*

"You two have already planned this all out, have you?" Livia accused, but there was no anger in her voice. Instead, Seth thought he heard approval.

"It seemed wisest to prepare, in case we had to act."

"If you go," Seth declared, "I'm going with you."

"Alas, I can carry you only so far, and you cannot swim from where I plan to go under the waves." Hrardorr sounded genuinely sorry about that, which mollified Seth somewhat.

"We could take my boat and approach from the far side of

the island. It'll take a little longer, but we could beach the boat and meet you on land."

"Absolutely not," was Seth's initial reaction, though he wanted some way to get to the island. He regretted his lack of knowledge about how to sail. If he could manage a boat himself, he'd have been all for the plan. "Besides, what could we do from land?"

"We could help treat the injured. And you can fight. You organized our harbor defense. You could do that there, as well. Or at least help those who are doing it with the benefit of your experience."

Her words had merit. If only there was some way to make it to the island without her help. Seth couldn't ask anyone else to put themselves in danger—especially since, if he did this, it would be without the Lair's blessing.

Hrardorr seemed deep in thought before he finally weighed in on the idea. *"Genlitha could watch from high above and help guide you to a safe spot on which to land your boat. Truthfully, I would prefer if Genlitha and Gowan were both safely away from the diamond blades we know the enemy still has."*

"You intend to take on the remainder of the enemy fleet all on your own?" Seth knew Hrardorr's abilities were more than adequate to deal with a few ships at a time, but how would he handle the rest of that massive fleet?

"With support from land, I believe it can be done," Hrardorr was quick to reply.

"And you could best organize that support, Seth, while I interface with the locals, like we did here." Livia reminded him. She was all too eager to put herself in danger as far as Seth was concerned, but she did have a point.

"This is all moot unless and until the Lair leadership makes a bad decision," Seth reminded them.

"Which is all too likely to happen," Hrardorr muttered.

"Which is why we should prepare our plan," Livia insisted.

Seth didn't like it, but he remained silent while Hrardorr and Livia talked through the best ways of implementing the plan they were devising. Livia was allowed to take her sailboat out twice a week. She would begin sneaking provisions down to the boat, as would Hrardorr. He could bring things from the Lair, with Seth's help, and deliver them to the boat when they met to go fishing. This way, when the time came, they would be ready.

If it turned out they wouldn't need to act, the supplies could be just as easily removed the way they had been delivered. Seth grudgingly agreed to assist because he was fairly sure Livia would be sailing off to Gryphon Isle without him if he didn't. If she was going to embark on the perilous journey, he would be right there, ready to protect and defend her should they run into problems.

"I suppose Genlitha is in league with you on all of this?" Seth asked after they'd hammered out the bones of the plan.

The basics, yes," Hrardorr allowed. *"I will fill her in on the details when I go back tomorrow. By then, we'll know more about what the leadership intends to do...or not do, as the case may very well be."* The dragon got to his feet and walked the few steps toward the edge of the deck on which he'd sat. *"For now, I'm going for a short swim and perhaps a longer hunt. I will return in an hour or two."* His head craned backward, as if looking at them, but of course, he couldn't see them. *"Do you plan to stay?"*

"If you don't mind the company, I need a few hours of freedom from my bedroom prison," Livia joked softly. "I have to be back there before dawn, but the night is mine, and I intend to keep it."

Hrardorr bowed his head as if in understanding. *"Then, I welcome your company, dearest Livia. Alas, I should have eaten before I left the Lair, but I had a taste for fresh fish tonight."* His attention turned to Seth. *"I suppose you will want to stay, even if I insist I am fine on my own?"*

Seth walked over to Hrardorr, making sure the dragon could hear his footsteps against the wooden decking. Hrardorr's head moved, following Seth's progress.

"My friend," Seth began, knowing he had to make the dragon understand his motivations. "I came here not to watch over you like a nursemaid, but to be here in case you needed a friend. I have lived a very lonely life in the Lair since I chose to follow the healer's path, and I'm receiving the same sort of odd looks and stilted speech you've been getting since the battle in the harbor. I think we surprised everyone with what we did and what we are capable of doing. Even ourselves." His voice dropped into lower tones as he made his admissions, but he knew the dragon could hear him. "We have a lot in common."

Seth considered his next words carefully. "In fact, I think I have more in common with you than with any other being I know. I want you to know that I am here for you, Hrardorr. Always. And unlike anyone else, I think I understand at least some of what you're going through now. I just want to be your friend. Not your crutch or helper or whatever other term you want to use for someone who thinks less of you. I know you aren't less than you were before you were blinded. I've known that from the first moment I met you. I only wish you believed it too."

Hrardorr didn't answer in words. He merely lowered his head and stepped closer, initiating contact for a dragonish hug. Seth put his arms around Hrardorr's warm neck, feeling the slide of his shiny scales and the healthy pulse of the fire beneath his armored skin.

"You are a good man, Seth," Hrardorr said finally. *"Never let anyone make you believe otherwise."* Hrardorr stepped away, and Seth lowered his arms, the moment over. *"I'll see you when I return."*

CHAPTER FOUR

Hrardorr lowered himself into the water without a sound, slipping away beneath the waves as if he had never been there. Livia watched him go, standing beside Seth at the water's edge.

It was only a moment before Seth's arm snuck around her waist, drawing her near. He seemed tentative, as if he'd let her go at the slightest hint that she didn't want him, but she snuggled into his side. Being near Seth was exactly what she wanted at the moment.

She'd missed him in the time since her father had come home and put her under virtual house arrest. She'd missed Gowan too. And Genlitha. But that couldn't be remedied right now. At least she had Seth with her...for the rest of the night, if she played her cards right.

She turned in his arms to face him, placing her palms flat against his chest as she looked up into his eyes. It was darker inside the boathouse without Hrardorr's scales and the light he somehow brought with him, but she could still see Seth in the vague reflections off the water.

"Do you think he was being circumspect, knowing we'd probably enjoy a little time alone?" she asked, smiling up one of the only two men on earth, it seemed, who made her feel truly alive.

Seth frowned just slightly. "You think so? The idea hadn't really occurred to me until you just mentioned it, but Hrardorr can be a very sensitive soul, though he doesn't like anyone to know it."

She walked her hands up to his shoulders, dragging him down for a kiss. It was a kiss of reunion. A leisurely exploration now that they knew they had a little bit of time they could spend together, with the dragon's blessing, it seemed. When they broke apart, Livia was warm, even though Hrardorr had taken his innate heat with him into the water.

Livia had a feeling that, with Seth around, she wouldn't feel the cold night air, at all. Seth had a way of making her blood boil with passion, and as long as they kept things a little quiet, they wouldn't be disturbed in the locked boat shed. Even her father didn't have a key. Livia had been sure to relieve the captain of his copy almost as soon as he'd come home. She was pretty sure he hadn't figured it out yet. He was more interested in the big ships than her little sailboat, and the boathouse that had been built specifically for it.

Livia wanted Seth. It had been far too long since she'd been with him. Far too long since that memorable night in her room, before her father had unexpectedly come home. That night spent with Seth...and Gowan.

Since being with them—separately and together—it was as if she couldn't breathe without them. She'd been pining for their touch, yearning for the fulfillment only they could give her. She didn't want to wait any longer to feel Seth's possession...his hard body against and inside of hers.

Livia backed him toward the wall of the shed, taking the lead in a way that almost shocked her. She had never been so forward with the few lovers she'd had before Seth and Gowan. And only with them had she ever even considered having more than one man at a time. But somehow...with them...it all seemed right. Felt right.

Only...her father's arrival had put the kibosh on it all. He'd grounded her, and the men had been busy with Lair affairs—each in different ways. If this unexpected interlude was all she could have, she was going to take advantage of it to the fullest.

His back made a soft thud against the side of the shed, and she gasped, stilling.

"You think anybody heard that?" she whispered.

"Too soon for your father's patrol to have come back around this way, but let's move away from the wall, just to be safe." Seth took her hand and led her through the darkness toward the spot farthest from the locked door, near a stack of sailcloth.

He let go of her hand only to unfold some of the thick cloth and lay it on the deck as a cushion against the cold. It wasn't ideal, but it would work. Livia definitely approved and moved to help him set up their temporary love nest.

When it was ready, she tackled him, taking him to the ground on top of the soft canvas. She pushed at his cloak, hoping he'd get the message that she wanted his clothing gone. There was too much fabric between them. She wanted skin on skin, and she wanted it now.

Luckily, Seth understood. Even as she joined her lips to his and kissed him with all the pent-up passion so many days spent alone had only increased, he removed his cloak and did the same for her. Little by little, his talented hands took away the impediments, removing one article of clothing at a time, until they were both bare and ready for anything.

Livia let him up for air occasionally, only to stroke her fingers over his hard-muscled body. Seth had always been built big, like his warrior sire, but he'd apparently been practicing his sword work a bit more since the last time they'd been together. His muscles were even harder than she remembered, larger and definitely even more of a turn on than before.

She'd probably grown a little softer in the intervening days while she'd been cloistered and not allowed to do much more than walk from home to work and back again. She wondered if Seth noticed. And then, she wondered if he liked it or not.

But then, he growled low in his throat as he turned the tables on her, flipping her over like she weighed nothing at all so that he was on top. *Oh.* She liked it when he got all manly on her.

"Tell me you're ready for this," Seth whispered, nipping her ear gently.

"I've been ready for days." She panted her words in between nibbling kisses all over his face and neck.

But he didn't just take her word for it. Seth reached between her legs, touching gently, probing to test her readiness and then increase her desperation as he slid his fingers inside. Stroking in and out, he added a finger, stretching her and bringing forth more of the wetness he'd apparently been seeking. A moment later, he replaced his fingers with his hard cock.

In a way, she felt a little cheated that she hadn't been able to get her hands on his dick, but in another, she was perfectly fine with the results. He began a quick pace that made her breathless in minutes and completely needy only moments later. It had been too long. She'd only been with him a handful of times, but he had already made her an addict.

She came once, and then once again while Seth held her tight, never letting her move beyond the small nest of canvas he'd made for them.

When it was over, he started again, slower this time, rocking her gently while he took his time with her pleasure. He brought her to climax over and over again before finally joining her once more in orgasm. It was a gentle loving, a less frantic joining than the first, and the pleasure went on and on.

They dozed for a bit, and at some point in the night, Hrardorr returned. Seth must have guided the blind dragon into position above water on the wooden deck of the boathouse, but she wasn't aware of the dragon's presence until she woke to find the small building warm with the dragon's breath.

Having Hrardorr nearby made her feel complete somehow. She didn't fully understand it, but she felt deep in her soul that Seth and the curmudgeonly dragon belonged together. The only piece missing now was Gowan and Genlitha, she thought sadly.

In her fantasies, they could all be together as one big family—if Hrardorr chose Seth as his knight and Genlitha as his mate. So much depended on Hrardorr coming around and seeing what could be…if only.

Livia knew it wasn't really fair of her to put it all on Hrardorr's shoulders. Certainly, his disability—and his insistence on retreating from life because of it—was a major problem, but there were other things in their way as well. Her father, for one.

And she had no real idea what Gowan thought of all this. He was still very new to being a knight. He probably would have to make some major adjustments to his thinking to accept the idea of sharing his wife. Trios weren't the norm anywhere in Draconia, except the Lairs. Seth had grown up with it, and so had Livia, to a certain extent. Gowan had not, and she didn't know exactly where he stood on the matter.

Many knights never married. Either they didn't find a woman to complete their circle or their dragons had not found mates of their own yet. So many things had to align for a family to succeed in the Lair. It was said the Mother of All guided the knights and dragons to the proper mates when the time was right, but still, many remained single.

After all, a dragon could have many knights during his lifetime. While partnering with a dragon allowed a knight to live hundreds of years longer than he would have normally, the dragon would still outlive the knight by many centuries. Unless they fell in battle. Unfortunately, that was starting to happen all too often now that open war had happened on at least two different fronts.

Livia put the troubling thoughts from her mind and snuggled into Seth's side. She had to leave before dawn, but she still had a little time to enjoy being with him…and the dragon who had changed her life.

Hrardorr wasn't surprised in the least when he returned from his late night swim to find Livia and Seth together. He couldn't see them, of course, but he could hear their gentle whispers and the brush of skin on skin as he settled down to sleep.

Though Hrardorr had never taken a mate himself, he thought he understood how hard it must be for the young lovers to have been together, only to be kept apart by the unexpected arrival of Livia's father. Hrardorr hadn't met the man yet, but he'd heard plenty. The captain had a larger-than-life reputation that was the topic of gossip even up at the Lair.

Hrardorr heard a lot of gossip. He didn't seek it out, but somehow, a lot of the beings in the Lair didn't always consider that he could hear as well, if not better, than he always had. It was only his vision that had been affected by his run-in with skith venom.

He tried not to spend a great deal of his time at the Lair, but he could only go fishing and swimming for so long. And his suite was fine, but lonely. He needed to be around others, even if he didn't really want to talk much. As a result, he spent a lot of time sitting curled up in front of the fire in the great hall, pretending to be dozing.

The great hall in the Lair was frequented by pretty much everyone who lived there at some point during the day. Communal meals were served there, and snacks could always be had at almost any time of the day or night. Those going on duty or those coming off would usually stop there before going wherever they were heading. And when they paused to eat, they talked. And Hrardorr often heard more than he'd bargained for.

He knew more about the inner workings of the Lair, and the town, than most. Nobody realized how much he'd learned through his silent observation, and he'd formed very definite opinions about most of the residents of the Lair— human and dragon alike. He wasn't too impressed with the leadership of the Lair, especially after the last battle.

Hrardorr had really thought his fighting days were over, but that last battle had proven he still had some fight left in him. Certainly, the opportunity to fight from the water wouldn't come along often, if at all, in the future, but he'd felt good to have been able to contribute again.

Livia had helped him recover, at least partially, from the deep depression he'd been in over losing not only his vision, but his last knight. Most dragons went into the mountains, to do their mourning in private, but even that had been denied Hrardorr with his injury. Livia had helped him realize that, while he may not be able to see like he used to, he was not as useless as he'd thought.

He felt bad for her now that her absentee father had decided to return. It was to the captain's credit that he'd come racing home the moment he'd heard about the threat to Dragonscove, but as far as Hrardorr was concerned, the captain's actions since had been too little, too late. He was trying to run his daughter's life as if she was still a child, or some kind of youngster on one of his ships.

She didn't need that. She wasn't doing anything wrong, from what Hrardorr could see. Sharing pleasure was a natural thing for humans. He'd seen it often enough in his centuries. Even if he hadn't been able to share pleasure with a dragoness yet—that was reserved for when he found his true mate and all the pieces fell into place—he thought he understood the human need.

Humans, after all, weren't as strong as dragons. A fighting dragon agreed at the outset that they would not mate unless and until their knight had found a mate. Technically, Hrardorr could seek pleasure with a female now that he was no longer bonded to a knight, but there were no unpartnered female dragons at the Lair who were old enough for him.

Not that he wanted to engage with just any female. No, Hrardorr was selective. If he ever got involved with a female, it would have to be a special one...like Genlitha.

But it was impossible. He was blind, and she had a knight now. He refused to take another knight. Not now. He wouldn't subject a fighting man to his sour humor and grief. It was too soon, and besides, he was blind. What warrior would want to swear his life to fight alongside a blind dragon?

Though if he was going to choose anyone, he probably would have picked Seth. The lad was noble and had proved himself an able leader of men in the last battle. He'd also proven that he was as courageous and fearless as his fathers, who were both exceptional knights. But Hrardorr wouldn't do that to Seth.

For one thing, Seth was already his caretaker. He wouldn't partner with him just to secure a nursemaid for the rest of his life. That would be unkind as well as unfair. For another, Seth had publicly chosen the healer's path long ago. Although he could fight, he wasn't really counted among the young warriors of the Lair.

"Thanks for giving me and Livia some time alone." Seth's voice came to Hrardorr as he began to doze off. *"I'm sorry if we invaded your privacy by coming here."*

"Nonsense," Hrardorr scoffed with good humor. *"The poor girl hasn't had a moment free since her father came home. I'm more than happy to have her company. And yours too, Seth. You both deserve a little happiness."*

"Thank you for understanding, my friend."

They slept through the night together, each watching over the other. And when dawn approached, Livia took her leave with obvious regret. Seth went with her to make sure she made it back into her room without incident. He returned a little while later, his mood contemplative and a little melancholy.

"You miss her already, don't you?" Hrardorr asked.

"Is it that obvious?" Seth asked, folding the sailcloth they'd slept on while Hrardorr stretched one wing at a time.

"Only to me, my friend," Hrardorr assured him.

"It's all quite impossible. She's destined for a knight pair, and I'll probably be condemned to watch it all unfold."

Hrardorr could hear Seth moving, sitting down to one side of the boathouse. The wooden walls held in the sound of his movements, allowing Hrardorr to know with much greater accuracy than usual where the human was and what he was doing.

"The future isn't written yet," Hrardorr reminded Seth, looking for something positive to say, though he didn't really think it was going to end well for the young lovers.

CHAPTER FIVE

Gowan wasn't completely surprised when Genlitha insisted on taking the small gryphon under her wing. She made sure Flurrthith was made welcome in the Lair and then insisted the youngster be made comfortable in their suite of rooms. In fact, she'd made Gowan find materials to make a nest of sorts for the young gryphon, where she could see him.

So, the spare room in their suite was now filled with blankets and pillows that had been scrounged from every corner of the Lair and formed into a circular nest for the gryphon. When Flurrthith slept, Genlitha's long neck was stretched over the side of her sand wallow so that her head could rest in the wide archway of the room where Flurrthith lay. Genlitha breathed over the child, gently stirring his feathers with a caress of warm air.

"He looks comfortable, doesn't he?" Genlitha asked Gowan, almost clucking like a worried hen as they both looked at the young gryphon.

Gowan stood beside Genlitha's head, leaning one shoulder against the stone arch that led into the guest room. Genlitha's head rested on the floor, her neck stretched to its full extent. All the rooms in the place had been built around the wallow, which was sized for a single dragon.

There were much larger suites in the Lair, reserved for

dragon couples and those with children. The size of the suite depended on the dragon's circumstances, and the knight was accommodated in the circle of rooms around the central cavern. Everything was carved out of the stone of the mountain, which meant arched doorways and rounded ceilings in most places. Air shafts were everywhere, allowing dragon smoke out and fresh air, and light, in. All had been created with the aid of magic, Gowan had been told, in the distant past.

"He's exhausted," Gowan commented silently, not wanting to wake the sleeping gryphlet.

"He needs friends," Genlitha surprised him by saying.

"There are few dragonets in this Lair, and they're all younger than Flurrthith," Gowan reminded her.

"I'm going to ask Hrardor if he'll take the child down to the town. I think Livia would be able to find some human youngsters closer in temperament to the child. Flurthith told me he was raised much as a dragonet, with two-footed brothers and sisters. They are likely fair folk, of course, but the fey are not so different from humans."

"Except for being the next best thing to immortal," Gowan observed wryly. *"Still, I think it's a good idea, but somebody will need to figure a way around Livia's father. The captain is formidable, and I'm afraid I can't help you. I'm probably the last person he'd listen to or help, even for the gryphlet's sake."*

"I know," Genlitha admitted, her mental tone mildly annoyed. *"The captain needs a good, stern talking to, in my opinion, but we're in enough trouble with the leadership of this Lair already. Still, I believe Seth could help us."*

Gowan caught himself before he could audibly scoff. *"Captain O'Dare is just as angry with Seth as with me."*

"Ah, but Seth works with the Lair's well-known and well-respected healer. I bet he could ask her to intercede with the captain. Even Captain O'Dare couldn't deny a simple request from a respected elder like Healer Bronwyn."

Gowan had to smile. *"It is a masterful and devious plan, milady. I like it."*

The very next day, Healer Bronwyn went in a well-sprung wagon down to Dragonscove in person, to visit the market and the trading houses of Captain O'Dare. Crafty lady that she was, she contrived to bump into the captain and have a rather pointed conversation with him about how she was just too worried about the young visiting gryphon.

Between the two of them, they somehow arrived at the idea that a young person such as the captain's daughter might be a suitable person to meet with the foreign—albeit young—dignitary. She managed to convince the captain that there might be some advantage to be gained in his daughter befriending a gryphon from Gryphon Isle.

After all, the captain ran a fleet of trade ships, and Gryphon Isle had just reappeared after centuries being hidden in magical mists called by the great wizard, Gryffid. The one and only wizard newly discovered to be alive after the wizard wars millennia ago. Who knew what riches could be traded for from and to his isolated home?

Further, it was said Gryffid had a thriving enclave of fair folk living there on the island with him and his gryphons, his greatest magical creations. The fair folk were well known to be craftsmen of the highest caliber. After all, they had very, very long lives during which to perfect their craft. Even an apprentice's work usually contained all the skill of many human lifetimes. The good captain, no doubt, understood the value in having friends on Gryphon Isle.

Gowan was duly impressed when Seth told him later the way Bronwyn had described the meeting. The elderly healer had enjoyed her mission to the town, and Seth was happy to report it had gone as well as they had hoped. The next day, they would introduce Flurrthith to Hrardorr, and then, Gen and Hrardorr would both accompany the young gryphon down to the town to meet Livia. It was all set up.

Flurrthith was looking much better the next day when Genlitha escorted him to Hrardorr's chamber. She had arranged that a meal of freshly caught fish should be waiting for the three of them, along with breakfast foods for both Seth and Gowan.

Seth was there before them, seeing to Hrardorr's ongoing eye treatments, though they seemed to do little good. The magnificent dragon still couldn't see, even if his pride had been restored slightly by the battle in the water where he'd taken out a good portion of the enemy fleet and sent the rest running.

Flurrthith walked into the chamber cautiously. He'd only been in the Lair a short while, but he'd already been told the story of how Hrardorr had almost single-handedly run off the pirates. Like any youngling, he seemed to be impressed by the tale.

"Greetings, Sir Hrardorr," Genlitha sent her thoughts formally to all the minds present. Gowan had accompanied her and the gryphlet from their chambers.

"Lady Genlitha, it is good to hear your voice. And who have you brought to my wallow this fine morning?"

Gen preened, glad Hrardorr had agreed to play along with her plans. He could just as easily have growled at them, but she'd talked him around earlier this morning.

"A visitor from Gryphon Isle," she said, though Hrardorr knew full well who she was bringing to meet him. *"And my knight, Gowan, of course,"* she added for good measure.

"Sir Gowan." Hrardorr bowed his great head directly in front of where Gowan was standing. He might be blind, but nothing had affected his other senses.

"Sir Hrardorr," Gowan replied aloud, in a grave voice, giving the male dragon a courtly bow for the benefit of the gryphlet. Gryphons, they had been told, lived in a very formal society with strict rules for interacting with their two-legged friends. "May I introduce Sir Flurrthith, from Gryphon Isle. He is the messenger who traveled so far and fast to our shore to tell us of the events transpiring on his island."

"Ah, Sir Flurrthith, I owe you my sincerest apology. Had I known the enemy would turn their remaining ships on your homeland, I would have followed them to hell and back." Hrardorr faced the smaller

creature, though he couldn't see him, and waited.

This was a moment of truth. A clearing of the air. Flurrthith would either prove his maturity or try to lash out at the dragon who could easily be blamed for the havoc taking place on Gryphon Isle at this moment. Everyone waited to see what the gryphlet would do.

"Iss it true that you are blind, Ssir Hrardorr?" came the gryphlet's hesitant voice, adding extra s sounds where his beak interfered with conventional speech, as all gryphons seemed to do.

"I am. I was hit full in the face by skith venom a few months ago and have not been able to see since, much to my disappointment."

Genlitha held her breath. This was the first time Hrardorr had spoken so calmly of his disability in her presence. It was a watershed moment indeed, though what it would mean for the future, she had no idea.

Flurrthith shifted on his front feet as if uncomfortable. "I'm ssorry you were hurt, Ssir. One of my teacherss at home hass only one eye, and it hinderss hiss flight greatly." Leave it to a child to speak so plainly, Genlitha thought, wondering how the gryphlet's words were affecting Hrardorr. "Iss it true you torched the pirate sshipss?" The gryphlet moved a slight distance forward, toward Hrardorr.

"I did. I rose from the water behind them and torched their sails. The ones in the harbor were trapped and burned. The rest ran away, though I got a few of them before they left. Had I known..." Hrardorr let his silent voice trail off for a moment before continuing. *"Had I known where they would go and what they would do, I would have tried harder to stop them all. I am truly sorry."*

"You didn't know they would turn on uss, Ssir." Flurrthith's little voice piped through the room, and Genlitha breathed again. This might yet turn out well. "I didn't think ssea dragonss could flame," he added in a puzzled tone.

"I am only part sea dragon," Hrardorr admitted. *"I can flame and fight on land, in the sky, and now, in the sea. Actually, the sea is all that's really left to me, now with my eyes the way they are. I do not need them in the water, you see. My other senses help me know where*

51

things are when I'm under the waves. It's only above them where my lack of sight hinders my effectiveness."

"Really?" The gryphlet moved closer, clearly intrigued. Genlitha knew things would be all right now. At least as far as Flurrthith and Hrardorr were concerned.

Hrardorr opened up a bit about how his senses worked underwater, which was an education to them all. The gryphlet hung on his every word.

"I didn't know ssea dragonss could do that," the youngster said several times. Finally, it was Gowan who addressed the question that should have been obvious to them all.

"Have you met many sea dragons, Sir Flurrthith?" Gowan asked.

Flurrthith turned his beak toward the humans, standing off to one side. "There iss a cove on the ssouthern end of the island where they like to come assshore. Ssome of the older gryphonss have made friendss among them, but I've only sspoken to one of the dragonss. Her name iss Sshanaraneth, but she said to call her Sshara for sshort. Sshe is older than me, but not too much older, and sshe was badly injured by a sschool of ssharkss a while back. One of our healerss, my older ssisster Lizbet, hass been working with Lady Sshara and letss me tag along ssometimess. Sshe iss very nice, though sshe wass very ssad when sshe wass sstuck on land healing."

Hrardorr sighed, sending smoke rings up into the vented dome above his head. *"It is a sad thing to be out of one's element. My ancestor was like your friend, a sea dragon injured and unable to swim like she used to, but she found happiness on land with a land dragon and went on to live many happy centuries with him in this Lair. They founded this Lair, in fact."*

Flurrthith looked back at Hrardorr, his feathers stirring with what looked like excitement. "I didn't know that, Ssir Hrardorr. If I may, I would like to tell Sshara about your ancesstor. The sstory might make her feel better."

"You certainly may, my young friend," Hrardorr agreed. *"Hope is a rare commodity. Your friend sounds like she could use some."*

After that interesting exchange, they all got to know each

other better. Genlitha broached the topic of flying down to the town to meet Livia toward the end of their meal. She told Flurrthith about how both Gowan and Seth were courting Lady Livia, seeing no reason to hide such information from the child. Perhaps Flurrthith could help the three humans in some way.

It was agreed that Genlitha would carry Gowan, and Flurrthith surprisingly volunteered to carry Seth on his back down to the town. It would be difficult for Hrardorr to carry anyone, since he planned to land in the water and then walk up onto land. While Gowan and Seth would stay well out of sight of Livia's father, they were hoping to get a few minutes to at least say hello to Livia. And if not, they each claimed to have errands to run in town anyway.

Genlitha doubted the veracity of those claims, but she wasn't going to say anything. She still had hopes for the threesome, even if circumstances were against them right now.

Seth couldn't believe he was riding on the back of a gryphon. Of all the things he'd expected when he'd awakened that morning, his backside being cushioned by a mix of fur and feathers while he glided almost silently down from the top of the Lair to the beach below the town had not been foremost in his mind.

He'd been taken aloft by his dragon parents on occasion, and this experience was similar, but also quite different. Gryphons were just...more comfortable, if he was going to tell the truth. They were soft where dragon scale was hard against human limbs. And their glide—or at least, Flurthith's immense wingspan—made the trip a dream.

They'd agreed to land on the beach in order to meet up with Hrardorr. The idea was to keep Flurrthith busy while the leadership up at the Lair made their decision. So far, Seth had heard through his fathers, the dithering was winning out over actually getting off their duffs and helping.

They'd sent a messenger to the capital *over land*, for

heavens sake. A lad on a horse, who would take days and days to get there. They'd used the recent attack as an excuse to keep all the dragon messengers here, regardless of the fact that they could have made the flight there and back in half the time.

Seth's entire family was disgusted, but his fathers were still trying to talk with the leadership, making their case through the proper channels. His parents were too old school to go against the leaders. At least not now, while the situation was still fresh. Perhaps, if nothing had been accomplished by tomorrow, they would actually *do* something. In the meantime, they'd asked Seth to keep an eye on the gryphon. Nobody wanted the visiting youngster to get the wrong impression of the knights or dragons of Draconia due to the pigheadedness of a couple of old men and even older dragons.

So this outing had been devised. It would keep Flurrthith away from the controversy at the Lair today, while affording Seth and Gowan the slight chance of seeing Livia out from under her father's watchful eye. Seth thought it was good for Hrardorr to socialize too. He'd been far too solitary since the battle in the harbor.

Flurrthith flew beautifully, and Seth took a moment to just enjoy the sensation of the wind in his hair, the sound of it sifting through the gryphon's feathers. The sun was shining, and there were no clouds in the sky today. It was a great day to be alive as far as Seth was concerned.

It started with an unexpected and probably once-in-a-lifetime gryphon flight and might result in seeing Livia. Things were looking up.

He'd missed her so much since her father's edict. The man was a tyrant and ruled his home like he must rule his ships, with an iron hand. The sea captain had a justly deserved reputation as far as Seth was concerned.

Flurrthith spiraled down from the high cliffs on which the Lair was built, flanked by Gowan and Genlitha. Hrardorr had gone on ahead, but they could still see him. In fact, Seth was watching his progress closely, ready to warn him if he should somehow run into danger. But it was clear. Hrardorr dove into the water quite a ways out into the sea, where there were no obstacles to hinder him.

His entry into the water was near perfect, without much of a splash. If Seth hadn't been watching closely, he wouldn't have noticed much of anything happening out there. The water truly was Hrardorr's second home. Seth was glad he had that at least. The dragon's spirits had been down since the battle, which had confused Seth at first, but he soon realized that the fight had brought back memories of Hrardorr's glory days. Memories that were hard to live with in his current condition, Seth figured.

As they made their way to the beach, Seth noticed another dragon already there. It was a dark blue. Had to be Xanderanth. He was a relative newcomer to the Lair, blessed with powerful wings. He and his young knight had been sent to the Southern Lair for their first assignment, partly because of Xander's youth and flying abilities, but also because his knight, Leonhardt—Leo for short—was from this region and still very close to his family. Rumor had it that his parents packed up his siblings and moved to be closer to the Lair once they found out Leo and Xander would be stationed here for a few years while they both learned the business of being a team.

Xander trumpeted a greeting when he saw Genlitha, and Seth felt Flurrthith tremble under him. But when Gen signaled back in a similar way, the gryphon seemed to relax again.

"We are in luck," Gen said into all their minds as they glided closer to their landing point and the young blue dragon. *"Xanderanth is only a little older than you, Flurrthith. His knight's family lives nearby, and he is visiting them, so Xander is at loose ends for a bit. He's a very nice dragon."*

There was no time to say more as they came in for the landing. Seth held on tight, expecting to get jostled around a bit because of Flurrthith's age and relative inexperience. Plus, he'd never been on a gryphon's back before and had no idea if they landed the same way dragons did. But Seth needn't have worried. Flurrthith set down with all the grace of the most elegant dragon, and Seth was just as comfortable as he would have been on dragonback—perhaps more so because of the fur, but he'd never tell a dragon that.

When Seth jumped down from Flurrthith's back, he was sure to go around and face the young gryphon, thanking him formally for the ride. Gryphons were formal. Everyone said so. Seth didn't want to be the one to mess up the budding relationship between gryphons and Draconia. No, he thought, holding in a grimace, he'd leave that to the idiots up at the Lair who were even now discussing ways to *not* help, in all likelihood.

"Thank you, Sir Flurrthith. I have never had a more comfortable flight," Seth said as he bowed, keeping his gaze locked with the gryphon's out of respect. He figured he could get away with that little bit of truth. The dragons would think he was just being polite.

"You are very welcome, Sseth. You ride well for one who hass no dragon partner of hiss own," Flurrthith surprised him by saying.

Seth rose from the bow and regarded the gryphon. "I was raised in the Lair. My fathers have dragon partners who raised me as their own. It was a great treat to be taken aloft, so I have flown before, just not very often. Thank you for the kind words. I am glad to have not caused you any difficulties."

The blue dragon's head appeared over Seth's shoulder, ending that avenue of conversation.

"Hello. I'm Xander," the blue dragon said to them all, not waiting to be introduced. He was still quite young to be in service, but he'd found his partner young, as well, and had been sent here to grow into his duties.

Seth stroked Xander's neck, already very familiar with the young dragon. He'd treated him for a sore wings after Genlitha put him through his paces a few times.

56

"Sir Flurrthith of Gryphon Isle, may I present Sir Xanderanth of the Southern Lair?" Seth said politely, hoping Xander's eagerness wouldn't somehow offend the gryphon.

"Hello, Xander. I like your sshiny color. You ssparkle like the ssouthern ocean beyond the Bay of Forgetfulnesss."

Xander seemed to preen at the gryphon's words. *"Thank you. I don't know where that is, but I'd like to fly there someday. I want to see everything,"* he declared with the enthusiasm of youth.

"That ssounds like fun," Flurrthith agreed.

Seth ducked out of the way while the two youngsters got acquainted. If he wasn't much mistaken, he believed he'd just witnessed the start of a friendship.

Hrardorr rose out of the water like a sea creature, stalking forward onto the sand with Genlitha's gentle—and silent—guidance, Seth knew. Steam rose from his hide, adding to the unearthly appearance. He really was something to behold when he came out of the ocean.

Gen and Hrardorr moved off to one side, talking amongst themselves for a bit when a newcomer joined their group. In fact, it was several newcomers. Xander's young knight had appeared over the dunes with some of his younger siblings in tow.

Seth knew Sir Leo and liked the lad. Leo had always shown great interest in learning all he could about how to help his dragon, which put him squarely in Seth's good books.

"Sir Leo, we didn't expect to find you here," Seth greeted him with a friendly outstretched hand. Leo was one of the few knights who had always treated Seth with respect, even before Seth had led such an effective defense of the harbor.

Leo came forward with all the enthusiasm of his more youthful age. If he'd seen twenty summers yet, Seth would have been surprised, but he wasn't rude enough to ask outright how old Leo was.

"Seth! Good to see you." Leo let his youngest sister off his shoulders and set her down on the sand before reaching out to share a warrior-like handclasp with Seth, a broad smile on his face. He then seemed to catch sight of the other knight.

"Sir Gowan." Leo's demeanor changed slightly, from open friendliness to slight wariness.

Gowan held a position of authority over Leo and his dragon, since Gowan and Genlitha were leading his fighting wing and Gen was tutoring Xander in the use of his exceptionally strong wings.

Gowan stepped up and offered his hand to Leo, breaking a bit of the tension. "It's my day off, Leo. I'm sorry we intruded on your family time. It was not our intent." Gowan shifted his gaze to the curious children gathered behind their older brother. One girl was nearly as tall as Leo, the rest ranging in size—and age—on downward from there.

"My day with the sibs," Leo explained. "And then dinner with the family. My brothers and sisters love Xander almost as much as I do."

Seth was pleased by the young man's candor about his feelings for the dragon who would share the rest of his life. Theirs was a very good match, indeed.

"Like Gowan said, we didn't mean to intrude. We came down to the beach so Sir Hrardorr could join us, and then, we were supposed to meet up with Mistress O'Dare to introduce her to our visiting dignitary from Gryphon Isle."

"Miss Livy's coming here?" a small girl asked, her eyes wide as excitement sparkled.

"Hush, Jenny," Leo told the small child gently.

Seth intervened, crouching down to meet little Jenny's gaze at eye level. "Do you know my friend, Miss Livy?"

Jenny nodded, her whole body moving up and down with her little head. "She gives us sweeties sometimes," Jenny admitted.

Seth dug into his pockets, remembering he had a few hard candies in there somewhere. Sure enough, he found the small parcel, wrapped in cloth. He unveiled the small sugar-dusted drops like he was unwrapping a magician's rabbit, enjoying the way Jenny's eyes widened as she watched.

The other children had gathered around him, and when he

offered the little mound of hard candy drops to them, the candies were gone in a flurry of little hands. They were polite about it, though, each taking one first, to be sure everyone had one, only then going back for more. They were happy, well-behaved children and Seth thought he understood a little better about Leo and how strong a family foundation he'd come from. No wonder he'd been chosen so young. He came from good people and would doubtless turn into the best of men, in time.

CHAPTER SIX

While Seth entertained the children, Gowan took the opportunity to have a quiet word with Leo. He gestured off to the side, away from the dragons and Seth and the kids, where they could talk privately. Leo followed, somewhat formal in his movements, since technically, Gowan was his superior.

That was good, as far as Gowan was concerned. It showed that Leo was aware of the chain of command and respected it, but it also made Gowan want to put the young man at ease. After all, they'd intruded on his time off with his siblings. Gowan wanted to make sure Leo realized it had been purely accidental that their paths had crossed.

Then again... The Mother of All worked in mysterious ways. Maybe their paths had been meant to cross all along. Maybe this group of youngsters was just what Flurrthith needed today, to keep his mind off the troubles in his homeland and the idiotic delay in responding from the Lair leadership.

"I'm sorry we interrupted your family time," Gowan told Leo, speaking plainly as was his usual habit. "It wasn't our intent. We merely wanted to get Sir Flurrthith away from the Lair for a bit and introduce him to Livia O'Dare in hopes that she could connect him with some younger people that he might enjoy meeting. He is very young to have been sent on such a mission, but you can see why." Gowan looked over at Flurrthith, talking with the dragons. "He is an amazing flyer for his age."

"I didn't realize he was young. I've never met a gryphon before. Are they bigger than that when they're adults?" Leo asked, his eyes on the gryphon, as well.

"The adult gryphons in the capital are larger, but I'd say Flurrthith's wings are even longer than the adults I've seen fly around Castleton. His wingspan is remarkable for any age—or so Genlitha assures me. I have not spoken to a gryphon before either. Flurrthith is my first, but I hope not last." Gowan frowned, thinking about the trouble facing the gryphon's island home right at this very minute.

"Then, you want us to go help the wizard and the gryphons?" Leo asked.

Gowan looked at the young knight. "I do." He had to sigh, thinking about the complications at the Lair. "But I very much fear our leadership is going to be…shortsighted, on this issue."

"You think they'd leave Gryffid in the lurch?" Now, Leo's expression took on an appalled cast. Good man.

"I don't know what they're going to do, but recent events have led me to doubt their courage." Gowan had just uttered a huge insult, but he couldn't find it in his heart to regret his words. They were the absolute truth, and he'd stand behind them if Leo went telling tales for some reason.

Leo's lips went thin as he clenched his jaw, looking from Xander to Flurrthith and back again. Then, his bright eyes shifted to Gowan again.

"Sir. Xander and I have been talking this over." That was a good sign, Gowan thought. The young knight was seeking the counsel of his dragon. "If it comes down to it and the leadership does something incredibly stupid, we're considering…"

Gowan put a cautious hand on the young knight's shoulder. "Do not do anything without telling me, son,"

Gowan advised, knowing Leo's strong heart would demand he and Xander race off to try to help the allies they had unknowingly put in danger from the pirates.

Leo met his gaze, a core of iron showing in his dark eyes. "Likewise, Sir."

Well. That was unexpected. If Gowan didn't misunderstand, Leo and Xander had just volunteered to go rogue with him and Genlitha if the leadership denied Gryffid's request for aid. Hmm.

There was no chance to take the conversation further since, at that moment, a cheer went up from the children as they were the first to spot Livia O'Dare making her way toward them from the direction of town. She had walked along the beach to get to them, much to Gowan's surprise. He'd thought the dragons and Flurrthith were going to walk into town to meet her, but apparently, she'd found a way to get free of her father's guards and come here on her own.

Then again, Livia was a very creative lass, with a mind of her own. If anyone could escape those who would try to keep tabs on her, it was Livia.

Livia had managed to escape her watchers for the day when she saw the dragons flying overhead with the small gryphon. It was easy enough to point out the fact that it would be simpler to go meet the dragons on the beach than to make them walk into the crowded town looking for her.

With a stern warning, her father had let her leave their place of business. He'd taken to letting her do the bookwork with him each day, since he'd found no fault with her bookkeeping while he'd been away. In fact, he'd been very complimentary about her running of the office.

He hadn't meant to leave her in charge of the whole thing, but when the man he had hired to run operations ran off with a saloon girl a few weeks after her father had set sail, there had been no recourse. Frankly, Livia was relieved the man had gone. Without him to get in the way, she'd been able to run the operation as she'd always known she'd be able to. It had been a challenge, and she had risen to it.

Luckily, her father agreed after some initial anger.

As she worked with him in the same office, she hoped to show him that she really was an adult, not the child he'd left behind. It was slow going, but if she was ever going to get out from under his thumb in a graceful manner, she had to prove to him she wasn't some silly child.

She loved her father and didn't want to hurt his feelings, but it was clear he had a very unrealistic view of who she was. There were times when he looked at her with such sadness in his eyes. Those times, when he thought she didn't realize he was watching her with such haunted eyes—when she probably reminded him of her dead mother...

It broke her heart too.

The portraits in the house confirmed that, as Livia got older, she began to look more and more like her. Livia knew that had to be painful for her father. He'd loved her mother truly and had gone a little crazy when she'd died.

He'd fled. Plain and simple. He'd fled to the sea, returning only intermittently to a heartbroken little girl who had grown up mostly without his presence.

Theirs was a sad tale, but she understood. She, too, had lost her best friend when she'd lost her mother.

While she didn't agree with the way her father had handled his grief, she had come to understand it over time. Livia was philosophical by nature—as her mother had been. She had long ago forgiven the sea captain for running away from the reminders of his loss.

Now, she just had to work to make him understand that time had not stood still here while he'd been off adventuring. Livia had grown. She was ready to step out into the world as, in fact, she had been doing all along while he hadn't been here.

He'd come around, but in the meantime, she had to be creative if she wanted to keep living the happy life she'd carved out for herself. It had been a challenge. Especially in regards to her two suitors.

That had been the most difficult challenge, in fact.

But there they were now. Her two favorite men, down on the beach, and she was unsupervised, for a change. The possibilities danced before her mind, tempting her to instigate a change of plans, if at all possible.

As she realized there was a crowd of children, as well as another knight and his dragon present, she began to hope that maybe there was a way to contrive some time alone with her guys. And they were hers. Since they had shared ecstasy together, she couldn't seem to think of either of them separately. Whenever she pictured being with them, she pictured them both. Oh, she'd happily take one of them to her bed, if the opportunity arose, but after knowing the total rapture of being with them both at the same time...only that would do for her fantasies.

When the children spotted her and cheered, Livia could only smile. She knew these tykes. They were all related. Brothers and sisters from a family that had moved to Dragonscove recently, with connections to the Lair and to her father's far-flung business enterprises.

Livia, in fact, had helped Mr. and Mrs. Stuart find their new place and had helped arrange their move. Mr. Stuart ran the supply side of her father's export business, coordinating shipments from various farms and craftspeople to the warehouses, there to be loaded onto ships and sent abroad for trade opportunities.

Livia had known Mr. Stuart for a while now. He'd come to town with every major shipment and had met with her to coordinate distribution of payment and planning for upcoming needs. He'd run his part of the business from the next port over for years, but when his son had been chosen by a dragon and stationed at the Lair above Dragonscove, he'd immediately asked if he could keep his position if he moved closer.

Livia had been only too happy to have such a capable manager closer to hand and had helped the family move. She'd also taken an immediate liking to his wife and children when she'd finally met them. Mrs. Stuart was a no-nonsense sort of woman who had a talent for cookery of all kinds. She'd been the head chef at a famous inn in Port Waymouth that was known far and wide, but she'd easily given it up to be nearer to her eldest son and his new dragon partner.

There were several establishments seeking Mrs. Stuart's advice, and more than one was trying to hire her, but she claimed to be enjoying being with her family too much to go back to working as hard as she had before. She did offer advice in return for payment and had become something of a consultant to inns all over the county.

Livia had plans to help Mrs. Stuart market her expertise on a wider scale, but she hadn't broached the idea with the good lady yet. Her father's return had made Livia put many of her side projects on hold, but she'd get back to them. Eventually.

"Hello, the Stuarts!" she called merrily toward the children who had been gathered around Seth. His golden blond hair shone in the sun as he rose and smiled at her.

The children ran to her, the littlest trailing behind until Livia scooped little Jenny up and carried her back the way they'd come. They were all talking at once, asking her questions and giving her little chance to reply. It was fine though. She loved their natural enthusiasm and inquisitive minds. This family was a model of what she wished she'd had growing up, and she admired them for it.

When she reached Seth, she put Jenny down and faced him, a broad smile on her face.

"It's good to see you, Master Seth." She felt as breathless as her voice sounded and hoped the children would blame it on her long walk.

"Lovely to see you again, Mistress Livia. Thank you for joining us here today to meet our visitor." Seth played the gallant, escorting her toward the gathered four-footed creatures, who were all watching them.

The children followed behind Livia, cautious but curious. Genlitha and Hrardorr stood together, with a slightly smaller sparkling dark blue dragon and their furred and feathered guest, the gryphon.

Gowan watched all from the other side, standing with a young man who must be the eldest of the Stuart children. She hadn't met the famous Leo yet, but she'd heard all about him from his brothers and sisters.

Livia had heard a great deal about the formality of gryphons and knew enough to greet the young gryphon first. She held the creature's gaze as she walked toward it, her heart fluttering a bit with nerves. She'd never met a gryphon before.

"Sir Flurrthith of Gryphon Isle, may I present Mistress Livia O'Dare of Dragonscove?" Seth said formally, stopping next to Livia as she faced the gryphon head on.

Livia sank into a deep curtsey, her eyes remaining raised as a sign of respect for the gryphon's great strength. The gryphon lowered one front leg by bending at the knee, also bowing, in its way, holding her gaze as if measuring her in some way.

Livia felt the impact of the gryphon's regard down to her toes. It wasn't really something she could put into words, but the way the gryphon looked at her, it was as if it was seeing down into the core of her being, measuring and considering before making some sort of decision about her. And then, it spoke, the audible words jarring her a bit.

"It iss good to meet you, Missstresss. Even on Gryphon Isle, we have heard of the daring ssea captain named O'Dare. Iss he your ssire?"

Shocked, Livia rose from her curtsey as the gryphon stood before her. "Why, yes. Captain O'Dare is my father."

"You are the sea captain's daughter the whole Lair is talking about?" The young dragon's shimmering blue head lifted and moved closer to Livia, eyeing her with deep blue eyes that sparkled even more than his scales.

"I guess so," she answered the new dragon. "I'm Livia," she said simply, introducing herself.

"Xanderanth, don't crowd her so," Genlitha scolded from the side. *"Livia is our friend. She is the one Hrardorr goes fishing with all*

the time."

"I'm Xanderanth, partner to Leonhardt," the young dragon
went on, clearly not cowed by Genlitha's gentle scolding.

Livia smiled. "Oh, I've heard great things about Sir Leo
from his siblings, and of course, I've known Mr. Stuart for
several years since he holds a very important position in my
father's trading company."

"I'm Leo," the younger man stepped forward, offering his
hand with a smile. "It's very nice to finally meet you,
Mistress."

When the greetings were finally over, it was quickly
decided that Flurrthith and Xander would be good
entertainment for each other, accompanied by Leo and the
Stuart brood, with Genlitha and Hrardorr to supervise. Livia
was included in their plans at first, but she coaxed the talk
around to the idea that she and Gowan and Seth had other
duties to see to before they could rejoin the group for a meal
later in the day.

The plans were quickly set, and Livia eagerly led her two
men away from the crowd, to a secluded spot she knew a
little farther down the beach, near the rocky part of the
shoreline.

"Lady Genlitha, is anyone following us or noting our movements?"
Livia sent silently to the dragon who had stayed behind with
the others. Genlitha had sharp eyesight and would be able to
tell if anyone was trying to follow them.

*"No, Livia. You made a clean getaway. And I will keep watch and
alert you if anyone comes near."* Livia swore it sounded like the
dragoness was amused more than anything.

"You're the best, Lady Genlitha. Thank you!"

Livia was leading them toward the rocks, and Gowan
knew from his aerial reconnaissance of the coast that there
were a few caves along this stretch of beach. Perfect
smugglers caves, he'd thought, when he'd seen them from
above, though none had seemed in use when he'd flown over.
Perhaps Dragonscove had more honest folk than most

towns, but he'd bet at least one of the caves had seen use sometime in the past for illicit cargoes snuck in at the dead of night.

Sure enough, the cave Livia led them to was perfect for smuggling. It had an entrance that was very close to the water, and anyone going from cave to water couldn't be seen from the beach. At high tide, a skiff could tie up very close to the mouth of the cave for unloading and never be seen.

The cave was tidy, free of the usual debris found in such places, which made Gowan think that maybe someone was still using it. There were no signs of cargo here at the moment, and no human footprints, but the place was just a little too neat for nature.

The sand was smooth, but it was still sand and would get messy if they were going to tryst here. First, he had to find out if she planned to dally with them, and if so, he had to devise a plan to keep Livia looking as if she hadn't been rolling around on the sand with two men. With her father back in town, they had to be careful. Not because he was ashamed of what they shared, but because he didn't want to make life at home harder for her than it was already.

Her father had put her practically under house arrest since he'd come home, and Gowan didn't want to be the cause of any further hardship for the lovely Livia. If he could, he'd ask her to marry him right now and take her up to the Lair, but marriage among knights wasn't such a simple matter. He'd learned, much to his annoyance, that it required the input and agreement of more than the usual two parties.

No, there were two dragons involved and another knight. And until Genlitha chose a mate, Gowan had no idea who the other knight might be.

It was a mess, to be sure.

As far as he was concerned, he'd made up his mind. He wanted Livia in his life. She was perfect for him in every way. But he had no idea if the other unknown knight would feel the same.

Genlitha tried to console him that the Mother of All had a

hand, more often than not, in Lair marriages, but Gowan was skeptical. And impatient. All he saw were the obstacles. He didn't see how they were going to overcome the biggest one—Genlitha finding her mate first, when she'd been unmated for hundreds of years already.

There was no guarantee that Genlitha would settle down in Gowan's lifetime. Although his lifespan would be expanded by a century or more, if he didn't die fighting, it was entirely possible Gen wouldn't mate for decades yet.

Which didn't bode well for Gowan and Livia's chances of being together long-term.

He hadn't known any of this when Genlitha spoke the words of claim over him. He wasn't sure he'd undo it if he could. Being with Genlitha was…pure magic. But not being able to give Livia the kind of commitment his heart yearned to have with her… That was pure hell.

Livia let go of their hands and walked farther into the cave, raising her hands and spinning in a slow circle. She looked so joyful his heart lifted. How could his bad mood last when faced with Livia's pure heart?

"Isn't this place amazing?" she asked them almost rhetorically as she explored the cave. "We used to come down here when I was a little girl. Father always said this was the pirate's cave. The dread pirate MacRobert's hidden hidey-hole."

"It might very well have been," Seth said, looking around, as well.

"It might still be," Gowan added, shooting them both a pointed look.

"Well, he's not here now, so I say this place is ours for the next few hours at least," Livia said, grinning as she walked closer to him.

"And what shall we do in our new domain?" Gowan played along as she put her hands around his waist and smiled up at him.

"We'll think of something, won't we?" Livia asked with that teasing light in her eyes that let him know exactly what she had in mind. Good. They were both on the same page.

But was Seth?

Gowan looked up to meet Seth's gaze. Blue sparks lit his eyes as he watched Livia rubbing up against Gowan. Oh, yeah. Seth was on board too.

It was time for Gowan to go to work.

"Seth," he said in a low voice. "Spread our cloaks on the softest sand you can find."

Command came naturally to him, even more so in this sort of situation. He was glad Seth was secure enough in his own right to play along with Gowan's dominant tendencies.

If only Seth were a knight...and his dragon partner was Gen's mate....

Yeah, right. Gowan might as well wish for the moon on a silver platter. But it would have been good. He knew that already.

So he'd enjoy it while it lasted and do his best not to think about the future. He'd also do his best not to let either Livia or Seth think about it either. This time was for them—as a threesome—stolen away from the world, wrapped up only in each other.

Seth moved to take the traveling cloak from Gowan's shoulders. Livia helped, untying the closures for him with her dainty fingers.

The cloaks Gowan and Seth had worn were specially designed to be both wind and water proof so that knights riding atop dragons wouldn't be frozen by the cold air that blew in lofty heights or drenched by clouds. They were made of stout fabric that had been treated with some sort of waterproofing substance. Seth probably knew exactly what was used and how they were made, but Gowan only knew he wouldn't want to fly without such protection.

The cloaks could double as a tarp while on the ground, and that's the purpose they'd use them for today. A nice big tarp under them, with Gowan and Seth's clothes on top to make it softer and warmer, while Livia's clothes lay folded neatly a distance away, safe. If Gowan had his way, Livia would leave this cave dressed as beautifully as when she'd entered. Nobody would know by looking at her what they had been up to—especially not her father.

After the cloaks were spread to his specifications, making a nice large solid foundation, Gowan nodded at Seth. Both of them began disrobing, placing their clothing in strategic layers on top of the cloaks, concentrating mostly on the area where their upper bodies would rest. Livia tried to help, but Gowan ordered her away with a look, and she smiled up at him, complying, which made him want to grin.

She was a biddable little thing when it came to pleasure. That was something that pleased him enormously. And he anticipated a lot more pleasure shortly.

Livia licked her lips as the two men revealed their gleaming muscles bit by bit. She'd died and gone to heaven. Her dreams were coming to life. She'd spent so much time thinking about the few times all three of them had been together, she almost tried to pinch herself to see if this was real.

But she couldn't have imagined the healing wounds and new scars on her boys. They'd both seen fighting during the battle for Dragonscove, and both had come out of it with injuries. Thankfully, none were too terrible, but they both had a few new scars. In Seth's case, he hadn't had many to begin with. He'd spent most of his life denying his warrior abilities.

It seemed he'd been making up for lost time since befriending Gowan, though, which had turned out well for the town. If not for Seth directing the cannons and leading the troops on the shore into battle when the pirates tried to storm the beaches, she didn't think there still would *be* a town.

Seth had done more than anyone had ever expected of him to defend Dragonscove, but Gowan, too, had been part of it. He'd fought his share of pirates during the battle and had been an instrumental part of the harbor's defense. Both of them were heroes—battered, bloodied, but going strong.

She had never been prouder of anyone in her entire life than she had been of them in the aftermath of the battle.

It had been some days since the fight, but both men were still recovering. A few of the deeper gashes would take some additional time to heal and leave only a scar behind. She looked her fill at each and every inch of their bodies as they were revealed, planning how she would caress them and kiss their hurts. If they let her. Or, more accurately, if *Gowan* let her.

She shivered, anticipating his orders. She'd never experienced such pleasure as that time the three of them had been together in the Lair and Gowan had been in charge. She liked his bossiness in the context of the bedroom. He didn't even try to order her around otherwise, but at certain times, in special circumstances—like when they were naked—she not only welcomed it but *wanted* it.

Like she wanted it now.

As she stood there, she realized her knees were trembling. Not in fear, but in anticipation.

Both men stripped to the waist, spreading their shirts out on top of the cloaks, and she realized they were sacrificing their clothing to make her bed. A warmth settled in her heart that was never far away when she thought about either man. Seth, with his blond good looks and boyish charm, had grown as she had, from the boy she'd loved from afar to this golden god of a man who now stood before her. A little battered from the fight he'd been in, but more handsome for it in her eyes.

And then, there was Gowan. A newcomer to their small world of Dragonscove. A compelling man in his own right. Hardened in ways Seth wasn't, she found it a challenge to make him laugh, each one of his smiles prized. He'd seen hard things in his life. He'd lost his home and created a new one with his dragon partner. He seemed adorably unsure of himself sometimes, though she'd never let him know that she noticed. He was so new to being a knight he didn't have that arrogance that some of the older knights from the Lair had.

Neither did Seth, though he took being around dragons for granted. It was clear that, to Gowan, being around dragons was still something new and magical. Not that Seth took any dragon for granted, but it was more like he was their kin...somehow. Like he loved them and understood them on a level Gowan didn't but was striving to learn.

As Seth taught Gowan about dragons, Gowan taught Seth in return about being a fighter—and a leader of men. She could see it happening before her eyes, though she doubted either man was fully aware of the changes they'd each wrought on each other. They were a good team. Good for each other. She felt a little pang at the idea that they would have made an amazing fighting partnership...if only...

But she understood Hrardorr was scarred beyond the obvious injuries. He wasn't ready for a knight. Most dragons went off alone after losing a knight and grieved for many years before returning to the fold to try again. Because of, first, his grave injuries and then blindness, Hrardorr hadn't been able do that. The loss of his knight was still a fresh wound in his heart and his soul. To ask him to take a new knight so soon, and with him still unsure of his place in the world as a blind dragon, was asking too much.

She pushed the sad thoughts from her mind as Gowan and Seth approached, one on either side of her, intent clear in their eyes. In silence, they began undressing her, inch by delicious inch, taking their time.

As her shoulders were bared, they each kissed one. Gowan stood to her left and slightly behind while Seth was on her right, slightly in front of her. He met her eyes but then looked to Gowan as if for direction.

Oh, yes. Gowan was in charge again, and Seth was playing along. This promised to be mind-blowing.

Her blouse lowered little by little, Gowan and Seth both loosening the ties that held all her clothing in place. Her skirt fell to the floor, and she felt Gowan dip down behind her, pausing to bite the curve of her butt in a playful way that made her squeak before he coaxed her feet up one at a time, removing the skirt. He rose, and she was peripherally aware of him folding her skirt neatly and putting it well out of harm's way while Seth freed her breasts and immediately began kissing and fondling them.

Gowan returned, and she watched him watching Seth sucking on her skin. The combination of Seth's expert touch and Gowan's dark eyes noting everything made her shiver...and want more. So much more.

Then, Seth moved to one side, and Gowan joined him, plying her body with gentle touches.

Seth went around to the back as he untied her drawers and took them off. He, too, seemed unable to resist biting her butt cheek on the way down. He lifted her feet gently, one at a time, and rose again, pausing to run his hands over her bare ass, dipping between her legs for a quick, almost ticklish, foray before he left.

He folded her clothing—the drawers and the blouse he held in his other hand—and placed them carefully down with the skirt.

As he walked back, he held her gaze, almost daring her to watch as he unbuttoned his pants and let them drop, along with his smalls. Her eyes widened as he closed the distance between them, his cock standing out at full attention, ready for her.

Gowan moved back when Seth moved in behind her. Seth lifted her hair away from her neck, bending to nibble on her ear and the soft skin of her neck while Gowan removed the rest of his clothing in front of her.

"Watch him now," Seth coaxed, whispering in her ear. "See how eager he is for you? Like I am. How much we both want you?"

Seth played with her taut nipples while his breath fanned the sensitive parts of her ear and Gowan stood only a few feet away, lowering his pants, his cock jutting out, hard and ready like Seth's, for her to see.

Seth pulled her closer, and she felt his hard cock against her skin. Then, Gowan moved closer, letting her feel his hardness against her lower abdomen.

"Are you ready for us, sweet?" Gowan asked in a low voice that made her want to purr. "I regret we don't have all day to play here. What time we have is stolen away, and we cannot go as slowly as I'd like."

He was apologizing? Now?

"It doesn't matter. I'm ready," she whispered, her voice ragged as her breathing went shallow with desire. "I want you now. Please don't make me wait."

"Is she ready, Seth?" Gowan asked, a twinkle in his eye as he looked at his co-conspirator over her left shoulder.

"I'll check and see," Seth growled, sliding his hand down over the curve of her ass and dipping his fingers into her wet heat.

She was more than ready. She was almost desperate. It had been too long since the three of them had been together in passion. She'd missed them so much. Her body had missed them…and wanted them.

"She's wet," Seth reported, in a rumbly tone that made her even wetter. He trailed his fingers up her back, leaving a cool line in their wake that mirrored the shivery sensation running up and down her spine.

"Is she?" Gowan asked, looking not at Seth now, but deep into Livia's eyes. "I'll have to see this for myself."

And when he said *see*, he meant it. Gowan kissed his way down her body, dropping to his knees in front of her. It might seem a submissive position, but she had no doubt that Gowan was very much in control of their every move in this passionate dance.

His fingers spread her, his tongue licking out to taste. Her knees gave out, and she would have fallen if not for Seth at her back, holding her up, his strong arms under hers, supporting her as her bones melted in pleasure.

Gowan took his time, despite the fact that they had to keep this encounter relatively short. He gave her several small climaxes that only made her want more. Seth watched the whole thing, making her even hotter.

By the time Gowan rose again to his feet, she was ready to beg. He must've seen it in her eyes because he smiled then, satisfaction in his gaze as he kissed her sweetly, letting her taste her own flavor, faintly, on his lips.

"I believe she's ready now, Seth. What do you think?" Gowan didn't wait for a reply. Instead, he bent slightly and placed his hands under her butt, lifting her high in the air and making her gasp at the unexpected movement.

What was he doing?

Seth helped, supporting her from behind while Gowan moved her again, sliding her against his torso until her open legs met his hard cock. Holding her gaze, he lowered her slowly onto him, impaling her gently, watching her with an intensity she savored.

Seth remained behind her, but this moment was all about Gowan as he took possession of her body...and soul.

He seated himself fully, and she caught her breath. It felt so good to be filled by him again. Like she'd come home. Like she'd been incomplete without him and was only now starting to regain her balance. Though...there was still a little something missing. A little something that was about six feet tall with blond hair, and he was standing behind her.

The strength of Gowan's arms impressed her. He was holding her as if she weighed nothing at all, though Seth was there, a safety net should he be needed. Or...that's what she'd thought until Gowan gave Seth a small nod over her shoulder.

And then, she felt Seth's hand move to her splayed cheeks, spreading something that smelled faintly herbal and felt deliciously slippery. Was he going to...?

Oh, bright stars in the heavens, he was. His fingers slipped inside, stretching her gently. First one, then a second followed, then a third. The sensations were indescribably delicious, making her want more, just as he removed his fingers and replaced them with something a bit more substantial...

Slowly—so slowly—Seth began to slide into the way he'd

made so accommodatingly slick. His breath was warm on the nape of her neck while he worked his way inside the tight spot, the fullness of Gowan's cock in her pussy making the fit exquisitely exciting.

She hadn't done this with anyone but them. Would never contemplate doing it with anyone else. This was strictly for the three of them. A perfect physical union made tragic by the fact that it could never be permanent. But while she had it, she was going to enjoy it. This was one of the few times she could really let go and be herself—and allow her boundaries to be pushed in a way that helped her grow into the person she was becoming.

Without these two perfect men, she knew she would never have dared this much. She cherished every moment with them, and yet, she knew their time together was finite.

Seth seated himself fully, and then, Gowan dictated a pace that made Livia mindless once more. There was no today. No tomorrow. No beginning. No end. There was just the three of them, joined as one. Scandalously enjoying the carnal delights she would only ever share with these two men.

She reveled in their strength as they held her between them. She marveled at their skill, and finally, she gave herself up to the ecstasy, chanting their names as they pushed her to levels of pleasure she had only ever felt with them.

She was theirs. Body, soul, pleasure and heartache. It mixed in a wave of indescribable emotion that made the world spin.

When it began to slow, she found herself lying on her side, between Seth and Gowan, on the pallet the men had made out of their clothes. They were in a tangle of arms and legs, and she had no clear recollection of how she'd gone from them holding her up to them holding her on the ground, but she didn't much care.

Her body was almost boneless in the aftermath of the brightest climax she'd felt in a long time. Not since their last trio session had she felt even close to what she'd just experienced.

She knew they couldn't linger too much longer, but for the moment, she was going to enjoy snuggling with her lovers.

CHAPTER SEVEN

Gowan was basking in the afterglow of pleasure when Genlitha's thoughts came to him. She was still down on the beach with the youngsters, but she'd kept lines of communication open with the Lair and the goings on in the Council session. The news wasn't good.

He got to his feet and began to move, unable to contain his anger.

"What is it?" Livia asked sleepily, still held in Seth's arms.

Gowan hated to ruin the moment, but the so-called men up at the Lair were responsible, and Seth and Livia deserved to know what had happened. He ran a frustrated hand through his hair, turning to look at her in the slanting afternoon light.

"After due consideration, the noble leadership of our Lair has decided to do nothing to help our allies on Gryphon Isle." Gowan was in a fine temper, his voice reverberating off the walls of the cave as he began pacing again.

Seth and Livia sat up. Their idyll was coming to an end, and they all knew it. Livia got up and walked toward the cave opening. She slid her hand across Gowan's shoulders on her way to the water.

Seth followed her in, both of them rinsing off quickly while Gowan tried to settle his temper. The others were taking the news much better than he was. While none were happy with the decision of the Lair's leadership, neither Livia nor Seth were letting their anger get the better of them.

Gowan realized he'd still held out some hope for the leaders. He'd hoped maybe their dragon partners could talk sense into them, but he shouldn't have been so naïve. The dragons were as stuck in the mud as their knights. They didn't want to force their knights' hands into a battle that could very well end them. The dragons were only protecting the knights who had shared so very many years with them.

They were old men. Men who had lived longer than most humans due to the magic of their dragons extending their lifespans. Gowan hadn't been with Genlitha long, but he thought he understood the bond. The dragons didn't want to lose their knights any more than the knights wanted to die, leaving their dragons behind. Gowan really couldn't blame the dragons, when he looked at it that way. They were protecting the ones they loved. They were trying to keep their families together just a little longer.

But the gryphons were in dire straits, and there was an alliance to uphold. Gowan knew that by the time word reached the capital and the order came back to aid Gryffid and his people, Gryphon Isle could be lost.

Livia came back and began to dress, as did Seth. Gowan went out and rinsed off quickly, then rejoined them. He'd made a decision, and he wasn't sure if he should tell the others or not.

"What are we going to do?" Livia asked quietly as they all got back into their clothing.

"We? Nothing," Gowan said, trying to be firm but kind. "Me? I'm going to go help them. Gen and I talked about this. If the Council made the wrong choice, we both feel we have no option but to go rogue and help the gryphons ourselves. We're going to fly out at first light."

"I'd like to go too," Seth said quietly. "I can help the wounded and the fighters on land."

"That you can, my friend," Gowan agreed, neither

encouraging nor denying Seth's words for the moment.

If it came down to it, Genlitha could probably carry two riders the great distance to the island, but Gowan hesitated to get anyone else in trouble with the Lair's leadership. Seth's family lived here, and Gowan didn't want to make trouble for them.

"Has anybody spoken to Hrardorr yet?" Livia asked, putting the finishing touches on her outfit.

She looked as fresh and beautiful as she had when she'd walked over the dunes to meet them, and Gowan was taken in again by her charm. She really was lovely. And kind. And generous.

If he wasn't much mistaken, he was falling madly in love with her, which was a new experience for him. He'd never felt like this before for any other woman. He didn't know how it could work long term, but he vowed to enjoy every moment he had with her and work to keep her in his life for as long as he possibly could. Hopefully—somehow—forever. Though he didn't really see how.

"He was the decisive factor in the battle for Dragonscove," Seth agreed. "He would be very helpful, if he was still inclined to lend a hand."

"Still?" Gowan asked, curious.

"We'd begun discussing this the other night," Seth told him. "But I'm not sure we really thought it would be necessary. We were hoping the leadership would step up and do the right thing."

"I haven't talked to Hrardorr recently," Gowan admitted, "but I think Genlitha has been speaking with him. We were both hoping—like you—that the leadership would make the right call." Gowan sighed, his anger having turned to disillusioned disgust. "We need to talk to Gen and Hrardorr."

Seth had picked up the last evidence of their interlude, and the cave looked much as it had when they'd arrived. Nobody would know they'd spent the most enjoyable hours Gowan had ever spent in a cave there. It would be a memory he would cherish forever.

They were ready to leave, and Livia struck out across the sand, the men following close behind. They could see the dragons in the distance. Genlitha and Hrardorr were huddled together, clearly deep in discussion, while the young blue dragon and Flurrthith played in the sand near the water's edge with the children and Leo.

Livia marched right up to Hrardorr and cleared her throat, gaining the blind dragon's attention.

"Have you decided what we're going to do?" she asked without preamble.

Gowan admired her straight talk. He didn't know many other women who were so direct and clear thinking. At least not any he'd ever bedded. His former bedmates tended to be a bit more fluffy-headed, which he thought was a shame now that he knew the value of a strong woman.

"Help them, of course," Hrardorr's thoughts came to Seth, Gowan, Livia and Genlitha.

"Good," Livia said, nodding in satisfaction. "I truly believe you are the only one who can, Sir Hrardorr. Like you saved Dragonscove. I have just one request. I'd like to be there. I want to travel to Gryphon Isle and help in whatever way I can."

"No!" Gowan didn't realize he was going to shout, but it came out anyway, drawing a stubborn look from Livia.

"Sweetheart, we don't want you in danger," Seth tried to explain, but from the firm set of her jaw, she wasn't having any of it.

"And I'm supposed to just sit here and worry while you're all out there fighting? It'll drive me mad. Better if I'm there and can help in some way, even if only just relaying communications. I can do that, at least." She was winning the argument, though Gowan didn't like it. "Besides, if you don't take me with you, I'll just set sail myself in my little boat, and come right after you, over the water. Flying with you would be much safer, I'm sure. Especially when I get closer to the island...and the pirate fleet."

"Dammit." Gowan had to concede that she had the guts

to do just as she threatened.

"There is one issue," Hrardorr put in quietly, his voice in their minds suspiciously calm. *"I cannot carry anyone on this journey since I'll be landing in the water some distance out and going right to work. And strong as dear Genlitha is, I doubt she could carry more than two such a long distance. Poor Flurrthith barely made it here unencumbered. He is too young to make the journey with a rider."*

"I can carry two. Gowan, of course, and I'm sorry, dear, but Seth would be the next logical choice," Genlitha said, her gentle azure gaze on Livia.

"I can carry Lady Livia." A new voice joined their conversation. It was deep and rumbly. A dragon's voice, but not as calm as Hrardorr or Genlitha.

Of course. Xanderanth.

Gowan looked at the big blue dragon, standing not too far away with his young knight.

"I didn't know it was possible for dragons to eavesdrop on each other," Gowan mused, not quite angry. He'd had an inkling that Xander and Leo would want to come along if they knew Gowan's intent, after all.

"It is possible, but most of us have better manners than to do it," Genlitha scoffed, tilting her head in adult disdain as she looked at the younger pair.

"Your pardon, milady," Leo said aloud, striding forward to meet Genlitha's gaze. "Xander meant no harm. We've both been rather anxious about the situation, and we want in on whatever rescue operation is mounted—whether official or not. Flurrthith's people need help."

"You'll get no argument on that from us, lad," Hrardorr said quietly, Genlitha appearing still too appalled to speak to the young knight. *"What we propose is not sanctioned by the leadership of the Southern Lair. You could get in serious trouble if you join us in this. We are all older than you, with much less to lose. Both you and Xanderanth have long careers ahead of you, and we would not wish you to jeopardize that by acting in haste."*

"Thank you, Sir, but we both feel it's necessary to uphold the alliances made by our king. And after meeting

Flurrthith… Well, Sir, there's just no way we could stay behind and not help him and his people."

Xanderanth stood right beside his knight, in unity with Leo.

"*I can carry two riders,*" Xanderanth put in. "*I'm the strongest dragon of my age group. Everyone says so.*"

Livia's face lit with a triumphant smile. "That settles it then. I'm going." She turned her smile on Xander. "That is, if you will be kind enough to consent to carry me, Sir Xanderanth."

"*It would be my honor,*" Xander replied, bowing his head slightly.

If they were setting off in the morning, Seth had a lot of packing to do. He advised the others on what to bring then rushed back up to the Lair to begin collecting medical supplies. He had to be discreet, of course, but Bronwyn soon figured out what he was up to. How could she not, when he was raiding their shared supplies?

She gave him a nod and a smile, though, assuring him that she'd hold down the fort while he went off to do what needed to be done. He was surprised that she stood behind his decision, but then realized he shouldn't have been. She was a woman of honor and had a very compassionate heart. She'd met Flurrthith and heard his report. She understood. Something had to be done, and the leaders were too old and cautious to do it.

So it fell to Seth and his small group of adventurers. It would either be a fantastic success or way too little, way too late. But at least they would try. Unlike the rest of the Lair.

Bronwyn made him sit down and write a note to his parents. She knew he was riding into danger, and while she might understand why he had to do what he planned, she insisted that he leave some message behind for his parents— both human and dragon—to explain in his own words why he felt the need to go. She claimed his folks would be proud of him for deciding to aid their allies in their time of need, but Seth wasn't so sure. His fathers hadn't been supportive of his decisions for a long time now. He didn't expect that to turn around overnight.

Although...they had been different toward him since the battle in the cove. Not enough time had passed since he'd taken up arms to defend his hometown to know how his fathers' new attitude would affect their relationship, but things had been much more positive since the battle than they had been in years.

Seth wrote the letter Bronwyn required and made her promise not to deliver it until he was missed. With any luck, that might not be until late tomorrow night or even the next day. By then, he'd be on Gryphon Isle, hopefully doing some good.

After that task was done, Bronwyn helped him pack. She also helped him come up with excuses for carrying multiple packs around the Lair. If anyone asked, he was to tell them he was operating on Bronwyn's orders, replacing supplies in the stashes she kept around the Lair for ease of access.

Nobody asked, though, so Seth was in the clear. They'd decided to put everything in Hrardorr's chamber, since nobody dared to visit him and he had a number of empty side chambers that would suit their purposes well.

Seth had a slightly harder time getting enough food for the journey to the island, but he managed it, and by midnight, he'd secured all the needed supplies he could think of in Hrardorr's side chamber. Seth would stay there that night, so as to be ready to go at first light. Actually, Hrardorr and Seth would sneak out before first light, with the supplies.

Hrardorr's coloration was so murky that he wouldn't be easily seen, and nobody really questioned his comings and goings anymore. Not since his prowess in the water had become common knowledge.

Hrardorr would carry the supplies and make a low, slow pass over the beach. Seth would drop the supplies and follow them down. He might take a few bumps and bruises landing on the sand, but it was better than getting dunked in the water when Hrardorr landed in the sea.

The others would meet them on the beach, and they'd take off from there at first light.

It had been up to Genlitha to tell Flurrthith of their plans—and of the Lair leadership's dithering. The leaders hadn't even had the decency to tell Flurrthith themselves. Instead, they'd merely sent a messenger to tell the gryphon that nothing could be decided until word had come from the capital.

Genlitha had calmed the young gryphon after the messenger departed. He was staying in her chamber for the night again, and Genlitha kept Hrardorr and Seth apprised of the gryphon's reaction and mental state. She had managed to calm him after a while, and when Hrardorr had spoken into the gryphon's mind himself, assuring the youngster that he would personally roast the enemy fleet, as he had done when they attacked Dragonscove, Flurrthith finally settled down to rest.

Genlitha watched over the young gryphon through the night. She had promised to alert Seth if he was needed, but Seth slept through the night in Hrardorr's chamber, his rest undisturbed. When Hrardorr woke him gently, in the hour before dawn, Seth was eager to get going.

He readied himself, using the chamber usually set aside for a dragon's knight in Hrardorr's suite, wondering just briefly how it would be if Seth actually was Hrardorr's knight. Or any dragon's knight, actually. He'd wake up in a chamber like this every morning, with a dragon partner of his own heating the entire place to a comfortable temperature, waiting for him just on the other side of the stone wall.

It was a lovely fantasy, but Seth knew Hrardorr would never choose another knight. Particularly not Seth. Still, it would be an honor and a treat to be aloft on Hrardorr's back this morning. He knew such a chance would not come again, and he planned to enjoy the novel experience.

Shrugging off his somewhat sad thoughts, Seth dressed in his dark cloak and got everything ready. He coached Hrardorr silently as they took off and glided down to the beach. The drop of the supplies went well. Seth's own tumble to the sand was about as bumpy as he'd expected, but he came out of it unharmed. Hrardorr set down in the water and walked ashore with Seth's guidance.

Now all they had to do was wait for everyone else to get here. Shouldn't be long now.

Livia had composed a note to her father. She didn't want him tearing apart the town or Lair looking for her. That would be irresponsible on her part, to create such an inconvenience for everyone. Plus, even in his fastest ship, her father could never get to Gryphon Isle before she did on dragonback.

He couldn't really come after her—at least not quickly—so she felt safe enough in telling him where she'd gone and why. Somebody outside the Lair needed to know how shamefully the leaders up there were treating their allies on Gryphon Isle. Maybe her father could get word to the king faster, though she didn't know how. Still, her father was an honorable man. Surely, he would understand her reasons for taking this action.

Maybe.

After he stopped shouting.

If he ever stopped shouting.

She shuddered just thinking about it and was glad she wouldn't be there to see it. If she lived through this adventure, she'd take her lumps if and when it came to it. But first, she just had to try to do the right thing by the gryphons.

She left the note with Rosie to give to her father only after he started looking for her. Rosie was making a lot of extra money these days with all the secrets Livia was asking her to keep, but the housekeeper had her own sort of twisted sense of honor. Livia knew Rosie wouldn't betray her, as long as she kept the extra cash flowing. Once Rosie's loyalty was bought, it stayed bought.

Livia climbed down the trellis from her room just before

dawn and made her way, with her small pack, to the beach. She felt very much as if she was going to meet her destiny. She could only hope it would turn out to be a good one...

Gowan and Genlitha didn't have to come up with any pretense as to why they were leaving the Lair so early in the day. They'd been assigned the far patrols for a while now, and nobody noticed their odd comings and goings anymore.

They left from the main landing ledge only a few minutes behind Hrardorr's departure from a much less-used portion of the Lair. There was no real way to camouflage Genlitha's sky blue hide in the darkness before dawn, so they winged away in the direction of their usual patrol, only veering out over the ocean after they'd lost sight of the Lair's sentries. By that time, the sun was starting to make an appearance, and Genlitha's pale blue scales began to take on their usual reflective properties, making her much harder to spot in the pale sky.

They looped back around to the beach below Dragonscove, finding Hrardorr and the rest of their party already there. Xanderanth and Leo had spent the night at Leo's parents' home, just past the dunes, so they had easily walked the distance to the meeting point, with no one the wiser.

Seth was already doling out the parcels of gear and supplies he and Hrardorr had smuggled out of the Lair. Xanderanth—strong as he was—would carry the lion's share, though Genlitha would take an extra satchel or two, as well. Hrardorr could not carry their supplies for the same reason he could not carry a rider. He would be landing and working in the water as soon as they drew close enough for him to reach the enemy fleet underwater but not be seen going into the sea. Genlitha would judge the distances for him and keep in touch with him if he needed intel from the surface.

Hrardorr's greatest value lay in being the surprise attack. Once the pirate fleet realized dragons were coming to help, they'd probably be looking more closely for the one dragon who had done such damage against them in their last encounter. They'd be watching the water as well as the air.

Flurrthith was the last to arrive, as they'd planned, but he wasn't alone.

Seth came to stand beside Gowan as they watched the familiar dragon and knight come in to land beside the gryphon. It was Seth's sire, Sir Paton, and his flame red dragon partner, Lady Alirya.

Paton jumped down from Alirya's back almost before she'd come to a complete stop, and walked toward his son. His expression was unreadable, but Gowan took some comfort in the fact that he wasn't fuming at them from the get go.

"Father," Seth greeted his sire.

There was no question that Seth was Paton's son, though Paton's fighting partner, Gerard, and the male dragon, Randor, had also been father to Seth as he grew up. But Seth and Paton both had the golden blond hair and good looks that marked them as sire and son. There was no doubt about it. Both were cut from the same cloth.

"Seth." Paton seemed at a loss for words, or perhaps he was trying to figure out where to start. After a false start or two, he finally found his tongue. "We understand why you're doing this, and we're proud of you."

Gowan was, frankly, surprised. Pleasantly so. He'd been half afraid that all the knights of the Southern Lair were frightened old men and youngsters too green to go against them.

"How did you find out?" Seth asked, suspicion in his tone.

"Your mother suspected something and cornered Bronwyn. To her credit, she still didn't hand over your letter until your mother told her that Gerard and Randor flew for the capital last night. They should be arriving there with the dawn."

Better and better, Gowan thought privately.

"Then, you'll come with us?" Seth asked in a hopeful tone, but Paton shook his head.

"We can't. Not until Gerard brings word from the king."

So the insurrection went only so far. Gowan wasn't all that surprised, but he admitted to a bit of disappointment. Still, they'd done the right thing in sending a dragon messenger to the capital. That should have been done in the first place.

"We swore an oath to follow the leaders' commands. We cannot gainsay that. Especially when they are claiming it would be treason to leave the Lair empty so soon after the Dragonscove attack. That's a position we can't argue with, since our first duty is to the people and protection of Draconia." Paton scrubbed one hand through his thick hair in an obvious sign of frustration. "If, however, the king sends other orders—as we expect—we'll be right behind you."

"By then, it could be too late," Seth said quietly, regret and anger in his stance.

Paton reached out and placed one hand on his son's shoulder. "I know, Seth. Which is why you need to go and make sure Hrardorr gets another crack at that pirate fleet. He's the reason Dragonscove still stands, and everyone at the Lair knows it." Paton stepped away from Seth to address the blind dragon directly. "Sir Hrardorr, you are the one who can do the most good for our allies. You have every knight and dragon's admiration for undertaking this task. Goddess go with you. Our reports to the king will detail your bravery and skill."

"I require no praise," Hrardorr said in a dry tone, including them all in his words. *"But I will take your prayers. I am not so cocky as to believe I can pull off the same trick a second time with the same results, but I will do my best."*

"That is all anyone can ask, Sir," Paton said quietly, waiting a moment before turning back to the human contingent. "You must go quickly, before anyone else gets wind of your plans. We'll be lobbying on your behalf every minute, and at the first word from the king, we'll be on our way to help."

"I pray, Sir, that you do not arrive too late," Livia put in, her tone suspiciously droll.

She was angry, Gowan knew, but too much the lady to say anything further. Or maybe she was just too angry to form more sentences. Either way, she turned on her heel and headed for Xanderanth, Leo skipping behind her to keep up.

"Thank you for coming to tell us," Seth said to his father, clearly surprised when Paton reached out and grabbed him into a fierce hug.

"Fight well and be safe," Paton said before letting Seth go.

"You too, Father." Seth clapped his father on the back and then headed toward Genlitha. Gowan followed behind with only a single rueful look at Paton.

Captain O'Dare wanted to hit something, but he resisted the impulse. Instead, he crushed the note his daughter had written in his fist, angry that she had taken matters into her own hands. There were things she didn't know. Things he couldn't tell her. Things that could very easily cost her life!

There was nothing for it now. He knew what he had to do.

Shouting for his second-in-command, he stepped aboard his flagship and was satisfied with the scramble he saw before him. He'd told the men to stay at the ready, and they had, but there was always some chaos before setting sail. He judged the level of chaos and realized they were very nearly ready to go. In less time than he'd hoped.

They would all get bonuses... If they all lived through the next few days.

O'Dare looked around the familiar harbor and noted the activity levels on the ships all around him. Those flying his flag were also in disorder, and he was glad to note most of the captains were visible on their decks, ordering their men around and making ready to sail.

The crossed sabers he'd chosen for his company's emblem were going to take on a whole new meaning after today. He hadn't intended to unveil the fleet he had been quietly building in quite this way, but the choice had been taken out of his hands. His impetuous daughter had made the choice for him, really. Which was another thing he'd have to chat with her about—if they all lived through this.

First, the knight and that young puppy from the Lair. Now this.

Livia was really much too independent for his liking. She wasn't the sweet biddable child he remembered. She only *looked* like her mother. Unfortunately for him, her character was just like his, down to the stubborn streak that ran a mile wide.

He loved her more than anything, but it was impossible to deal with her now. He wanted to keep her safe, and yet, by nearly imprisoning her in the house, he seemed to have driven her into even more dangerous pursuits.

He knew he was at fault, at least partially. He saw it clearly now, after the fact, when it was too late to fix things between himself and his only child.

If she died in this foolish exercise, he would have only himself to blame. Himself and those two upstarts who dared to court her. Captain O'Dare would have his revenge on those two men—dragons be damned. If one hair on Livia's pretty head was harmed, both Seth and Gowan would be answering to the captain.

He gave the order to set sail with grim determination, knowing his other captains were following close behind. The harbor would be almost empty that night. All the O'Dare company ships would be at sea…heading at full speed for Gryphon Isle.

CHAPTER EIGHT

The flight was long, but uneventful. Seth had packed provisions, and the humans snacked along the way. They also threw a few tidbits—fruits and a fish or two—to the fliers. Flurrthith especially thought it was great fun to try to catch a fish hurtling through the air. The little game helped distract the youngster from what lie ahead. At least for a little while.

When the sun was a long way past its high point in the sky, Genlitha spotted the first signs of the island. As they drew nearer, she flew higher, her body camouflaged against detection from below. She orchestrated the flight paths of the others, sending Xanderanth and Flurrthith out to the east, making a wide loop to land on the far side of the island, which was free of the pirate menace from what she observed. She sent Hrardorr lower, to skim the waves before finally signaling him to dive beneath them before anyone on the ships could see him.

The plan was working so far. Now, Genlitha would land—hopefully without being seen—then Gowan and Seth would see what help they could be on the island while Gen went back up to act as high guard. The idea was that either Gowan or Seth could act as liaison between the inhabitants of Gryphon Isle and the dragons.

If they needed more fighters, Gowan would use his sword.

If they needed more healers, Seth would ply his trade. Of course, both men could fight, but one or the other needed to liaise, so that was the division of labor they'd come up with. Livia, meanwhile, would be making her way overland from the secluded cove where she had landed with Xanderanth and Flurrthith. The gryphon and Livia would travel together while Leo and Xander fought under Genlitha's direction.

Flurrthith might be too tired to fly after the long trip to the island, but if he could, he would carry Livia on his back and fly to the wizard's keep. If he couldn't fly, they would walk. Livia would watch over the young gryphon, and he would take care of her on his home island.

Gowan thought it was as sound a plan as they could come up with for now. Everything might change once they got on the ground and met with Gryffid's people, but they would adjust on the fly, if they had to. They were all adaptable, and for now, at least, Livia was as safe as Gowan could make her on this island.

Genlitha was spiraling tightly, making her descent as quickly and stealthily as possible. She kept the sun behind her so nobody looking up could really see her. But at the final approach, she had to pull up sharply so as not to smack into the land too forcefully. She could break bones, as well as kill her two passengers.

Gowan didn't interrupt, letting Gen do her thing. She was the expert flier here. He could only cause problems if he spoke at the wrong moment.

But there was one thing they could do, and that was try to let someone below know that they were coming. In all likelihood, nobody would attack a dragon—especially since Gryphon Isle had sent Flurrthith to bring dragons back—but it wasn't good to startle those below. Some might act without thinking and fire upon Genlitha.

As Gowan thought about it, Seth was already broadcasting a call to those below, carefully shielding Genlitha out of his thoughts, Gowan noted.

"Ho, the island! I am Seth of Dragonscove. A dragon is coming in.

A light blue dragon from high above, at great speed. Hold your fire. We come to help."

"Who is this?" came a rather perturbed voice from somewhere far below.

"Seth of Dragonscove. Apprentice healer from the Southern Lair. We've come to help," Seth repeated.

"You are not a knight?" The voice sounded suspicious now. It was time for Gowan to intervene.

"Seth is a healer and a swordsman. I am Gowan, knight partner to Lady Genlitha, the dragon now on approach. If you act hostilely toward her, she will have no choice but to defend herself. We come in peace, to help defend your island."

He knew he sounded a bit belligerent, but Gen was picking up speed, and he was truly worried about this breakneck approach.

"Where is Flurrthith?" A new voice broke into the conversation, female, worried and gryphon, if Gowan wasn't much mistaken, though he'd never talked mind to mind with a gryphon before.

"Landing on the other side of the island, away from the pirate ships with another dragon," Gowan answered quickly.

"Thank you! Thank you, Sir Knight!" The female gryphon's voice faded, and Gowan suspected she was already flying away toward the far side of the island. If he had to guess, he'd say that had probably been Flurrthith's mother.

"Where are you?" the first voice came back.

"Hurtling toward the keep courtyard too fast for comfort," Gowan replied truthfully. *"We will be down shortly. Do not be alarmed. Genlitha is sky blue and very reflective."*

"I see her now," came a new voice. A gryphon voice. Male, Gowan thought. *"She flies like a mad thing."* The tone was complimentary, though the words were questionable.

"That's Genlitha. The newest flight instructor at the Southern Lair," Gowan said, feeling the need to brag on Gen a little.

"I can see why," the gryphon responded. *"We will clear her path, though she is threading the needle quite well without our help."*

There wasn't any more time to communicate with those

below as Genlitha started backwinging like crazy. The strain on her wings was enormous, and Gowan grew concerned for her wellbeing after this absurd landing. Would Seth have to treat her for muscle strain before they even got into battle? He hoped she knew what she was doing.

Dust rose from the courtyard, but not much. The place was tiled in hard stone and kept conspicuously clean. Probably because gryphons landed here all the time, and the wind generated by their wings would be about the same as a dragon's. It would be dangerous to have debris flying everywhere every time a flier landed. Every Lair was kept clean of debris and sand, as well, Gowan had learned, for just that reason.

Genlitha came to a much softer stop than Gowan expected, her wings out for balance as she came to an abrupt halt on the flagstones of the courtyard. She held her head high, scanning those around them, holding absolutely still, leery of what would come next.

Gowan slid off her back, as did Seth, each of them going to either side, their swords remaining sheathed at their sides, their stances wary. Gowan waited to see what would happen next. The moment was tense while the gryphons all around the courtyard looked hard at the newcomer trio.

Finally, a large mottled brown gryphon came forward to meet Genlitha face to face. He stood a moment, striking a strong pose, then dropped in a gryphonic bow, holding her gaze. Genlitha returned the gesture, meeting him as an equal.

"I have sseldom sseen ssuch magnificent flying, milady," the gryphon spoke aloud, though Gowan instantly recognized his tone as that of the gryphon who had spoken mind to mind with them. "I am Ferator, Captain of the Home Guard Flight."

"I am Genlitha of the Southern Lair," Gen replied, including them all in her speech. *"Thank you for your kind welcome, Captain Ferator. With whom can I trade battle information?"*

"I coordinate defensse of the keep only, milady. For the battle againsst the piratess in the water and on the beachess, you need to sspeak with General Falthith. Or the maker himsself. He comess."

Ferator stepped back, making way for a tall man in a brown robe. He was old, but not decrepit. His eyes sparkled with energy, and his gait was that of a man half his apparent age. Was this the great wizard himself?

"Excellent flying, milady!" the man in the robe said without preamble. He was grinning up at Genlitha, his expression one of admiration and welcome. "I have seldom seen the like."

Genlitha bowed her head respectfully, and Gowan realized this must indeed be Gryffid. Genlitha only showed such respect in the presence of the king or royal family…or the last of the great wizards, apparently.

Gowan looked over at Seth and nodded. They moved as one, as if they had rehearsed, which they most definitely had not. It was just that, after training in sword work together for so long, Seth had begun to pick up on Gowan's non-verbal cues. They would face the wizard together and see where this led.

Gowan wasn't sure what the protocol was in dealing with a wizard. Nothing in his life prior to this had prepared him for such an occasion, but he'd been born of nobility. He remembered the courtly dance. A bit. And Seth could help too. He understood politics far better than Gowan, he freely admitted.

"I am Sir Gowan of the Southern Lair, and this is our healer's apprentice, Seth. We have come to render what aid we can, in whatever capacity you see fit." Gowan bowed respectfully, as did Seth, just on the other side of Genlitha's head. They had moved forward a few paces to meet the man in the robe.

"I am, as you have no doubt guessed, Gryffid. Be welcome in my domain." The man answered their introduction, but did not bow in return. Gowan figured wizards were like royalty in that respect. "Tell me, what news have you brought and what reinforcements?"

Now came the tricky part. Gowan looked at Seth and the younger man stepped a pace closer to the wizard, taking the lead on breaking the news.

"As you know, Dragonscove was attacked recently. The main reason we were able to repel the pirate fleet was a very special dragon named Sir Hrardorr. He is part sea dragon, which means he swims like a fish, but he can also flame like the dragons of our homeland. He crept up on the pirates from below and behind, rising out of the water to flame their sails before they knew what was happening. He is out there, even now, doing reconnaissance below the waves. He will check in soon and tell us exactly what we're up against."

"Genlitha and I function best as the high guard," Gowan put in. "Nobody can see her from below when the skies are in our favor, as they are now."

Gryffid looked at Genlitha with an appraising eye. "I can see that. You have remarkable coloration, milady, and impressive flight skills."

"Thank you, sirrah," Genlitha answered in as meek a voice as Gowan had ever heard out of his dragon partner. If he wasn't much mistaken, Gen was nearly overcome at the idea of speaking with an actual wizard.

"I will not stand in the way of your plan," Gryffid said quietly. "Lady Genlitha, if you wish, you may resume your overwatch." Gryffid stepped back, and both Seth and Gowan worked quickly to take the packs from Genlitha's back so she could fly unencumbered by the supplies for her human friends.

Within moments, she was free of all physical burdens and had launched herself neatly into the sky once again. She seemed relieved to be out of the wizard's presence, which Gowan found surprising, but he'd talk to her about it later.

Gryffid watched her take off with an admiring look, then closed in on Gowan and Seth who were standing together, near the small pile of baggage. The wizard made a quick motion with one hand and three servants moved out of the shadows by the courtyard wall to pick up the luggage and whisk it away, within the walls of the massive keep.

"You will have rooms here, during your stay," Gryffid announced, motioning for Gowan and Seth to fall into step with him as he began walking toward the main archway that led into the keep. "I assume your dragons will be doing reconnaissance for a bit longer before going into action. That gives you just enough time to refresh yourselves from the long journey and learn what's been happening here on the ground so you can share the information with the dragons. How many more dragons are you expecting?"

"Sir..." Seth spoke while the three came to a halt. Gryffid turned to face them, an expectant look on his face. "Sir, the problem is, the leadership of the Southern Lair is waiting to hear from the capital. One of my fathers went to talk to the king personally, but it will be a day at least before orders come back to the Southern Lair. For now, it's just us. Genlitha, Hrardorr, Gowan, me, Lady Livia, who is with the gryphon, Flurrthith, and one other knight-dragon pair—a dark blue dragon named Xanderanth, with his knight partner Leonhardt."

Gryffid frowned. "Where are these others you speak of?"

"They landed on the far side of the island to avoid being seen by the pirate fleet. Flurrthith and Livia are making their way here now, over land if need be. It was a very long flight for young Flurrthith. Sir Xanderanth and his knight will fly at Genlitha's direction once we know where best to place him."

"I see." The wizard looked troubled and a little angry, if Gowan was any judge.

"But Sir, you must understand," Gowan tried to mitigate the damage. "Hrardorr alone is the reason Dragonscove was not overrun. He is worth an entire Lair full of regular dragons. His abilities in the water are unmatched."

Gryffid turned that cunning gaze on Gowan, and he felt a moment of apprehension. What did he know of wizards? He was a simple soldier. He knew sword work and strategy. The politics of wizards and gryphons was beyond him.

Although...he knew dragons now. Thanks to Seth and

Genlitha, he was learning more and more every day. But did that qualify him to meddle in the affairs of wizards?

"If not you, who else?" Genlitha put in, her presence a comforting shadow in his mind, as she had been since the day she'd spoken the words of claim over him.

Buoyed by his dragon partner's faith in him, Gowan felt once again up to the challenge. He hoped.

"Thanks, Gen. I'll do my best."

"That's all we can ask of ourselves, in the end. Your best is better than most people's, Gowan, else I never would have chosen you."

"A sea dragon who can flame, you say?" Gryffid once again had all of Gowan's attention. The wizard's expression was thoughtful.

"More like a land dragon who can swim like a fish," Seth put in helpfully. "Hrardorr is mostly land dragon, but one of his ancestors was a stranded sea dragon who mated with one of ours in Draconia centuries ago. He has very muted coloring, unlike most of our dragons, and more webbing in his claws, which helps propel him through the water. I've never seen an actual sea dragon, but I suppose he gains those attributes from his sea dragon ancestor. But other than that, he is all Draconian. He flies well, flames with the best of them and was a fierce fighter on the border."

"Was?" Gryffid asked, his eyes narrowing in suspicion. "Is he old then? Retired in the seaside Lair like the others?"

"Oh, no, Sir. He is Genlitha's age. Not old at all, for a dragon," Seth was quick to say. "But he did come here to recover. He was injured in the fighting on the border and lost his knight."

"A tragic thing," Gryffid said, compassion in his mutable gaze. "But is he still badly injured? Is he fit for this duty?"

"Sir, the worst injury was to his head. He was hit full in the face by skith venom and could not break free to wash it off for far too long. His eyes..." Seth swallowed, visibly looking for the right words. "He is blind, Sir. But underwater, he isn't. I don't understand how it works, but he can sense things underwater in ways that allow him to see, in a fashion.

It's only above water that he is…somewhat…crippled."

Gryffid breathed a sigh. "Echolocation," he said, the word meaning nothing to Gowan. "It is the way sea dragons see underwater. They emit a pulse of sound, and it comes back to them, telling them the distance to things. It is complicated to us, but natural to them. It seems your dragon friend inherited that aspect of his sea dragon heritage as well. Lucky for us—and for him." Gryffid began walking again. "Come, we have much to discuss. I have a map in the hall that you need to see."

Walking beside the gryphon over the green hills of Gryhpon Isle would have been pleasant if not for the dire circumstances that brought them to this foreign land. Flurrthith had given his all flying back to his homeland and simply couldn't fly another yard. That was fine. Livia liked walking along the countryside. Gryphon Isle was lovely and like no other place she'd ever seen before.

They'd landed in a small cove surrounded by cliffs, out of sight of the enemy ships that nearly surrounded the entire island. Only small sections of coast were free of them—those sections that were either sheer cliffs or those that had dangerous hazards making it impossible for a ship to approach, such as sand bars or rocky outcroppings in the water that could destroy a hull.

The cove they'd chosen was one of the latter. Livia could see the navigation hazards sticking up out of the water all around the mouth of the secluded cove, and some way out into the ocean. And that was just what she could see above the surface. She knew without having to look that there would be even more unseen rocks just below the lapping waves. No way could a ship of any size run that gauntlet and make it to shore in one piece.

The cove was surrounded on both sides by cliffs, so that stretch of coast was free of ships, luckily for Livia and her friends. Xanderanth had landed first, scouting for Flurrthith, who looked completely exhausted. Leo and Xanderanth had stayed for a while to make sure Flurrthith was all right, but after Livia and Flurrthith had made it safely to the top of the sloping cliff face, Xanderanth had launched skyward again, to patrol the far side of the island until called for.

Livia knew he would be called for sooner rather than later. The element of surprise was one of the main things they had going for them and delaying too long would jeopardize that small advantage. She tried not to think too hard about it, concentrating on her task, which was to make sure Flurrthith made it back to his people safely. For all his bravery, he was still a child who might need some help, and Livia was it for now.

"You did so well flying here, Sir Flurrthith," she praised him, hoping to raise his flagging spirits.

She wasn't sure if he was just tired or also depressed. He'd accomplished his mission, but he hadn't brought back a dragon army. She knew he had to be disappointed with that. She was too. She was more than disappointed. She was downright angry with the leaders of the Southern Lair, and if she ever got a chance, she would tell them so in no uncertain terms.

"I'm happy you think sso, Lady Livia. I had hoped..." His words trailed off, but she knew what he was thinking.

"I had too, my friend," she replied, daring to reach out one hand and stroke the long feathers of his wing, folded on his back. He was very soft compared to dragon scale. "But you did your duty and got word to us. That some did not respond as they should is not your fault. Have faith. I know the king will not let his allies suffer alone. Once he hears what's happening here, he will send whatever help he can spare. I know he will. Roland is a good and just king."

"I jusst hope it'ss not all over by then," Flurrthith answered dejectedly.

"Take heart, Sir Flurrthith. You did not see what I did when Hrardorr sent the enemy running from my home town. If Hrardorr lets loose on the pirates, I doubt they will stand against him, even after knowing what he can do from the last time. No, *especially* after last time," she amended her words. "They'd be wise to run at the first sign of him."

"I hope you are right, Missstresss."

Poor Flurrthith. It seemed nothing she could say would raise his spirits. They continued walking along until the crested the hill in front of them, and Livia paused. Below them lay a sloping plain that led downward to a town. A lovely town built in a style she had never seen. Each house was ornate with carved wood and worked stone. There were many marvelous statues and works of art everywhere. In fact, the entire place looked like something out of a fairy story.

And maybe it was.

Livia had heard that only fair folk lived on Gryphon Isle. Fey were the next best thing to immortal, and their artisans were said to be the finest in all the lands, for they had many years during which to perfect their skills.

And then, she noticed a dot in the sky, slowly growing larger.

"Is that a gryphon?" Livia pointed into the distance as Flurrthith raised his head, following the direction of her finger. Despite the name of the island, Livia hadn't seen any other gryphons yet, besides her companion.

Flurrthith didn't answer, but took off running across the grassy plain, as if to meet the newcomer. There was no way Livia could keep up. Once his cat body got going, he was bounding away faster than her human legs could manage. She watched him go, concerned, but she realized when the faraway dot resolved itself into a large gryphon that Flurrthith was happy to see his friend.

The flying gryphon landed and then enfolded Flurrthith in her wings, holding him close for long moments. Livia could see the older gryphon was female now that it was closer, and she looked enough like Flurrthith for Livia to think maybe it was his mother.

A tear came to her eye at the happy reunion as Livia continued jogging toward them. She didn't want to intrude on the moment, but she also didn't want to get left behind in case Flurrthith was so overcome with rejoining his people that he forgot all about her. She could always get help in the town below, but it was still very far away, and she'd have a heck of a time explaining who she was and how she'd arrived there. She'd much rather stick with the gryphons, if at all possible.

CHAPTER NINE

What Gryffid had called a map was a thing of magic. A glowing, transparent representation of what was happening in real time on the waters and beaches of his coastline. Seth had to consciously shut his mouth, his jaw having dropped open in astonishment at first sight of the wizard's so-called map.

Gowan seemed less impressed with the wizard's magic and more troubled by what it showed him. He had a scowl on his face as he watched the movement of the ships and the deployment of the gryphons.

"The red ships are the ones we've already seen shooting diamond-bladed weapons. They seem to have an endless supply of the things," Gryffid said, sounding extremely put out.

"Skithdron was being supplied with diamond blades by the Northern barbarians. We believe the pirates got them from Skithdron," Seth explained.

"I wouldn't be surprised," Gryffid replied, grimacing.

"The orange ships have only used more conventional weapons to this point. They may be hiding diamond blades somewhere aboard, but have not used them yet. And the yellow ships have not yet engaged with weapons. They're either scouts or reserve. Or both." Gryffid summed up the action on his living, glowing map.

"Seth?" Hrardorr's voice came to him suddenly.

"I'm here. What news?" Seth said quickly, eager to know what the dragon had found.

"I believe I've identified all those ships holding diamond blades," Hrardorr reported. *"There are quite a few."*

"We are with the wizard, Hrardorr," Seth told the dragon. *"He's got this amazing map of the ships they have confirmed shooting the blades, and those that have not."*

"It would be good to compare notes," Hrardorr said.

"Sir, I'm talking with Hrardorr—" Seth began, but Gryffid held up one hand.

"I heard," Gryffid said aloud, then switched to silent speech. *"Sir Hrardorr, this is Gryffid. First, thank you for coming here to help us. Now, can you see this?"* Gryffid opened his eyes wide and concentrated on the glowing map. Seth could only assume he was somehow sending the image to Hrardorr, though Seth wasn't sure how such a thing could be accomplished.

"You are a mightily gifted wizard if you can make me see through your eyes, sirrah." Hrardorr's tone was full of emotion, coming through to all of them. *"Some of those yellow ships carry the blades,"* he said in a stronger voice as he seemed to regain his equilibrium.

"As I suspected. Can you show me which..." Gryffid's eyes unfocused for a moment, then he came back. *"Yes, I see."* He waved his hand, and several of the yellow ships turned red, as did a few of the orange ones. *"Thank you, Sir Hrardorr. My generals have a duplicate of this map in their meeting place, and it, too, has been updated. Now, what is your plan?"*

"I would gladly fight at your direction, sirrah." Hrardorr's tone was as awed as Genlitha's had been, though he didn't seem quite as cowed by the wizard's presence.

"And I bow to your superior ability and knowledge of the enemy, Sir," Gryffid said in a respectful tone. *"You have faced them before. We will support your action, whatever course you decide to take."*

"I will start by flaming them, then work from below where I can see. I can disable their ships from beneath in many ways." Hrardorr

sounded as if he was looking forward to the battle, which made Seth happy for the dragon, even under such circumstances.

"When the ships start to become disabled, the men on them will make for the shore," Gowan put in. *"That's what happened in Dragonscove. Your fighters will have to meet them on the beaches."*

"We have already been engaging them in such ways, though not in great numbers," Gryffid said.

"That will change," Seth told him. *"Once Hrardorr begins his work, many men will make for shore all at once. Your people must be ready for it."*

"I can help there, Sir," Gowan volunteered. *"Genlitha can report from above, and I can help deploy the teams to the right spots with her input."*

"Then, that is what we will do." Gryffid stood to his full height and seemed to gather his resolve. "Captain Ferator will assign one of his gryphons to take you, Sir Gowan, to the front lines. There is a headquarters set up just beyond our widest stretch of beach. You will work with the captains of our fighting forces there. When you are certain all is ready, you may begin the operation, at your—and Sir Hrardorr's—discretion." The wizard's eye fell to Seth. "Now then, what about you?"

Seth gulped, facing the great man. "I was going to be the liaison between your people and Hrardorr, but if you can communicate with him as easily as a knight, then there is no need. I am a healer of dragons, Sir, but I would be happy to help your gryphons or anyone else, if there is need."

"He is also the swordsman who led the defense of Dragonscove from the cannon batteries in the harbor," Gowan put in helpfully. "If you need more fighting men, Seth could definitely help. And he can coordinate with Hrardorr, since they are close friends."

Gryffid's eyes lit with interest. "Then, that is what he shall do. We have enough healers for now. Goddess willing, we will not have too many more serious injuries, and your services in that area will not be needed." Gryffid looked worried for a moment, but turned to a servant who had been standing in the shadows. "Alert Captain Ferator that these two will need fast transport to the beach."

Less than ten minutes later, Gowan was settling in with the tall blond warriors who led the two-legged fighters of Gryphon Isle. Gowan pointed Seth toward the leader of the winged contingent, and Seth understood his role. He would deal with the winged creatures—liaising between Hrardorr and the gryphons where needed.

Frankly, Seth thought he got the better end of the deal, but then again, Gowan seemed right at home among the fair-skinned warriors of the fair folk. They spoke the same language—that of warriors the world over—and were soon fast friends.

Meanwhile, Seth approached a gryphon who had been pointed out as the general of the fighting wing with caution. He made his ritual bow and waited to be noticed. The male gryphon was huge, much larger than Flurrthith, but they shared a bit of coloration.

Seth couldn't guess too much about his wingspan, since both wings were folded neatly across the general's back at the moment. Still, just going by his body size, those wings must be quite broad and powerful. Suddenly, the beak turned, along with the rest of his face, and the gryphon's eyes were set on Seth. Was it wrong to feel like prey?

Seth swallowed hard and did his best to stand his ground. It would not do to show fear or weakness to such a strong and intelligent predator.

"You are the healer they've ssent me, eh?" the general asked rhetorically.

"I am Seth, apprentice healer of the Southern Lair. I am your liaison to Sir Hrardorr, our best weapon against the pirates," Seth introduced himself, giving credit where it was due, to Hrardorr.

"I look forward to sseeing thiss weapon in action," the gryphon replied, and Seth couldn't tell if his tone was impatient, annoyed or just factual. Seth wasn't great at interpreting full grown gryphons' moods yet—if he ever would gain such a skill. The gryphon general's gaze dropped to the sword and sheath strapped around Seth's waist. "You carry a blade? Odd for a healer, no?"

"I'm also a student of the sword. Sir Gowan taught me and gifted me this blade just before the battle of Dragonscove," Seth replied honestly.

"It hass been blooded?" The gryphon looked skeptical.

"Yes," Seth said quietly, remembering the lives he'd been forced to take and the many injuries he'd inflicted on the invaders before it was all over.

"Ah." The gryphon nodded sagely. "Well, then. Perhapss you will be of ssome usse, after all. Tell me, when doess thiss ssecret weapon plan to sstart working?"

"Hrardorr?" Seth sent his silent message quickly, hoping for an update.

"I am nearly in position," came the reply just as fast. *"Is the beach defense ready? I'm going to start on the eastern point and work my way down the beach."*

"We're ready on the beach," Gowan told them, Hrardorr having brought him into the conversation.

"Sir Hrardorr is nearly in position, and Sir Gowan reports that the two-legged defenders are ready on the beach," Seth said, reading surprise in the way the gryphon general reared back a bit. "Hrardorr wants to know if the winged contingent is ready."

"We are," the general said. "Though we cannot do much about the sshipss with thosse evil weaponss, we are more than able to defend the land. The two-legged, asss you call them, are the firsst line of defensse, and we will block any that might get through a weak sspot."

Seth relayed the gryphon's words to Hrardorr.

"Good. Keep the gryphons away from the water for now. I don't need their help just yet, but if they are able to drop boulders from great heights with any accuracy, that could help later, once I'm clear," Hrardorr told Seth in return.

Seth passed on Hrardorr's words to the gryphon, drawing an unexpected laugh from the giant cat-bird.

"That we can do," the general agreed. "When your dragon friend hass cleared the sscene."

"I'm starting my first run," Hrardorr told Seth at that moment, and a split second later, Seth saw the dragon erupt from the water, shooting flames into the sails of the ships at the far end of the beach.

"There he is!" Seth pointed as a cheer went up from the two-legged defenders down on that end of the long, wide beach.

The gryphon's beak clacked open in what Seth thought was surprise. "I never thought to ssee the like."

Hrardorr felt alive again as he hadn't since the last battle. He was a warrior. This was what he lived for. If dragons could grin, he'd have been wearing the widest smile in the universe as he flamed the sails on a half dozen ships on his first run.

He dove back down into the water, preparing for his next flame run. He'd have to hit them hard and fast before they could turn those dragon-killer weapons on him.

He leapt out of the water and did a second run, farther down the beach. He'd targeted the most dangerous ships for his first few runs. If he destroyed their catapults and sank the stores of diamond-bladed weapons, so much the better for everyone with wings.

On his third flame run, a blade nearly clipped him as he dove back down into the water. The enemy had adjusted. No more flame runs just yet. No, now, he would go to work below the water line, as he had in the cove, to disable the most important ships—those with the most deadly armament. He would ruin their rudders so they couldn't steer. He'd poke holes in sensitive places with his talons. He would sink what he could and damage the rest.

He could *see* underwater, after a fashion, and stars knew he could navigate in the depths much better than in the air. This was his battleground now. If he could, he would have made it his home, but the one thing that he hadn't inherited from his sea dragon ancestor was the ability to breathe underwater.

Hrardorr had no gills. Oh, he could hold his air for a long, long time. Nearly an hour, if he'd judged it right, but at some point, he had to surface to get a gulp of air into his lungs. True sea dragons, he believed, didn't have to do that. Although…he'd never met a real sea dragon, so he was just going by the old tales he'd heard of his ancestor.

Hrardorr set to work on the hull of the nearest ship—one that was loaded with deadly diamond-bladed spears. He attached himself to the underside of the ship like a giant barnacle, trying to crush his way through the thick wood with his talons.

Something brushed past his tail, making him bleed, and Hrardorr realized archers were shooting diamond-tipped arrows down into the water. He'd have to be more careful about his wings and tail. He'd have to keep all of his body directly under their hulls while he worked and dive deep before moving on to his next victim.

As it was, he was bleeding, but it was only a flesh wound, as far as he could tell. Seth would fix it up for him when this was all over, Hrardorr thought fondly. Seth always set him right. He was a good lad.

"What are you doing?"

Hrardorr stilled as an unknown voice came to him…from below. He turned his head, using that underwater sense he had to distinguish several large bodies swimming directly below him. Dragon-shaped bodies, if he wasn't much mistaken.

"Hello. I'm Hrardorr. I'm helping those living on Gryphon Isle to defend their shores from the men in these ships. They have been shooting at dragons and gryphons and have killed several with their deadly spears."

"Killing dragons?" came the curious voice again in his mind, tinged with concern now. *"And gryphons?"*

"And people," Hrardorr confirmed, letting go of the hull

he'd been menacing and swimming a little deeper. *"Are you sea dragons?"*

"Of course," the melodic voice answered. *"Aren't you?"*

"I'm only part sea dragon. One of my ancestors was of your kind, but my other forbearers were fighting dragons from the land of Draconia."

"I am Salwinalia," the soft voice continued. *"I've never met a land dragon before. Can you really breathe flame?"*

"Isn't that what drew you here? The light from above? Those are my flames, torching the invading fleet right now. But they have deadly weapons on these ships, and I cannot chance another flame run right now, so I'm working from below."

"How? Can we help? We like the people and gryphons on this island. They have always been kind to us. We would like to help, if we may, but we have never battled people in ships before. Mostly we just leave them alone, and they do the same."

"I would be grateful for your help. It is a lot for one dragon to disable an entire fleet. I am coordinating with those above, who are fighting the invaders on the surface, but if we can disable their ships, it will be a major step in the victory. It is dangerous, however. I have already been hit by one diamond-tipped arrow on my tail. You must keep all of your bodies hidden by the ship you are working on, then dive deep before coming out of its shadow to move to the next. Understand?"

"Yes, Hrardorr. We're fast learners. And a little impetuous. There goes Neri."

Hrardorr sensed one of the pack of sea dragons break away, heading for the closest hull. He wished he could see her with his eyes, but underwater, his other senses were almost as sharp as his sight had been above. He sensed when the small sea dragon turned its tail on the hull, using the sharp points on its tail to poke massive holes in it.

That ship was destined for the bottom of the sea, no doubt about it. When two-legged bodies started jumping off the sinking ship, the sea dragon created a wave under them that swept them onto the beach. Hrardorr wasn't sure how the dragon had generated the wave, but it was definitely a handy trick.

The small sea dragon called Neri came back to the group and was congratulated by the others. They seemed a happy bunch, game to try the same trick.

"Was that all right?" Salwinalia asked Hrardorr, a bit of amusement in her tone.

"That was fantastic," Hrardorr told her, glad of the chance to meet actual sea dragons and even happier that they were willing to help him, and the inhabitants of Gryphon Isle. *"And sweeping the men into shore is a good thing. If we don't have to kill them, we should not,"* Hrardorr told them solemnly, not sure what ethical standard sea dragons lived by, if any.

"What will happen to them?" Salwinalia asked, sounding curious.

"The people on shore will make them prisoners, question them, and then send them back to their homelands when this is all over, if at all possible."

"That is a good fate. I can see why you ally yourself with the creatures on the island. I have always thought the gryphons were noble beings, and the fair folk must be, as well, to be allied so closely with the gryphons."

"So you'll help me then?" Hrardorr wanted to get back to the business of sabotage, though this interlude hadn't taken long at all.

"Oh, yes. It looks like great fun."

"Dangerous fun," Hrardorr reminded Salwinalia.

"We are not unfamiliar with danger. Living in the sea is not all fun and games, though we try to make it that way."

Hrardorr thought he had just gained a small insight into the way of sea dragons, but he wanted to learn so much more. Still, this was an amazing start and a fortuitous encounter.

"Excellent. Then, let us begin."

"Lead the way, Hrardorr. We're with you and will follow your lead."

Seth almost didn't believe it when Hrardorr told him and Gowan that the underwater campaign had just found a few unlikely recruits. He passed along the information to the gryphon general and wished he had time to discuss the new development with Gowan, but things were going to happen really fast from here on out. The speed with which the sea dragons took out a large part of the attacking fleet was simply astounding.

And the sea dragons did something to usher the swimming men onto shore. The defenders had their hands full, trying to corral those who came ashore. Some wanted to fight. Many just wanted to surrender and have their feet on solid ground, without fear of drowning or being eaten by whatever was macerating their ships.

The carnage of splintered wood and sinking ships was incredible. Even having seen what happened in Dragonscove, Seth was impressed by the massive scale of the destruction happening now. Hrardorr's sea dragon friends were pretty amazing, and Seth hoped he might catch a glimpse of one of those elusive creatures when this was all done. He'd love to see where that special part of Hrardorr had come from. The part that made him so much more than the other dragons Seth had grown up with.

Hrardorr was special. Seth had felt that way from the moment he'd first seen the blind dragon being led into the Lair.

"Your dragon and his friendss are doing a great job," General Falthith said to Seth, between sending his people out in pairs and squads to deal with the prisoners and the few who kept trying to fight on land. "Perhapss it iss ssafe enough now for uss to fly and help from above?" the general asked, cocking his beak to the side in what Seth interpreted as a gryphon expression of a question.

"I'll ask," Seth replied quickly, relaying the question to Hrardorr. But the dragon was quick to reply in the negative. "Too many of those ships still have dragon-killing weapons aboard, Sir. The best use of your strength is here on land for now, or so Sir Hrardorr advises."

The gryphon seemed disappointed but resigned. Seth felt

he was getting better at interpreting the lay of his feathers and the slight ruffle of his wings, not to mention the position of that dangerous-looking beak. The more Seth was around the gryphons, the more he recognized certain traits they had in common with dragons.

Just at that moment, Hrardorr broke the surface, flaming for all he was worth toward one of the larger ships that had been resistant so far to the attack from below. Bright orange and yellow flames shot from his mouth as he arced through the air in a sideways dive that brought him out of the water only long enough to loose his fiery breath on the enemy. They barely had time to get a shot off at him, so fast did he move, but Seth saw the arrows follow Hrardorr back into the water and grew concerned. The tips of those arrows gleamed and sparkled in the firelight.

"Are you all right?" Seth held his breath waiting for a response from the dragon.

"Mostly," Hrardorr said after a slight delay. *"A couple of those arrows hit me, but I don't think it's anything serious. You can take a look when we're done here."*

Seth frowned. He had no idea how much longer the battle would take. He didn't like the idea of Hrardorr continuing to fight while injured. Hrardorr couldn't see to really assess his injuries, and he'd fought while in agony before. That's how he'd become blind in the first place. Seth wanted to tell the dragon to break off and come ashore so Seth could take a good look at him, but he knew he could not.

For one thing, Hrardorr was enjoying this too much, and Seth would not take it away from him. For another, Hrardorr was needed. He was the only one who could really *do* something against these pirate ships. And he had somehow gotten sea dragons to help too. If Hrardorr left the battle, would they abandon it too? Seth wasn't sure, but it was important to keep all the allies they could working on the problem, while they had them. Which meant Hrardorr's injuries would have to wait.

Seth tried to console himself with the thought that he

would take the best care of Hrardorr any dragon had ever received when he was finally free to be treated. Seth would find him the best meal he could and set up Hrardorr in as comfortable a wallow as he could devise, waiting on the dragon hand and foot. If Hrardorr let him.

Seth would make sure Hrardorr let him. Somehow.

"There are sshipss on the horizon, coming from the direction of the mainland," the general told Seth, shaking him out of his reverie.

Seth realized that the gryphons had eyesight like dragons—maybe better, considering their bird-like heads. They could see things mere humans could not.

"Can you see what flags they are flying?"

Seth knew the emblems of most of the ships that frequented Dragonscove. If the approaching ships were friendly, they would be flying their colors. The pirates, by contrast, flew no flags at all, and some had the black sails of those who crept about at night, not wanting their movements tracked.

"They all fly the ssame flag in different ssizess. A dark flag with crossssed ssaberss," the gryphon general reported.

Could it be?

"Sir, that is most likely the flag of Captain O'Dare. He is a resident of Dragonscove, and his daughter is the one who is even now making her way to the keep over land with your envoy, Sir Flurrthith. It's just possible that her father decided to sail here to help." *And to chase after Livia,* Seth thought privately.

"We musst have confirmation," the general snapped out. "If it iss the enemy, other planss will have to be made."

"Understood, Sir. I believe I know how we can confirm this. We have another dragon and knight aloft who have been holding off until Sir Hrardorr could take out the most dangerous weapons to dragonkind. I propose we send Sir Leo and Sir Xanderanth out to meet the oncoming ships. They will recognize ships from Dragonscove, and Sir Leo knows Captain O'Dare personally."

"A good plan. Ssee to it." The gryphon general turned away, consulting with his lieutenants.

They gryphons were helping contain the prisoners, but there were a lot of them, and the situation was highly volatile. Some of the prisoners were trying to sneak away, and the gryphons and fair folk were having to chase them down.

Captain O'Dare fumed as they raced toward Gryphon Isle. The place was too damned far away. He used his spyglass to help him see, but all he could make out were the masts of many ships surrounding the island. Some looked too low in the water—as if the ships were sinking—but he didn't see any dragons or gryphons flying above to explain it.

Perhaps the blind dragon was doing what reports said he'd done in Dragonscove. If he was attacking from below to spare the flying targets those diamond bolts, he was making good progress.

A dark spot in the sky caught the captain's attention, and he focused on it. It was a dragon, growing larger as it flew toward him. It was dark blue and powerful, its wings propelling it quickly through the sky.

Captain O'Dare watched it come. He thought he recognized the dragon as one that had been frolicking on the beach with the Stuart children, the eldest of whom had been chosen as a knight. If so, that would make this Sir Xanderanth and his knight was Sir Leonhardt. O'Dare knew of them. He had employed Leo's father since before the lad was born and trusted him to oversee the land-based side of his trade business.

The dots began to join together in O'Dare's mind. Livia had been working with Stuart and had helped the family resettle nearer to Dragonscove when their eldest son and his dragon partner were assigned to the Southern Lair. No doubt Livia knew Sir Leo and the dark blue dragon. And now, that same dragon was approaching his ship. O'Dare planned to ask that young upstart knight a thing or two, if he got the chance.

And it looked like he would. The dragon approached, flying around the fleet O'Dare had put together. Now, O'Dare could see the small figure of the knight atop the dragon's shoulders. It was Leo, the eldest son of his long-time employee.

"Ahoy, the *Olivia*," the knight called out as the dragon made a slow, spiraling pass around O'Dare's flagship, named for his late wife.

"Ahoy!" the bosun called back, acknowledging the hail.

"Permission to come aboard?" the knight shouted on his next pass.

O'Dare didn't believe the cheek of the youngster. How in the world did he expect to board? They were under full sail. If he splashed into the water, they'd have to stop and turn around to get him. There was also no place his dragon could land aboard the ship by the captain's judgment. And if he tried to jump onto the deck, he'd go splat more likely than not. What was the young pup thinking?

"Captain?" the bosun looked up at O'Dare, seeking how to reply.

"If he can manage it without killing himself, he's welcome aboard," O'Dare said, wanting to shrug, but resisting the impulse. Fleet captains did not shrug.

"Permission granted!" the bosun shouted upward to the circling dragon.

The bosun was in charge of the men in the rigging and on the deck. This particular officer—a fellow named Penwith—had the most penetrating voice in O'Dare's crew, so he was also the one who answered hails. He was fourth in line for the captain's job should something happen to O'Dare and his other officers, so he had quite a bit of authority on the vessel.

What followed was the craziest thing O'Dare had ever seen. First, the dragon matched pace with the ship, gliding between wing beats until he was traveling at the same speed as the ship. O'Dare watched between the sheets of the sails, which were fully extended, as did everyone else who could spare a glance in the entire fleet.

Then, the dragon maneuvered lower...and lower still...until he was so close to the masts and the crow's nest he could reach out and touch them. Which he did, much to everyone's surprise. The dragon reached out to touch the tallest mast, on which the crow's nest sat, and O'Dare held his breath. If the dragon exerted too much pressure, the mast could snap, and they'd all be done for.

But the massive dragon had more finesse than O'Dare would have credited. He merely touched the mast, still matching speed with the fast-moving ship. And then, the knight sprang into action, in the most daring move yet.

Sir Leo stood on the back of his dragon partner, then began to walk, calm as you please, down over the dragon's shoulder and onto his outstretched forearm. He fairly danced across the dragon's slick scales, right to his talons and then dropped, light as a feather, into the crow's nest, next to a startled young crewman.

The dragon let go and veered away from the ship, but didn't go too far, still keeping pace, while he also kept a watchful eye on his knight. The knight didn't stop in the crow's nest, but worked his way down the rigging as if he'd been doing it all his life. Perhaps he had. O'Dare would have to ask Leo's father where the young man had apprenticed before being chosen as a knight. He'd bet the youngster had gone out on at least one sea voyage, judging by the way he climbed down the rigging.

The crew was stunned by what they'd just seen, and several nodded to Leo as he passed them when he finally made it to the deck. They knew talent when they saw it, and who didn't appreciate such a show of daring and bravery? Not to mention the absolute trust between knight and dragon. O'Dare hazarded a guess that he'd never see the like again.

"Welcome aboard, Sir," Penwith said to Leo as he arrived below the quarterdeck.

Only a select few were allowed on the quarterdeck with the captain when the ship was under sail. O'Dare noticed that

Sir Leo hesitated, looking to the captain to give him the nod. He was sure of it now. The lad had been aboard a sailing ship before.

O'Dare gave him the signal, and Sir Leo bounded up the steps to the quarterdeck, making a slight bow of respect when he greeted the captain and his officers. O'Dare returned the gesture. Leo might be young, but he was a knight and deserved respect on that basis alone. Dragons did not choose their knights lightly and Leo must've had something special in him to make the magnificent blue beast still flying above pick him.

CHAPTER TEN

"Captain O'Dare, sir, I was sent to make sure it really was you on approach. The gryphons spotted you a while back and were concerned your ships might be more pirates," Leo reported in a rush as he faced the famous Captain O'Dare.

"What news of my daughter?" O'Dare got to the heart of the matter first. Everything else could wait.

"We left her on the far side of the island with Sir Flurrthith. She is accompanying him over land to the wizard's keep." Leo was surprised the captain, who had a reputation for being hard as nails and somewhat neglectful of his family, chose to ask after Miss Livia first.

O'Dare merely nodded, giving nothing away of his reaction to the news. "How goes the battle?"

"Sir Hrardorr is destroying the pirate ships with the unexpected aid of a group of sea dragons," Leo reported, still stunned by the idea himself. He and Xander both wanted to get a look at a real sea dragon, but they were very hard to spot, swimming so deep. "The fair folk and Sir Gowan and Seth are battling on the beaches while the gryphons are seeing to the prisoners, staying out of range of any potential diamond-bladed arrows or spears. Which is why they ordered Xanderanth and me to come out here. No fliers are being let within range of the dragon killers."

"A wise precaution," O'Dare agreed stiffly. He'd twitched one eye—perhaps involuntarily—when Gowan and Seth were mentioned. Leo didn't really know why, but the captain seemed to hold them in dislike. "What of the wizard?"

"He coordinates the battle in his keep," Seth answered. "Though his gryphon general oversees his own forces, as the Captains of the Guard have charge over their troops. The main force is on the beach you see before you. It is the largest swath of shore that is able to land ships. There are, however, several smaller incursions on other parts of the shoreline. Once Sir Hrardorr and his new friends finish with the main portion of the fleet, I believe they intend to do the same in the other areas. If I might suggest, sir, your ships could be of help in those areas, if you have come to join the fight."

The cheeky puppy. Sir Leo was nothing like the timid child O'Dare remembered meeting on occasion when he dealt with his father. He was growing into his knighthood well. His father must be beaming with pride.

O'Dare was inclined to like the young knight, if for no other reason than his feat of acrobatics and the courage he'd demonstrated just coming aboard. After talking with him a bit, he was even more disposed to befriend the young man.

Why couldn't Livia find a nice boy like this to get involved with instead of those two imbeciles? One was a soldier thug, it was plain to see, and the other a wimp who had chosen the safe healer's path instead of what he should have been doing all along—fighting to protect his homeland, like young Leo here.

Of course, Leo was probably a few years younger than Livia, come to think of it, so that probably wouldn't work out. It still seemed strange to O'Dare to have left his daughter a child and come back to find her a young woman, bred in the image of her mother...and with all of her father's character faults, apparently.

"It shall be as you suggest, Sir Leonhardt. Will you communicate with the others on land and find where best to place us? We will sail at the wizard's command."

Leo really shouldn't have been so surprised. Or, if he was, he should have hidden it better. But that would come in time, O'Dare supposed. The young knight had many years—if he didn't fall in battle—to learn his craft. The fine art of diplomacy would be among the things his elders, and time, would teach him.

O'Dare watched Sir Leo's face closely, noting no real change in his ability to focus even as he held a conversation, purely in his mind, with either his dragon or the others on shore, O'Dare wasn't sure which. A few seconds later, Leo blinked and refocused on the ship.

"Is it possible to split your group in two, sir? There are two areas of concern at the moment, on nearly opposite sides of the island." Leo waited with seeming patience for O'Dare's reply.

"Lieutenant Freistan," O'Dare called to one of his officers. The man was at his side in a moment. "Send signal to Captain Livingstone. We're flanking."

They'd already drilled for such situations. Livingstone was a capable commander who stood next in line to be commodore of the entire fleet O'Dare had put together. He could easily take half the force and work independently of the rest of the fleet.

Within a few minutes, signals had been sent back and forth between the two ships, and in consultation with the land contingent through Sir Leo, they came up with a workable plan. A few minutes after that, the fleet split roughly in half, one portion heading for the east side of the island, the other for the west.

O'Dare swung around to the east, since Leo claimed that was the side closest to the wizard's keep. If at all possible, O'Dare planned to go ashore when the battle was done and retrieve his wayward daughter.

Though, if what he suspected was true about the pirate fleet, he might be obliged to leave her in the wizard's company. That might just be the safest place for her.

It was as he swung around the eastern side of the island that Captain O'Dare saw something that sent a cold chill down his spine. It was a ship, speeding away under full sail, already almost beyond visual range.

O'Dare had to use his spyglass to see if what he feared was true. With a sinking heart, he recognized the ship he'd never wanted to see again.

None of the masts he'd seen so far in the enemy fleet sported a flag, which was strange in itself. Every ship flew something to identify itself to its fellows—unless it was up to no good. But on this side of the island, that escaping ship was one O'Dare recognized. A ship that bore the scars of previous battles.

It was O'Dare himself who had given the orders for his cannons to let loose on his enemy. O'Dare had put those scorch marks on the timbers and caused the patchwork of new wood beams to be added after his cannons had blasted holes in the ship time and time again. And still it sailed—the thrice-damned rival O'Dare had been fighting this past decade and more.

Fisk. Former friend, frequent partner until O'Dare had finally realized what Fisk was up to—no good. The traitor Fisk continued to sail, some said, because he'd made a deal with a demon. O'Dare didn't know for sure, but he knew he would keep hunting Fisk as long as one of them still breathed.

He owed Fisk a deadly debt. He would repay the bastard in kind. The lying, cheating bastard who had turned Captain O'Dare into a pirate.

With the unexpected aid of Captain O'Dare's fleet of ships, the tide of the battle soon turned. Between the sea dragons and the mighty roar of ship-mounted cannons, none of the winged creatures had to take chances with those diamond blades. Gowan suspected Hrardorr would do the same as he'd done in Dragonscove, collecting the weapons off the sea floor and bringing them ashore to be disassembled and made into harmless stones.

Judging by how many of the ships were thought to be carrying the deadly weapons, the haul in diamonds would be enormous. Gowan hoped the wizard would be willing to share some of the loot with the merchant ships who had come to their aid. A small fortune might help ease Livia's father's anger a bit. Maybe.

Speaking of which, the fair folk had things well in hand when Gowan and Seth were summoned back to the keep to meet again with Gryffid. Livia had been in touch, as well, telling them all that Flurrthith's mother had come to meet them and had given Livia a ride to the keep, her young son having recovered enough by then to make the short flight the remaining distance to the keep.

Genlitha was still running high patrol, reporting the enemy's retreat directly to Gryffid. She seemed to have lost a bit of her awe of the wizard, though she still spoke of him with obvious reverence. Xanderanth was escorting Livia's father as he made for the shore and the keep. It seemed the sea captain had come for his daughter and would storm the wizard's keep to get her.

Gowan wondered how that would go over. If Captain O'Dare insisted on being an ass to the last of the great wizards, he could very well end up turned into a toad. And wouldn't Gowan pay to see that.

Livia ran into his arms when Gowan entered the keep. Seth wasn't far behind Gowan, but he'd have to wait for his hug and kiss. Gowan was enjoying having Livia in his arms again too much to let her go quickly.

A throat clearing rather pointedly somewhere in the great hall made him look up. He met the twinkling eyes of the wizard, Gryffid. He seemed indulgent, but only to a point. Caught, Gowan let Livia go with a final kiss, leaving her to Seth. Gowan, meanwhile, went to greet the wizard, who was smiling.

"Sir Gowan, your dragon friend is everything you claimed and more. How he got the sea dragons to help, I would love to know, but I won't interrupt him while he's working so diligently on my island's behalf."

"I'm not sure how he managed it either," Gowan admitted, shaking the wizard's hand. "But it was a blessing. The force that came against your island was larger even than that which attacked Dragonscove. It felt like they were making an all-out assault here."

Gryffid frowned. "Yes, I believe you are right, but I have not yet figured out why or what they could possibly hope to gain here. I thought everyone realized it was my home and that the fey and the gryphons would defend it vigorously."

"Aye, Sir. It seemed a strange attack to me, and most of my life has been one battle or another." Gowan sighed, scratching his head while he tried to puzzle out what could have been driving the pirate fleet to such lengths.

"Which is why I asked you here. My people are questioning the prisoners as we speak, but you have seen this fleet of brigands in action before. I was hoping you and your fellows might be able to shed more light on what could have motivated them."

Gryffid ushered them all toward a table to one side of the great hall that had been laid with food and drink, along with plates and utensils, buffet style. He invited them to take what they wanted and then sit with him at another table, in a group of empty tables with chairs, off to one side.

Only then did Gowan realize how hungry he was. Adrenaline had kept him going all day and throughout the battle, but he hadn't eaten since the snacks they'd snarfed down while flying, many, many hours ago. The sun had set, and bonfires were lighting the beach, lanterns and candles providing light inside the keep. Gowan was dusty with grime from the battle on the beach, though he'd been able to wash off the worst of the blood and sand before answering the summons to the keep.

He was presentable, but famished. As was Seth, it seemed, from the way he piled food on his plate. Gowan followed suit and then joined Livia and the wizard at table.

They went through every facet of the battle for Dragonscove at Gryffid's urging. The wizard asked pointed questions, leading the three of them through their actions and that of the fighters and then the prisoners who had surrendered to the king's judgment.

Gryffid asked Gowan and Seth to compare the behavior of the enemy in Dragonscove to what they'd just witnessed. What they came up with was confusing. In Dragonscove, they'd been after riches. A few establishments along the shore had been obvious targets, a small amount of looting had even taken place before the enemy was defeated.

On Gryphon Isle, the enemy hadn't made it ashore, though small groups had fought their way through the lines, making for the lands beyond the beaches. They'd met up with the gryphon guard there, of course, and were stopped before they could go any farther, but their destination wasn't clear. The beach was wide and the village far inland. Only small shepherd's huts dotted the hillsides leading down to the beach, and only flocks of very frightened sheep lay in the direction most of the fighters had been trying to go.

The obvious target on the island was the keep, but the beach where the main battle had taken place was quite a distance from it. The secondary attack, however, had been much closer, but foiled by Captain O'Dare's fleet— specifically, the portion of it that was under his direct control at the time.

Which made Gryffid look quite eager to talk to the captain. Gowan would be just as pleased not to cross paths with Livia's father, but it seemed there was no help for it. Just as he thought this, the doors to the great hall opened once more, and the man himself strode in as if he owned the place.

The bastard had bravado to spare, Gowan would give him that.

"Father!" Livia stood from her seat at the table and made a start toward him, then seemed to remember she was at odds with him at the moment.

O'Dare's heart clenched. He didn't care that she'd run off—not at the moment anyway—all that mattered was that she was safe and unharmed.

He walked right up to her and pulled her into his arms, hugging her tight. He loved her deeply, though he'd been unable to express it and had, in fact, run away from home, in essence, to avoid the painful memories of Livia's late mother. That he'd avoided Livia at the same time was something he would always regret.

But there had been reasons... Good reasons. Reasons that had come to fruition today.

O'Dare opened his eyes to find every eye in the room on him. He was used to people watching him. He was in command of a fleet of ships, after all, but he wasn't used to displaying any emotion in front of his men. To show that you cared for someone was to expose your greatest weakness. He'd learned that the hard way, at the expense of his wife's life. He wouldn't make that same mistake again.

Captain O'Dare let go of his daughter and set her slightly away from him. There was much to discuss, and he had yet to meet the owner of this impressive keep. If rumor was to be believed, it was the wizard Gryffid himself, back from the magical mists of...wherever. O'Dare wasn't sure if he believed in all that hocus pocus horse shit, but whoever owned this keep, he commanded a hell of a lot of power between the fair folk and the gryphons.

"Gryffid, I presume?" O'Dare said, walking up to the only one around the table that he didn't know. Much to his annoyance, the two jackasses who wanted to bed his daughter were there too. O'Dare heard Livia gasp behind him, and he realized he was being a bit rude, but it had been a hell of a long day.

The older man didn't appear to take offense. He merely bowed his head slightly in acknowledgment. This was the guy going by the name Gryffid. O'Dare wondered if he really was a wizard or merely a very clever charlatan cashing in on the fame of the long lost wizard.

"I'm O'Dare. Livia's father. Captain of the smaller fleet of ships this day, much to my chagrin. Fisk caught me off guard. A large part of the fleet I've been putting together for the past several years is either on its way to Dragonscove or still at anchor in other ports, having not yet received my orders." O'Dare figured he'd just lay it all out there. The time for secrecy was over.

"Regardless of the size of the fleet you commanded today, Captain, they were essential to our victory, and you have my thanks," the purported wizard replied. "Please, make yourself a plate and join us. We are discussing what may have motivated the attack. You said a name... Fisk? Is he the enemy leader?"

Livia had made a plate up for her father while he'd been talking and brought it to him so he could sit at the table with the wizard and the others. Such a thoughtful gesture touched him deeply. Not since her mother had been alive had anyone done such a small kindness for him. He thanked her, wishing he could say more, but there were too many eyes watching. He would not expose her to even more danger if the wrong set of eyes saw how much he truly cared for his only child.

"I recognized Fisk's ship as he ran away. I've known for some time that he was collecting the somewhat questionable loyalty of the worst cutthroats and cheats that ever sailed the seas. In response, I began forming an opposing fleet in secret, made up of my trade ships and allies, which have been quietly upgraded and outfitted with cannons and men who could fight as well as trade, over the past several years."

"You took this task upon yourself?" Gryffid asked with a shrewd look in his eye.

"There was no one else to do it and nobody who knew how much of a devil Fisk truly is. He skates very close to the law and has a decent, if not good, reputation. But I know the evil in his heart." O'Dare looked down at his plate, knowing he needed to tell them all of it, but dreading having to say the words. "At one time, he was a business partner. I trusted him, and he learned many of my secrets, and my greatest weakness... My wife, Olivia. Fisk murdered her, and I have been hunting him ever since."

Silence greeted his words, and he didn't dare look at Livia. She hadn't known how her mother had died. He'd deliberately kept it from her, not wanting to hurt her any more than she already had been by the loss of her mother. She'd been guarded all her life, though she probably didn't realize the full extent of it. And he'd stayed away to protect her, as well as to collect his fleet. He'd done nothing for the past decade or more but work toward the goal of killing Fisk and ending the threat he posed not just to O'Dare's family, but to the world in general.

"Is it true?" Livia's whisper worked its way into his heart. He felt her pain, but he couldn't expose his ongoing grief to the world. Not yet. Probably not ever.

"Yes, daughter," he acknowledged her question, trying to remain as unemotional as possible. "It's all true. This is why I haven't been home in so long. I've been working to build the fleet to protect you—and everyone else—from Fisk." That sounded a bit grander than the real reason—that he wanted to hunt Fisk down, cut him into tiny little pieces and feed him, bit by bit, to the sharks.

"Well, I, for one, am glad you took the initiative, Captain O'Dare," Gryffid said, breaking the tension in the room. "You will all stay the night in the keep. Rooms have been prepared." Gryffid stood briskly from the table and looked around at everyone. "I will see you all at breakfast, here in the hall, an hour past sunrise, if that is convenient. I wish to speak with each of you again, once you've had a chance to rest and recover from the events of the day."

Murmurs of assent followed the wizard out the doors as he left them.

O'Dare turned to lace into the two men who had caught his daughter's eye when the door opened again and the dragon and knight that had accompanied O'Dare's ship walked in. Their pace was urgent, their expressions troubled.

"Seth, Sir Hrardorr has been trying to reach you, but

believed something about the wizard's keep was preventing him getting through," the young man said. "Lady Genlitha and Xander tried to reach you, too, but their voices were blocked."

"Not anymore," Seth said, rising to his feet, his face grim. "Hrardorr just told me. I'll be with you in a few minutes. I have to get some supplies from my baggage." Seth raced out of the room without further explanation.

"What's going on?" O'Dare asked Sir Leo as he approached.

"One of the sea dragons was cut badly by the diamond blades they are gathering from the sea floor. Sir Hrardorr wants Seth to look at her injury, since he is the only healer on this island truly familiar with dragons of any kind. Sir Hrardorr asked Xander and me to come get Seth and bring him to the little cove on the other side of the island where they say the sea dragons like to sunbathe." Leo's report was helpful in shedding light for Captain O'Dare on just how involved Seth was with the dragons. Very.

"Genlitha reports the same thing. She couldn't get through to me for some reason while Gryffid was here," Gowan said, scowling.

"Could he have blocked them somehow?" Livia asked, clearly concerned.

"I have no idea if that's even possible, but it seems likely given the evidence we have. The minute he left, we were back in communication. But why would he block them? It seems odd. He didn't do it earlier, when we first arrived."

"Maybe it wasn't him," O'Dare put in, thinking of the possibilities.

"Who then?" Livia asked, her gaze reminding him so much of her mother, yet her independent spirit was more like his own. His late wife, Olivia, would never have challenged him in public. She was far too refined to do such a thing. But her daughter, Livia, was more irreverent. More independent. He liked that about her, but it was also trying at times.

"Fisk has been known to dabble in magic. It is said he

131

made a deal with a demon to remain hidden from my vengeance for so long, and I'm half inclined to believe it, though I don't generally hold with talk of magic," O'Dare told them. They all seemed to ponder his words as Seth skidded back into the hall, a bulging pack slung across his back and another in his hands.

Xanderanth lowered his neck for Seth to slide the strap of the bigger pack around his long neck, settling it against his broad chest. Then, Seth and the dragon left the great hall, followed closely by Leo, who shrugged and waved to them all on his way out.

CHAPTER ELEVEN

Seth talked with Hrardorr about the sea dragon's injury on the short ride to the other side of the island with Leo and Xanderanth. With Xander's powerful wings, they arrived in no time at all, and Seth slid down off of Xander's back, approaching Hrardorr, who sat quietly next to a slightly smaller dragon that shared Hrardorr's dark coloration, but was just slightly different. She leaned more toward the dark blues than the deep greens that were the base of Hrardorr's multi-hued hide.

"Hrardorr?" Seth asked, uncertain how to approach the unknown dragon who was eyeing him with a shy sort of suspicion.

"Seth, this is Lady Shara. She has been injured by a diamond blade and is in need of your expertise," Hrardorr said formally, introducing the sea dragon.

Seth bowed as well as he could with the pack on his back. "Lady Shara, I am Seth, apprentice healer of the Southern Lair. Will you let me have a look at your injury? I promise to do all I can to help you."

Her jewel-like gaze went from Seth to Hrardorr and back again.

"You may approach," came her tentative voice in his mind. It was like a shushing whisper of waves against the shore, unlike

any other dragon's voice he'd ever heard. He found it pleasant.

Seth went to work, inspecting the long, thankfully shallow, gash that still wept blood on her foreleg. Seth sensed Hrardorr's frustration in being unable to see what was going on, so he began to talk about what he was seeing and doing.

"It is a shallow but long cut, Lady Shara. I will apply a special salve that will stop the last of the bleeding and begin helping your scales knit together. You may have a slight scar after this, but it will disappear in time when the affected scales shed in the natural course of things. Sea dragons do shed your scales like land dragons, right?"

"Yes, Seth. Not often, but we do it from time to time," Shara answered, her voice a little stronger as Seth applied the salve that he knew would also deaden any pain she might be feeling.

"As do we," Hrardorr put in. *"I always know a patch is going to shed when it becomes unbearably itchy."*

Shara seemed to giggle. *"The itch is the* worst,*"* she agreed with Hrardorr as Seth continued his work.

"Lady Shara, is it possible for you to remain out of the water for a few days? I only ask because the salve may dissipate in water, and I fear infection could set in. It might be best if you kept the wound from getting wet while it is still healing."

"We sea dragons can spend time on land," she admitted. *"It is not our preferred place to be, but the wizard allows us the use of his beaches and caves. We like the ones in this area best, and the gryphons mostly leave us alone. I can stay in the cave over there for a few days if that will help in the healing. I have done so before."*

Seth looked over to the darker area in the cliff she'd gestured toward. Sure enough, he could just make out the opening of a cave that he hadn't really noticed before. Night had fallen, and Xanderanth and Leo had set up a bonfire so Seth could see. Seth noticed the way Xanderanth was watching the sea dragon, as if mesmerized.

"Have you met Sir Xanderanth, Lady Shara?" Seth asked

while he worked, hoping to distract her a bit from her injuries.

"I have not," she replied rather shyly.

"Xander, come closer and meet Lady Shara," Seth said familiarly. He liked Xander and Leo—especially since they'd proven their worth by insisting they come along on this mission.

The dark blue dragon shuffled slowly forward, as if he, too, was shy. Seth was surprised. Xander was usually one of the more self-assured young dragons.

"Hello," Xander said, approaching slowly. *"I'm Xanderanth, but my friends call me Xander."*

"I'm Shanaraneth, Shara for short. Pleased to meet you."

Was it Seth's imagination or were the two dragons exhibiting the initial signs of being smitten with each other? Could a land dragon and a sea dragon even *be* mates? There had been only one case that Seth knew of—Hrardorr's famous ancestor—but nobody in Draconia had even seen a sea dragon since then, and that had been centuries ago.

Seth finished up with the cut on Shara's scales while she and Xander exchanged pleasantries. Yeah, they were definitely intrigued by each other, though only time would tell if anything would—or could—come of it. They were both quite young. Seth judged them to be somewhere around the same age, which put them both at just coming out of their adolescence into adulthood. That was very young for a dragon to find a mate.

And there was the complication that Xander was a fighting dragon. He'd bonded fully with Leo and could not take a dragon mate until Leo found a wife, lest the spillover from Xander's amorous activities drive Leo mad. At such times, only a true mate would do for the human side of the family because the bonds ran too deep for a casual bed partner to be able to satisfy.

Seth sat back, having finished with the cut when the gleam of blood in the firelight caught his eye. He stood, walking around to the back of the dragon and had to stifle a gasp. She had another injury—a much more serious injury—to her wing that she was either unaware of, or trying to hide. He had no idea why she would do such a thing, but he had to try to help her.

"Lady Shara, may I look at your wing?" Seth asked gently.

Shara shied away from him. Not good.

"I only want to help you, milady," Seth tried to reassure her.

"I prefer to wait," Shara said softly.

Wait? Seth had no idea what the dragoness was waiting for. It didn't make sense. Why wouldn't she let him help her?

And then, the answer came clear when a tall blonde woman came down the treacherous path from the cliffs and walked into the firelight. Seth frowned. He couldn't see her that well across the dancing flames, but as she drew closer, he saw that she held a satchel much like his own.

"My dear Shara, what have you got into now?" asked the woman, clearly familiar with the sea dragon.

At this, Shara extended her bleeding wing, trembling badly. Seth moved to support her, knowing she could use his help.

"I will hold your wing, if you allow it," he offered to the dragon, not wanting to touch her without her permission.

Shara looked at him in surprise and nodded her great head just once.

"Thank you, Sir…?" the newcomer asked, moving closer.

Seth could see her a lot better now, and she was definitely one of the fair folk. If he hadn't been convinced by her melodic voice, her lithe blonde beauty made a believer out of him. She was stunning.

"I'm not a knight," he told her. "I am the apprentice healer from the Southern Lair, milady. My name is Seth."

"My mistake. I'm Lizbet, a fellow healer. I mostly work with gryphons, but some of the sea dragons allow me to help them when needed." She approached Shara on quiet feet, her hands moving gently over the dragon's scales in what Seth recognized as a thorough examination. "Oh, Shara, sweetheart, what happened to you?"

"It was the diamond blades," Shara admitted in a small voice. *"Sir Hrardorr warned us all, but I got too close to Mattie when she was tugging one of the big blades free of the wreckage, and it sliced me up."*

"Is she badly hurt?" Hrardorr asked Seth privately.

"The web of her wing is sliced open between the third and fourth joint," Seth told Hrardorr honestly as he got his first good look at the injury.

Hrardorr winced. *"A flight-ending injury if not healed correctly."*

"Don't worry, my friend, I'll see to her," Seth promised. He would make sure this young dragon didn't suffer permanent effects from this injury if at all possible.

"I have not dealt with many wing injuries on dragons," Lizbet admitted, coming up behind Shara's wing, near Seth.

"I have," Seth replied confidently. "This is bad, but not impossible. It can be healed, but we'll have to stitch her up, and she cannot go in the water until the cut is knit together properly."

"You have a needle that will go through dragon hide?" Lizbet looked at him with wide eyes.

Seth nodded. "I brought along my kit. I have all the tools we'll need, and Sir Leo and Sir Xander can help us." He remembered to address his patient. "Milady, will you allow Sir Xander to support your wing while we work on it? I have more of the ointment that will numb your wing so you will not be hurt further by our work, and I promise you that, in time, you will be healed, though this will leave a permanent scar, I'm afraid."

The young dragoness looked scared, her head swiveling from Lizbet to Hrardorr, and then to Xander, surprisingly, before she turned back to look at Seth.

"Have you done this before, truly?" she asked, clearly frightened. He had to remember that these sea dragons did not interact with people much.

"Yes, milady. I grew up in the Lair with three human parents and two dragon parents. I apprenticed to the healer at ten years old and have worked on almost every dragon in the

Lair at one time or another, including my dragon parents. The Southern Lair is different from most Lairs in that we have a lot of older dragons and knights and many young ones, like Leo and Xander, who are gifted fliers that need the training of the more experienced dragons like Sir Hrardorr and Lady Genlitha. The changeable winds along our coast are exceptionally good for learning, from what I understand, but training means pushing oneself to one's limits and often results in injuries until skills are mastered. As a result, I have seen and treated many different kinds of injuries."

"Seth sewed up my wing when we first got to the Lair," Xanderanth put in helpfully, spreading his right wing out to show Shara the jagged line that had healed well. *"I tore it doing something stupid and was very afraid I would not fly again, but Seth fixed me up, and as you can see, the rip was a lot crazier than your straight cut. Seth does good work. You can trust him."*

"We are taught to fear humans and stay far away from them," Shara admitted. *"But maybe that is wrong. You seem like a nice human, Seth. And your touch does not hurt."* She looked over at Xander and Hrardorr. *"And land dragons like you and vouch for you."* Shara lowered her head to the sand. *"Please proceed. I want to fly, even though I spend most of my time underwater. I like sunshine on my scales more than they say is good for a sea dragon."*

Seth had to smile at her declaration. "So then, you're a bit of a rebel, eh, milady? That's good. So am I." He lowered her wing into Lizbet's care with gentle hands and went to fetch what he'd need from his pack. With a nod, he motioned Xanderanth over to help support Shara's wing. Lair dragons were used to helping each other in such situations, and he knew what to do.

"How are you a rebel, Seth?" Shara asked as she watched him take things from his pack, a few feet away from her on the sand.

"My fathers are knights. Everyone expected I would be, too, but I gave up the training and apprenticed myself to Bronwyn, our healer. She is very old, and her joints ache almost constantly. She needed help, and nobody else was offering. I could not let her suffer alone, so I started to help her instead of going to fighting practice. My family was not happy, but I insisted. Bronwyn meant more to me than doing sword drills."

Seth kept talking as he bathed the wound in a liquid that would both clean it and numb the area. The pungent scent of the herbs it was made from almost made him sneeze, but he kept on working. Lizbet was at his side, helping once she saw the way of it.

Seth opened the small metal case in which he kept his most precious tools. Diamond needles in various shapes and sizes. Diamond was the only thing that would easily get through dragon hide, and each Lair had one set of the precious instruments.

This new set gleamed and was Seth's newest and most prized possession next to the sword Gowan had given him. Livia had ordered these tools crafted by her artisans— probably without her father's knowledge—from the diamond blades Hrardorr had recovered from the bottom of the harbor after the battle of Dragonscove.

Most of those diamond blades had been slated to be cut up into ornaments and jewelry, then sold on to pay for the damages to the town and to re-equip the harbor defense cannons with newer models and supplies. But Livia had set aside a few of the longer blades, earmarking them to be made into tools that could help heal dragons instead of kill them. Several sets had been made and sent to the capital for dispersal to various Lairs around the country, but one had come by special messenger with a handwritten note from Livia, delivered into Seth's hands with the grateful appreciation, or so the note said, of the entire town.

He hadn't had a chance to use them yet, but now was as good a time as any, and he knew the diamond cutters who worked for Livia's father were among the best in the business. Seth had checked and rechecked these wondrous tools, and they were sound. He was sure of it.

And now, they would be put to very good use indeed.

He lifted out the slightly curved needle that was about the length of his hand. This would be perfect for the job ahead.

"You have done this before," Lizbet commented at his side. "I've never seen such tools. Gryphon hide is not nearly as tough as dragon scale."

"Each Lair has a set of these diamond-tipped tools for exactly this purpose, but this set is mine. It was a gift from a friend. The diamond slides easily through the patient, allowing the sutures to cause as little additional damage as possible, and when numbed with the potion I just used, the dragon shouldn't feel anything in the area of the wound for a few hours. The potion also cleans the wound and removes any contaminants."

"We have something similar, but I'd love to compare recipes," Lizbet said softly as she watched Seth thread the extra large needle.

"I would be happy to," Seth agreed. "But for now, would you hold the cut together while I stitch it up?"

"You said this won't hurt, right?" a worried Shara asked them in a small voice.

Sea dragons were definitely more timid than their land brethren. It was a shock to Seth, but he'd better get used to it.

"Do you feel anything near the cut now, milady?" Seth asked calmly, leaning back to look her in the eye.

"No," she answered tentatively. *"The fire went out when you doused it with that smelly water."*

Seth tried not to laugh though he couldn't hold back a small grin. "That was a numbing potion. It will relieve the pain in the area for a few hours," Seth said again, trying to sound reassuring and confident. "But if you feel anything at any point, just tell me, and I'll stop, all right? You're in control here, milady. I want to help you. I don't want to cause you any further pain. You have my word."

She held his gaze for a long moment and then sighed and set her head back down on the sand. *"All right. Proceed."*

She didn't sound happy about it, but Seth was confidant she would be reasonable. She was probably still scared, though.

"Xanderanth," Seth sent his message privately to the big blue dragon. *"Can you help her feel less scared?"*

"I'll try," Xander immediately replied.

He adjusted his position so that he held her wing aloft with his hind feet, stretching and twisting his neck to lay his head next to hers. Her eyes blinked open in surprise, but then warmed, if Seth was any judge of dragonish expressions.

And then, the dragons began talking among themselves. Though Seth didn't hear any of their conversation, he could tell by the attitudes of their heads and the look in their eyes that they were communing silently. His dragon parents got just such a look on their faces when they were talking together.

"Leo?" Seth said quietly, calling to the young knight who was watching his dragon partner with a concerned gaze. "Would you help with the supplies while Lady Lizbet holds the wound together for me?"

"Happy to help," Leo replied at once, coming closer and positioning himself next to the supplies and close enough to hand things to Seth when needed.

All knights received training in how to help care for dragons both when they were well and when they became injured, so Leo knew what to do. Seth set to work, sewing up the long cut with precise stitches. He realized at one point that Leo was staring rather pointedly at the fair Lizbet, but she didn't seem to notice. Or if she did, she was too polite to say anything.

"Lady Lizbet, this is Sir Leo, Sir Xanderanth's partner," Seth made the introductions quietly.

"Oh, yes, Flurrthith told me about you all. Thank you for accompanying him home. He is part of my family unit. His parents are partners to my parents, and we were raised together," she explained.

"He's your gryphon-brother." Seth nodded as he continued working. "I understand completely. I come from a family like that, only with dragons instead of gryphons. And two human fathers, of course." Seth spared a second to look up at Lizbet and wink.

"Trios are not unheard of among my people, but it is not the norm, I will admit," she said, surprising him with her frankness.

"It's not the norm where we come from either, but the soul-deep bond between dragon and knight makes it necessary. And it all seems to work out. Many say the Mother of All has Her hand in the dragon pairings, taking personal interest in the knights and dragons' happiness. I don't know for sure, but it certainly seemed that way for my family."

"It's a beautiful thought," Lizbet admitted. "Though my people believe the Warrior Goddess helps those who first help themselves. She is a bit harsher than the Mother aspect of the many-faced Goddess."

"You come from a warrior household then?" Seth asked, truly interested.

"Yes. My parents are both warriors, and you've already met my gryphon-father. He is General Falthith," she told him.

Seth was impressed. "A warrior among warriors," Seth complimented the winged general. "I didn't realize Flurrthith was his son."

"None of the gryphons in my family are boastful. They are all high achievers, but do it quietly, with as little fanfare as possible." Seth could tell she was very proud of her feathered relations.

He set to work in earnest, spending many minutes carefully sewing up the gash in the sea dragon's wing. Both Leo and Lizbet were of great help, and Seth found himself answering astute questions as he worked, showing them both how to do what he was doing and explaining the why of it. He was happy to pass along his knowledge—especially to Lizbet who was the de facto healer for the sea dragons who frequented Gryphon Isle.

When he finished stitching and applied healing salve and a dressing over the stitches, the other two helped. Xanderanth had kept the pretty young sea dragon busy with their silent conversation, and when she was told it was over and she could move again, she seemed truly surprised. She looked at her bandaged wing for some time before lowering her head to Seth's level. She looked him in the eye and thanked him in a gentle voice, her polite words and tone touching him deeply.

Xanderanth volunteered to escort her into the cave she'd chosen, and the two went off together, walking slowly, Xander supporting the sea dragon's injured wing when necessary. Seth cleaned his tools while Lizbet helped. They talked about the tools and how she wished she had a set.

"Livia can have some made on the mainland and sent to you, or even better, if you have diamond cutters among your people, I might be able to show them these before I leave. I can't leave them here, I'm sorry to say, but I'd be happy to let your people look at them and perhaps trace their patterns."

"That's a really good idea, Seth. Thank you. We do have craftsmen who I'm sure would be able to make such things, but they'd need to see a working set to know what they're supposed to look like." Lizbet sounded enthused about the idea of having her very own set of dragon healing instruments.

"And you'll soon have an abundance of diamond in need of reshaping," Seth agreed. "That's how I got these." He put the last needle back in its metal case and closed the lid. "Livia had them made from the diamond blades Hrardorr retrieved from the bottom of the harbor. The rest of the blades were cut down into jewels and other harmless things, but she had a number of them made into sets like this for dispersal to Lairs throughout the country. Until she did that, last week, there was only one set per Lair. Now, most have two sets, which is a boon with all the fighting our dragons have been facing lately."

Seth would have said more, but Leo came back from checking on the dragons in the cave. His gaze seemed troubled.

"Xander doesn't want to leave Lady Shara tonight. He says

he'll stay in the cave with her, to make sure she's all right," the young knight told Seth, Lizbet listening too.

"To be honest, that's a relief," Seth told Leo. "She seems somewhat timid and afraid of me," Seth knew his disbelief sounded in his voice, but he couldn't help it. He'd never had a dragon be afraid of him—or of any human, actually. "I'm staying here tonight, though, in case she needs me. And I still have to see to Hrardorr. I know he got hit a few times during the battle, but he's been on the move since then and hasn't wanted me fussing over him. I'm about to put my foot down, though."

Seth looked over at the dozing dragon a few yards away, near one of the bonfires they'd lit. Hrardorr had done a yeoman's work today and was justifiably tired, but Seth would treat his wounds while the dragon slept if he had to. There was no more reason to put Seth off. The sea dragon had been seen to, and now, it would be Hrardorr's turn. Seth would abide no further argument.

That tough stance would work, too, since Hrardorr was so tired he could barely lift his head. If not for his huge expenditure of energy today, the dragon could easily have escaped Seth indefinitely, and they all knew it.

"I'm staying too," Lizbet surprised Seth by saying. Her voice was musical, but firm. "Shara and I are close. I often spend time here with her when she comes ashore. I will see to my friend's recovery."

"Then I suggest you two see to the bonfires. We'll need them later tonight," Seth said quietly, seeing the way Lizbet and Leo's gazes seemed locked in the firelight. "I'm going to treat Hrardorr."

"Do you need our help?" Lizbet asked kindly, but Seth was already shaking his head.

"Thanks, but I think most of his wounds are relatively minor. If I find anything I can't handle, you'll be the first to know." Seth walked toward the other fire and the dark dragon dozing next to it.

They'd set up several stacks of dried wood at various

points along the beach and set them to blaze, lighting the area. There was one near the mouth of the cave, one where they'd treated Lady Shara and this one around which Hrardorr had settled, liking the warmth after having been submerged most of the day.

Hrardorr didn't put up any argument when Seth started checking him over, finding a few arrow holes in his wings that needed stitching, along with a gash on his tail that required a pot of salve and a dressing. Seth worked steadily, taking his time and making sure Hrardorr was as well treated as any hero who had just saved an island full of people and gryphons, should be.

They didn't talk much—both being bone weary—but Seth did manage to tell his dragon friend how incredibly proud he was of Hrardorr's actions today. Hrardorr didn't put up too much of an argument, and he surprised Seth by talking to him a bit about his encounter with the sea dragons. They chatted off and on while Seth put Hrardorr's wounds to rights, and then, Seth guided his weary dragon friend toward the cave where the other dragons had settled. It was plenty big enough for all three dragons and their two-legged friends.

Seth watched Lizbet and Leo covertly as they worked quietly together. It was clear there was an attraction between the two, but Seth had no idea how it would all work out. Leo was a knight, and he'd become a great knight in time. The signs were clear.

If Seth felt a small pang of envy, it was understandable…wasn't it? He still liked Leo, but he almost missed what he knew he, himself, would never achieve. Seth would never be a knight, but being Hrardorr's friend and being healer to a Lair full of dragons was good enough. Wasn't it?

Seth wasn't so sure anymore.

CHAPTER TWELVE

Leo sat on the beach as the night wore on. They had plenty of light from the bonfires Xanderanth had lit before going into the big cave to sit with the sea dragon, Lady Shara. Hrardorr was in there, too, sitting slightly apart from the other two dragons, already sleeping. It had been a big day for them all.

Leo and Lizbet had added fuel to the fires, keeping them going from the piles of driftwood he and Xander had gathered earlier. Leo talked silently with Xander, checking on the sea dragon. Xander told him she was resting easily now, warm and secure, though very drained from her ordeal. She seemed to be taking comfort from Xander's presence, and the young male dragon refused to leave her side.

Leo wondered about that. He and Xander had only been paired for a short time, but Leo had never seen his partner take such an interest in a female dragon.

Of course, the sea dragon was something special. He and Xander had talked about how awesome it would be to actually see a sea dragon. Now, not only had they seen one, but they'd helped her during a crisis, and Xander showed every sign of befriending her. If not more.

It was the *more* that was worrying. What if Xanderanth wanted the female sea dragon for his mate? How in the world would that work?

Leo wondered if he'd be the first knight in known history to be left behind by his dragon partner. It wasn't a pleasant thought. And he was probably just making that up anyway. He and Xander were joined on a soul-deep level. Leo had no idea if such a link could be severed by anything other than death, and he didn't really want to find out. Leo poked the fire he was sitting in front of with a long stick, rearranging the logs, lost in depressing thoughts.

"Shara's asleep, finally," Lizbet said, settling onto the long log Leo had reserved to use as a seat until it was needed for fuel. She held her hands out to the fire, rubbing them together as if chilled. "I think she'll be all right now. She just got a hell of a scare."

"I'm glad she's doing better."

Was he, though? Really? When that innocent female dragon could spell doom for Leo's partnership with Xander?

Leo shook off the negative thoughts. Of course he was glad that the dragoness was out of danger. It had been uncharitable to even let such thoughts cross his mind. Leo was better than that. He *wanted* to be better than that.

"How are you holding up?" Lizbet surprised him by asking.

The fey healer had been with the dragoness most of the evening, working alongside Seth to sew up an incredible gash in Shara's wing. Leo had noticed Lizbet, of course. He'd have to be dead not to notice such a beautiful woman. But he'd assumed she hadn't given him a second thought. Had he been wrong?

"I'm fine," Leo said quickly. "Are you warm enough? You could wear my cloak if you're cold." He got up and retrieved the special cloak knights used when flying that was both warm and weatherproof. He stepped behind Lizbet and leaned down to place it around her shoulders.

She looked up as he bent down, and their eyes met. Time stood still.

Did he move or did she? He would never know who

moved, but the next moment, her lips met his, and the world as he knew it changed forever.

"What are you doing?"

Leo stood, breaking the kiss as his mind spun. He realized almost instantaneously that the question hadn't come from his guilty conscience. It was Xanderanth, wanting to know what his partner was up to.

Sweet Mother of All.

"Just a sec, Xan," he told the dragon silently, trying to figure out what to say to the beautiful woman he'd just kissed.

"I'm sorry," Lizbet said shyly, pulling his cloak tighter around her shoulders and turning away from him, facing the fire. "I didn't mean to do that."

"Milady, it was not all you," Leo had to admit. "I apologize if I overstepped my bounds."

"No, it's..." She turned her head quickly to look back up at him, and then, it happened again. Their eyes met, and time stood still.

"Well, I think Lady Shara should be comfortable enough for now," Seth said in a brisk voice, coming out of the shadowy mouth of the cave, rubbing his hands together.

Time began running again, and Leo shook his head, stepping back from Lizbet. The moment had passed, but it had left him...unsettled.

What in the world had possessed him to kiss her? Was she upset with him? Had he just created some kind of international incident by accosting a fey citizen of Gryphon Isle?

Terrible thoughts raced through Leo's brain as Seth walked closer to the fire. Thankfully, the other man seemed unaware of what he had interrupted. Either that, or he was good at dissembling.

"Now that we've made the dragons as comfortable as possible for the night, I think it's time we set up something a bit more camp-like for us. What do you say?" Seth's voice was almost too loud in the darkness of the night. Too jovial.

Shit. He did know what he'd interrupted. Leo took a deep

breath and met Seth's gaze, finding a question in the other man's eyes that he couldn't answer. He had no idea what he'd been doing kissing Lizbet. Except...maybe...that she'd been irresistible.

Leo knew that lame excuse would never fly. A knight was supposed to have honor and courage. He was supposed to be able to resist temptation when necessary. Leo had failed at the first test, and he felt ashamed. Ashamed and really, really confused.

How could something that had felt so right be wrong? Was it, really? Or was he making more of this than he should? And what in the world was Lizbet thinking? That was the most important of the unanswerable questions racing through his thoughts.

"Hush, Leo," Xanderanth's voice came into his mind, soothing him. *"I'm not sure what has you in such a tizzy, but we're all right. You're all right. Everything will work out. I'm here for you."*

That his dragon partner had sensed his turmoil wasn't surprising. They were joined in spirit and soul. But though he calmed a bit, Leo still worried...for how much longer?

Lizbet's head was spinning from the unexpected kiss. What in the world had possessed her to kiss the handsome knight? To be sure, Sir Leo was easy on the eyes, but she knew many handsome young men, and few had ever turned her head. And if they had, it didn't stay turned in their direction long.

Lizbet had been searching for the kind of loving partnership she saw her parents share. She wanted a life mate, not just a quick tumble or a relationship that lasted a few years out of mutual convenience, then petered out.

She was young by her people's standards, but she wanted love in her life. She had felt it was just around the corner for a long time. Could it be? Had her true mate arrived in the form of this most attractive *human* knight?

"If you like him, you should act on it," Shara said in her mind, the dragoness's advice unasked for, but welcome. *"He is joined*

to Xanderanth. The dragon magic will keep him alive almost as long as you, so the difference in your race isn't an impediment. You won't lose him early because he's human, though he is a fighting man, and there are no guarantees he won't die in battle." The dragon paused as if musing. *"Of course, that's all the more reason, to my mind, to grab for happiness while you're both here and feeling the pull."*

"Like you and Xanderanth?" Lizbet dared to send her thoughts back to the dragoness. If Shara was going to butt into Lizbet's love life, turnabout was fair play.

"Maybe," Shara said, considering. *"I do like him an awful lot. But there's Leo to consider. The land dragons bond to their knights and make certain sacrifices to do it, or so I've been told. I'm not really sure how it all works. That is something I will need to ask Xanderanth about…if we decide to move forward. I mean, I only just met him."*

"But you feel the attraction, don't you?" Lizbet didn't wait for an answer to her question. *"I thought so. I felt little sparks around the two of you all night. Even when you were in so much pain from the wound and apprehensive of the humans. They turned out to be nice, though, right?"*

"You sound as surprised as I was," Shara said, humor in her tone.

"I've never met a human before," Lizbet confided. *"Though I've heard many tales about them. Some are good, like Leo and Seth, but some are very bad indeed."*

"Just like your folk. And mine, too, if truth be told." Shara sighed, and Lizbet could hear the gentle exhalation even outside the cave. *"There are always a few bad squid in the sea."*

"We call them bad apples, but I get your meaning."

The easy rapport with Shara was unlike anything Lizbet had ever experienced. She and Shara were friends, but it went deeper than that. Somehow, Shara always sensed what Lizbet was thinking, and when she wasn't with her friends at sea, they spent a lot of time together here on the far side of the island, away from both Lizbet's and Shara's people. They were happy together, as they weren't among their own kind, which was odd, when Lizbet stopped to think about it.

But she didn't question it much, really. They enjoyed each

other's company too much to wonder the why of it. Lizbet had just come to accept the fact that the being most close to her heart—other than her family, which was a different sort of bond altogether—was Shara. Their friendship was like a family link, but closer, because they each had *chosen* to be the other's friend. They hadn't been forced together by an accident of birth.

They may wear totally different skins, but they were sisters at heart.

Lizbet sat quietly by the fire, warming up while Seth took Leo off somewhere. When they returned, they each held a big pack in their hands. She watched while they both bent to open the packs and pulled out the makings of a campsite.

She was amazed, really, at the ingenuity of some of the items. They folded up to almost nothing but, when open, were useful items. Bedrolls. Even a tent. A pot for cooking. Foodstuffs and other supplies.

Lizbet offered to help, but both men told her to sit and relax. They claimed to have everything well in hand, and watching them, she believed the claim. Although Seth wasn't a bonded knight, he certainly shared all the skills Leo displayed in unpacking and using the supplies that seemed to be standard among dragon knights.

When Leo stepped up to the fire to set up a small metal grate over the top of the burning coals, Lizbet offered to help once more. This time, Leo smiled at her, giving her the pot and water skin, along with the makings for tea. Lizbet boiled the water and herbs as she watched the men move around, setting up tents and creating a little home away from home for them.

The two tents were set up just inside the mouth of the cave, one on each side of the entrance, tucked behind the outer wall for both protection from the wind and anything that might try to sneak up on them in the night. One wall of each tent was against the inner wall of the cave, while the entrances to the tents had been situated a few feet back from the cave opening.

With the dragons inside, between the two tents, there would be plenty of warmth. The dragons also made for fierce guards, even with Shara injured. She still had sharp claws and teeth, along with a mobile tail that was one of her wickedest weapons. And Xanderanth could fry anything approaching that had nasty intent. They'd be safe enough.

Leo walked back to the fire, and she handed him a cup of tea. There were three cups. Seth had put one of his potion cups into use along with the mug that had been in his camping gear, so they could all drink at once.

"You can have my tent, Lizbet. The one on the right. I've also set up my bedroll for you, so you can sleep comfortably. Seth and I will switch off on watch," he told her as he sat down beside her. "We'll share his tent and bedding since only one of us will be sleeping at a time."

"I can stand watch too," Lizbet offered.

She'd been raised in a warrior family. She understood the need to keep watch in uncertain situations. The island had been attacked. Everyone would be posting watches all around the island for the foreseeable future, just in case it happened again.

"That's all right," Leo told her. "I doubt I'll be able to sleep much anyway. This is my first real adventure with Xander...and maybe our last. The leaders of our Lair didn't exactly sanction our trip out here. When we go back, there will be some consequences to face, I'm sure."

"Really?" That was the first Lizbet had heard of it. "I'd wondered why there were so few of you. It's just the three dragons and four humans, right? I thought you had a lot more dragons and knights in your land."

"We do," Leo told her. Seth was inside the tent the men would share, fixing something, so for the moment, it was just her and Leo by the fire. "We have almost a hundred at the Southern Lair alone, and we're not one of the real fighting Lairs. The Border Lair has more, and the Northern Lair has been fortified since all the fighting started up there. I think the largest concentration of dragons and knights, though, is probably in the capital."

"What do you mean about your Lair not being a real fighting Lair?" she asked.

Leo made a face. "Some call it the *retirement* Lair. Where old knights go when they're too old to fight and want to spend the rest of their days in the balmy weather by the seaside. It's also where they send the really good young fliers to learn how to skate on the tricky air currents we have along the coast. That's part of why they sent me and Xanderanth here. He's going to be one of the best fighters in the land one day. He just has to grow into his powerful frame and learn how to best utilize his strength, and his wings. Plus, my family is from the Southern shores. My parents actually picked up and moved closer to Dragonscove when they heard I was going to be stationed there for the first part of my career. We're very close."

"Do you come from a big family?" she wanted to know. She was intrigued by the things he was telling her about the land of men.

"I'm the oldest of a brood," he said, laughing. When he smiled, his whole face lit up, and she could tell he really loved his big family. "My folks thought it best if I could still see my younger siblings on my days off, and Xanderanth is a big hit with the little ones. They climb all over him, and I'm always surprised how patient he is with them. Of course, Xander's young, too, for a dragon. I'm his first knight. We're learning together."

"That's really beautiful," Lizbet said, and Leo felt a flush run along his cheekbones. "It must be so amazing to share your life with Xanderanth."

"I'm truly blessed," Leo agreed, feeling a bit more comfortable seeing that she wasn't making fun of him. Far from it, she seemed truly impressed, which swung his emotions back the other way, from embarrassment to pride.

They talked a bit about the bond between dragon and knight. Lizbet seemed very interested in how it all worked, so

Leo did his best to explain it, though some of it was beyond his ability to put into words. It just...*was.* The bond that had formed between Xanderanth and Leo was stronger than anything he'd ever felt before and joined them on a level he hadn't known existed until Xander had come into his life.

Lizbet was a good listener, and when Seth returned to share a snack with them, the talk turned to her life on the island. She told them about the small villages and towns dotted around the island and how everyone deferred to Gryffid's rule, though the wizard seldom interfered much in anyone's lives. The fair folk lived and worked alongside the gryphons in much the way the knights lived and worked with their dragon partners, only on a much larger scale. There were almost as many gryphons on the island as there were fair folk, and not all were suited to be warriors. Some were artisans in their own right, and some were strategists, teachers and poets.

Leo was fascinated by talk of the gryphons and listened raptly, even after Seth excused himself to check on the dragons one last time before turning in for a short sleep shift. Leo was on first watch, and Lizbet seemed to want to share it with him. Leo didn't object. He liked her company and figured she would turn in when she got tired enough.

Oddly, she didn't. She sat with him for the long hours of his watch and didn't leave until Seth came back to relieve Leo. Only then did Lizbet get up and go into the tent Leo had set up for her, but not before leaving him with a parting peck on the cheek.

Leo held one hand to his cheek long after she disappeared into the tent, marveling at the strange turn of events. He was wildly attracted to the fey woman, but he had no idea how—or even *if*—such a thing could ever come to fruition.

Still, he was smiling as he lay himself down on the bedroll Seth had vacated, in the tent just across the way from Lizbet's. Leo lay his sword within easy reach and then shut his eyes, knowing he would dream of the fey woman who had captured his imagination...and just maybe...his heart.

Livia snuck out of her bedroom deep in the night and tiptoed next door, where she knew Gowan would be. They'd only just arrived back at their rooms after a long discussion of the day's events with the crowd still in the great hall. It seemed the battle had made more than one fey warrior unable to sleep. Many were talking and sitting quietly all around the hall, which Gryffid seemed to keep open at all hours for guests.

Discreet servants kept food and drink flowing, but few drank to excess, and those that did were cared for quietly by their brethren. Livia had been impressed with the way the fey handled themselves. A few bards played quietly in one corner. Calming tunes. Sad tunes, to remember the dead and mark their passing. The fey seemed to be respectful even of their enemies' deaths. There was no joyful celebration. Only sober remembrances and quiet comradeship.

Livia and Gowan had stayed late into the night, talking with the fey. Livia thought she understood better now why they seemed to want to spend time in each other's company after such a tumultuous day. She felt better for having shared time with those somber warriors.

But now, she wanted to spend time with Gowan. Nobody saw her in the corridor, though she suspected her father would have set a watch had he been allowed to bring any of his men into the keep with him.

As it was, Gryffid's people had put her father in a guest suite in another section of the massive keep, and she felt secure enough to sneak over to Gowan's room for a few hours. She didn't want to be alone. Not after all they'd been through today.

More importantly, she didn't want Gowan to be alone. She couldn't help the fact that Seth was on duty, his healing skill much needed in the aftermath of battle.

She opened his door, sneaking in quickly, lest someone come down the corridor and see her. Leaning against the closed door, she caught her breath. Gowan was looking at her, and it was clear she'd startled him a bit, though he reacted well. He was shirtless, wearing only his trousers and socks. It looked like she'd interrupted while he was caring for his sword, honing the edge and inspecting the dully gleaming blade.

She had an entirely different sword in mind to care for herself this night, but she had to admit, he posed a dashing picture, standing there, one foot resting on the chest at the foot of the bed. His blade rested on his knee, his muscles gleaming in the candlelight as he bent over the sword, inspecting it. He had a cloth in one hand, a sharpening stone in the other, but he put both aside when their eyes met.

He straightened, placing the blade carefully on the lid of the chest before he walked toward her. She felt very much as if he was some exotic mountain cat, stalking her…in the best possible way.

"Should you be here?" he asked in a low, rumbly voice.

"There's no place I'd rather be," she replied, giving him what she hoped was a sultry smile. She felt like her insides were melting into a puddle of need as he prowled closer. Her mouth went dry as she watched him, knowing that, in mere moments, she would be in his arms.

She'd missed him so much since her father had come home. The stolen moments on the beach had been incredible, but she missed talking to Gowan and just being around him. He'd become a needed presence in her life in such a short time. It almost scared her to think about it, because she knew the whole situation was difficult, at best…impossible, at worst. And since her father had returned, it had been the pits most of the time.

"What about your father?" Gowan persisted, closer now, taking his time as he crossed the large room.

"He's in another wing of the keep. It seems either Gryffid has some sympathy for our situation or luck is on our side." She tilted her head to look up at him as he stepped into her personal space, only the width of a heartbeat separating them now. Thank the stars!

"Or perhaps a little of both," he mused, smiling in that

lopsided way that lit her on fire. He was too sexy for his own good. Too sexy for her peace of mind, to be sure.

He leaned closer, and then, his lips were on hers, possessing gently, like the first time they'd come together on the sunny cliff top above Dragonscove. They'd been on a picnic. No hint of the danger that was to come. And Gowan had been the perfect gentleman—until he hadn't—and she'd practically pounced on him, making love to him in the soft grass, his dragon partner sleeping nearby.

She'd only been with the men she was coming to think of as *hers* together and separately a handful of times. Each was a glowing memory in her mind, brought out in the dark of night when she was alone, wondering where they were and what they were doing.

Tonight, she wouldn't have to wonder. At least not about Gowan. And she knew where Seth was and what he was doing. He was safe, in the company of dragons and gryphons, where she knew he loved to be. He had genuine affection for all dragons, and they seemed to respect him in turn, from what she had observed.

She came up for air when Gowan raised his head.

"How long can you stay?" he whispered.

"A few hours, but I should leave before dawn, just in case. My father was always an early riser, and I wouldn't put it past him to come find my room to make sure I was in it."

She felt very naughty defying her father, but it couldn't be helped. He insisted on seeing her as a child, when she hadn't truly been a child since her mother's death.

Gowan reached behind her as he held her gaze, and she heard the click of the lock catching on the door. "As you say then, just in case, we'll throw the latch so we won't be disturbed."

She smiled up at him in total breathless, eager agreement. His head dipped lower, and he was kissing her again, taking his time with her. This promised to be a thorough loving, where neither of them would have to rush. They had hours to spend together, and the stresses of the day to work through.

She needed to be held so desperately. She needed to feel alive after all the death and danger that had been visited on this island today. And she'd heard about how soldiers got keyed up during a fight and needed the release of sex after.

She felt the same tension in her own body. The need to be close to someone special. To reaffirm life in the most basic way. To enjoy the time they had together, for life—as had been proven over and over today—was uncertain, at best.

Gowan continued to kiss her as her head spun, and then, she realized he'd lifted her up and turned with her in his arms, giving the appearance of the room rotating around her. She felt a moment of giddy dizziness, brought on by the combination of Gowan's most excellent drugging kisses and the unexpected motion.

Then, he began walking, slowly, toward the large bed on the other side of the room. Livia rubbed her palms over the hard muscles in Gowan's chest and arms. He was built like a god from some ancient pagan cult. His body had been honed, like the sword he'd been working on, until it, too, was a fine-edged weapon of war, but it could also be used to protect and defend, not just attack.

Gowan, for all his warrior-like ways, was a man of peace, and that part of his complex personality appealed to her. He trained and kept himself in optimal condition so he could protect the people of Draconia, and—as he had done today—allies and innocents who suffered an unprovoked attack. He had a noble streak a mile wide, and she admired him as well as desired him.

Gowan placed her gently on the bed and helped her remove her clothing, placing her garments carefully aside as each piece came free. Once again, he was showing his care for her, knowing she might be seen in the hallway when she left in a few hours and making sure her things would be presentable.

He was such a sweet man. So protective of her. And if he'd known she was thinking of him as *sweet*, she knew he'd scoff, but it was true nonetheless.

He lowered her blouse and freed her breasts, his large hands covering her, his calluses rasping against her soft skin in a way that made her shiver. He played with her nipples, watching them, then watching her expression as he squeezed and tugged, as if gauging her reaction and learning what she liked.

They'd never really had the opportunity to make love at such a leisurely pace. Not alone, without Seth. And though Livia felt Seth's absence, she also relished this time alone with Gowan. She loved them both, strange as it seemed. Livia thought maybe she understood how the Lair families made such a different arrangement work. If love bound the triad, then it felt like nothing was odd or wrong with it.

But she knew her own little trio was missing a very key ingredient. In her case, the dragons were not part of it. She assumed the dragons were what bound the whole thing together, but she didn't really understand how or in what way. It seemed—judging by Hrardorr's refusal to take another knight so soon after being blinded and losing his previous knight—that she would never find out. At least not with Seth.

For in her heart, she knew that if Hrardorr was going to choose anyone as his partner, it would most likely be Seth. It didn't matter that Seth had consciously chosen to follow the healer's path. In his heart, he carried everything noble and necessary to being a knight. He would be a fine knight. A credit to his family and his land. But Livia couldn't see him partnered with anyone other than Hrardorr, which they all knew was improbable if not impossible.

"What are you thinking about?" Gowan whispered, his gaze boring deep into hers.

She knew honesty between them was the only way, which is why she told him. "Seth."

Gowan stilled, removing his hands from her body. His knees lay on either side of her hips, straddling her, but he still wore his trousers. She was the one who was almost completely naked.

"Do you miss him? Do you want him here?"

"Yes and yes, but that doesn't mean I don't want to be here, making love to you, Gowan. I just…" She rolled away and he let her go, moving off her to sit on the wide bed while she clutched her petticoat to her bare body. "I was thinking about Seth and Hrardorr and how it would be so perfect, if only—"

"If only Hrardorr were Genlitha's mate and Seth his knight," Gowan finished her thought for her. She looked up at him in shock. Had he really been thinking the same things? Gowan gave a short bark of laughter at her expression. "It's fairly obvious, isn't it? I mean, that would be the perfect solution for us all, but I have to be honest. I just don't see it happening. Hrardorr's got too much to work through, and I don't even know if Genlitha thinks of him as a potential mate."

"You don't?" Livia was surprised.

She'd thought a knight would know everything about his dragon partner. She'd heard they shared minds at times. Wouldn't that mean he'd know if Genlitha was attracted to Hrardorr as a mate?

"In my experience, most females are inscrutable. Dragon females even more so than human ones." He laughed, and she realized he was sort of joking, but also somewhat serious. He didn't seem to understand Genlitha as well as Livia had thought he would. "It would have been nice, though, wouldn't it?" he went on, musing as he looked away from her.

"It would have solved a few problems for me," she admitted. "Particularly with my father. He couldn't object to our relationship if it was sanctioned by the crown, and we could go live in the Lair. He wouldn't have any say in the matter at all since the needs of dragons and their knights overrule almost any objection he could've made. Especially since, in the eyes of the law, I'm an adult entitled to make my own decisions."

Gowan sighed. "I think your father will always see you as his child. He'll want to protect you. I mean, if a man sets sail with a fleet of ships ready to do battle at great cost to himself and his business, simply because he knows his daughter is in danger... Well, that says a lot about him."

She hadn't thought of it quite that way. Gowan had just opened her eyes a bit. "Yeah. You know? I think you may have something there." She moved closer to Gowan, wrapping her arms around him from behind. "You almost sound as if you admire him."

Gowan covered her hands with his, over his heart. "After today, I think I do. At least a little. I don't like hiding our relationship from him—or from anyone—but I can't do the noble thing here and leave you alone, Livia." He turned, taking her in his arms, her petticoat slipping away to the floor.

"I don't want you to leave me alone, Gowan." She smiled at him, looking into his eyes. "I want quite the contrary."

He kissed her then, and it wasn't the polite, gentle foray of before. No, this was raw need. Bare emotion. Sizzling attraction.

This was more like it. An honest, open need that raged between them. She realized then that he'd been holding back before, trying to give her a different sort of experience. While she was touched by his gesture, now was not the time for such gentility.

They'd both been through a lot that day. Gowan had fought alongside the fey. He'd wielded his sword and spilled pirate blood in defense of an ally of Draconia. He'd faced death and come out on top.

She, too, had been asked to do things quite out of her ordinary experience. The desperate flight, the walk over land into an uncertain situation. Meetings with gryphons and wizards. Magic and mayhem. It was more than her usual boring business day, and it had left her feeling rough in places...especially those close to her heart.

Tonight, she needed complete openness between her and her lover, and Gowan was giving it to her now. Just what she needed from him.

No time to think. Only to feel. To give and receive

pleasure in its most basic form.

She turned the tables on him, tackling him to the bed. He let her. She climbed over him, tearing at the trousers that separated them. He helped.

Finally, when he was freed, she took him almost brutally. Surging down onto him, claiming him for herself. Wild with need, potent with emotion, she began rocking on him, wanting...needing...desiring all he had to give.

And he was with her. Blessedly so.

When she came in a fast, hard climax, he held her. When she collapsed onto his chest, almost sobbing with each breath at the intensity of her feelings, he comforted her. And when he rolled them over, carefully maintaining the connection between their bodies, he began to seduce her all over again.

Gowan was a powerful man, and he used his strength wisely that night, bringing her to climax after climax, letting her rest for short periods before he started it all again. They rarely spoke, but they were always touching, speaking in caresses and murmurs of skin on skin.

He took her hard and fast, then soft and slow. Languorous, one minute; hectic, the next. He gave her everything and demanded all she had in return, which she gladly gave. She was raw emotionally, but his loving presence put a balm on her inner turmoil. When the night started to fade into the next day, she felt renewed in spirit and soul.

He'd done that. He'd restored her. His loving embrace had rebalanced her battered emotions, and she felt she could face whatever the new day brought them in better spirits.

When she left his bed, reluctantly, she was a little sore, but Gowan—for all his hard use of her body that night—had been careful not to harm her. He'd taken exquisite care of her in every way, and she loved him all the more for it.

She hadn't thought it would be possible to love the man any more, but she'd been wrong. Every time they were together, he burrowed a little deeper into her heart.

She left him with a last lingering kiss, wishing she didn't have to go. They both knew, however, that she had to be careful. Gowan had told her that he didn't want anything ruining the memory of the night they had just shared. He got up and opened the door to his room, checking the hall before he let her out.

She made her escape back to her own room just as the first bird began to sing in the darkness. Collapsing onto her own bed, she sighed in bliss and couldn't stop the smile that curved her lips. She fell asleep that way, still smiling.

CHAPTER THIRTEEN

Sir Leo was on watch again when dawn broke over the ocean to the East. Lizbet had not reappeared when he'd gone back on watch, and he was both glad and sad. Glad because he wanted her to rest, but sad that he didn't have her company during the long lonely hours before dawn.

In the pearly light, Leo saw a gryphon approach. It looked like he was making directly for the beach and the bonfires that had died down to mere coals. Sure enough, a few minutes later, a proud gryphon of noble bearing walked soundlessly into camp, giving the glowing coals a wide berth, Leo noticed. Feathers and fur didn't do well with fire, he supposed, unlike dragons who could bathe in the flames with impunity, their flexible, armor-like scales protecting them.

Atop the gryphon was a man. Not a fey. A dark-haired older man. The wizard.

"Hail, Sir Leonhardt," the wizard called as he jumped down from his seat astride the gryphon's massive shoulders. "How is the patient this morning?"

"Greetings of the day, milord," Leo answered politely, standing to face the last of the great wizards of old. "I believe Seth is already at his work, checking on Lady Shara's wounds," Leo told him, unsurprised when Gryffid strode right past him and into the cave without hesitation.

Leaving Leo, of course, facing a rather fierce-looking gryphon. Leo tried to keep in mind the proper etiquette when meeting a gryphon for the first time. He didn't want to do anything that might offend such a fierce creature.

"I am General Falthith," the gryphon said to Leo, surprising him.

"Greetings of the day, General. May I offer you breakfast? Or a snack? I have apples in my pack that Xanderanth often enjoys." Leo wasn't quite sure what to offer a gryphon. They might be roughly the same size and shape as a dragon, but they were quite a different beast altogether.

"No, thank you," the general replied. "We have been touring the island, looking to ssee the sscope of the damage for oursselvess in the light of day." Falthith turned suddenly, looking toward the water. "Ah. Company comess."

Seth looked to where the gryphon was gesturing and saw at least a dozen dragons walking out of the waves and onto the beach. Sweet Mother of All, the sea dragons had come to visit their injured friend. Or maybe they'd come to see the wizard...

As it turned out, the sea dragons had come to do both. Several went into the large cave to check on Shara. A few went to visit with Hrardorr. Leo noticed that Xanderanth stayed by Shara's side, even when her fellow sea dragons came to see her. Xander seemed almost possessive of the female dragon, and he was definitely protective to a degree Leo had never before witnessed—except maybe when Xander was watching over Leo's youngest siblings.

About half of the sea dragons gathered around the wizard when he came out of the cave. Leo heard only a small a portion of their conversation, but he got the idea that Gryffid was thanking the sea dragons for helping to defend the island and offering them a more involved role in future. They walked off a short distance away and seemed to be discussing things in earnest when Seth came out to sit by the small fire Leo had kept burning, and over which he was cooking breakfast.

"Is Lizbet still sleeping?" Leo asked, trying to sound nonchalant.

"*Lady* Lizbet is with Lady Shara," Seth answered, stressing the fey woman's title as if reminding Leo just how out of his league the beauty truly was. Seth sighed heavily and walked around the cook fire to face Leo. "Look, just be careful, will you? She is fey. The next best thing to immortal. Not human, you know? I just...I just don't want to see you get hurt."

Leo felt his face flush with heat, but he appreciated that Seth was trying to be a good friend.

"Thanks, but...it really is none of your business. Don't take that as a rebuke, Seth. I appreciate your friendship, but in this matter, I will have to find my own path."

Seth regarded him for a long time, then finally nodded. "Stars know I'm no one to give advice on romance. Just know I'm here for you if you need a friend."

"Thanks." Leo was truly touched by Seth's concern, but he knew he'd said the right thing.

This felt too important to allow anyone to influence the turn of events—even well-meaning friends. This *thing* between Lizbet and himself would have to prove itself strong enough to stand in the light of day, or peter out like last night's coals.

Seth took his breakfast, and nothing more was said of the matter. Instead, the men discussed the plan for the day ahead as they ate together, saving a portion for Lizbet when she finally emerged from the cave that had become a temporary home to a now-sizable flock of dragons.

Lizbet saw Gryffid come in and chose to stay by Shara's side. She would remain unless, and until, Gryffid asked her to leave. Thankfully, he didn't. He merely smiled at her in that fatherly way he had and looked speculatively between her and Shara while he examined Shara's wounds.

He spoke a few words of magic that seemed to help Shara feel even better than Seth's potions, for which Lizbet was grateful. Anything that helped Shara—be it magic or medicine—was more than welcome. Lizbet hated seeing Shara suffer.

Gryffid surprised Lizbet by staying to chat a while after he'd checked over Shara's wounds. He even invited Lizbet to ask some of the questions that had been bothering her.

When Leo entered the cave, coming over to stand near Lizbet, she saw a knowing look in the old wizard's eye that said all too much. He knew there was some sort of spark between them, and he seemed to be waiting for Lizbet to work up the courage to ask him what she wanted to know.

It was Leo who started the conversation, though, much to her surprise, as they walked the wizard out of the cave. Leo had more courage than she'd thought, to question the last of the great wizards.

"Milord, are sea dragons and land dragons really so different?" Leo began. "I confess, I was expecting them to be much more different from each other, but besides the ability to flame and the webbing on their feet and hands, they seem more alike than they are different."

"At one time, there was no distinction between the types of dragons we know today," Gryffid said in his thoughtful way. "Ice dragons, snow dragons, sea dragons and all the others were all brethren of the dragons who remained in Draconia in the beginning. Most stayed there, but those that branched off turned into these separate enclaves over the centuries."

"So then, it's possible that Xander and Shara could be mates?" Leo asked the question Lizbet had not dared to voice, his brows furrowed.

"It is very possible," Gryffid nodded. "But that leaves you in a quandary, does it not? Because of the way you are joined to Xanderanth, you must find your mate before he can take his."

"But Shara isn't a fighting dragon. She hasn't bonded to a knight—or to any person," Leo said in a glum tone, clearly upset by this idea.

"Hasn't she?" Gryffid turned his knowing gaze to Lizbet.

"I'm not sure…" Lizbet hedged. She was bonded to the sea dragon, but was it the same kind of bond the knights shared with their dragons? She had no idea.

"Aren't you?" Gryffid challenged her again in the same tone. He shook his head. "Come now, you are joined on a deep level with your dragon friend. I see the same link between you and Shara as I do between those two." Gryffid pointed to Leo and Xanderanth, who had followed them out of the cave and onto the beach, leaving Shara's side for the first time since the night before.

"You do?" Leo blinked a few times and looked at Lizbet, then he looked back at the wizard. "Could that work? Would we not need a third?"

"A third in the relationship is something you knights have faced due to several factors, including the scarcity of human women who can bespeak dragons or even tolerate living with dragons, and the fact that only males are chosen as knights. Back in the beginning of dragon knight pairings, many things were tried, and the triad was proven the most stable arrangement and has become the method of choice over time, but I see no reason why your situation couldn't work just as well." He had taken on a sort of lecturing tone, and Lizbet was glad Gryffid has put some serious thought into his answer. "Furthermore…" he went on, "…I am too old and wise not to acknowledge the hand of the divine often stirs the pot where you dragon knights are concerned. Although I am a man of science and magic, even I bow to the Mother of All's wisdom."

Lizbet was shocked, but also pleased by his words. The idea of mating with a human—albeit a dragon knight—was scary. Leaving her homeland was an even more frightening thought. She had never been to the lands where humans ruled. She had never wanted to leave Gryphon Isle. But if she joined with Leo…

Dear, sweet, irresistible Leo…

How could she?

How could she not?

The conflict within her heart made her head spin. She didn't know what to think. What to do. She wasn't sure of anything at the moment, only that she felt something when she was with Leo that she had never experienced before. Something that told her this was significant. *He* was significant.

"You must contemplate many things, young ones. And you must be patient while decisions are made on your behalf in faraway places." Gryffid took on that mystical tone he used when imparting information about future.

Lizbet perked up. Gryffid knew more, but he wasn't telling. She would have to think hard on his words and look for every possible nuance of meaning, for when the wizard decided to keep his own counsel, he did just that and not even a herd of rampaging gryphons could make him budge.

*

Later that morning, Seth arrived back at the wizard's keep while breakfast was still being served in the great hall. He'd left Leo and Xanderanth with Lizbet and Shara. Hrardorr had allowed Seth to guide him in for a landing in the keep's huge courtyard because he wanted to meet the wizard, if at all possible. When asked why, Hrardorr only replied that it was a once-in-a-lifetime chance to converse with someone who had walked among the ancient dragons and designed the gryphons.

The respectful tone Hrardorr used when talking of the wizard surprised Seth, but also pleased him. It seemed there were still a few things in the world that could rouse the interest of the blind dragon. Seth took it as a good sign. To him, it meant that Hrardorr's attitude toward the world—while still bleak, at times—was improving.

Each success built on the next, and Seth hoped that, at some point, Hrardorr would come to accept his blindness and move on with his life. There was still so much he could do—so much he had done since coming to the seaside Lair. But all he saw was his disability, instead of the incredible gifts he could still give to the world and all the beings in it that wanted to give to him in return. Friendship, love, laughter and happy times could be had, if he was willing to accept them.

That was something Hrardorr was going to have to figure out for himself and accept...or not...as time went on. Seth was impressed with how far Hrardorr had come in such a short time, but he still had a ways to go, and Seth vowed to be there for his friend, every step along that journey, if Hrardorr would allow it. And even if he wouldn't. Seth was stubborn, too, and would be there with the dragon's permission or not.

Thinking those somewhat militant thoughts, Seth joined the others in the great hall, guiding Hrardorr with silent instructions. The hall had been built large enough to accommodate gryphons, so even a dragon of Hrardorr's size easily fit within. Seth directed him to an area that seemed tailor made for large four-footed folk near one of the huge fireplaces.

Hrardorr sat comfortably and lowered his head to one of the cushions that seemed to be set there just for that purpose. Once Seth was sure Hrardorr was settled, he greeted everyone, gathered some breakfast from the buffet table, and sat at the table with everyone else.

Livia was there, as was Gowan, but so was Captain O'Dare, sitting between them and making more intimate conversation with Livia impossible. Seth nodded a greeting to her, sending her a little wink when her father wasn't looking, but any other familiarities were strictly curtailed by the captain's glowering presence.

Seth elected to sit near Gowan, who just happened to be in a chair very close to where Hrardorr had settled. The open seat next to him would put Seth right by the dragon, which seemed a good place to be when Livia's father was giving him the evil eye.

A number of fair folk had joined them this morning. Seth recognized some of them from the command tent when he'd been there the day before. Gowan introduced him to a number of the fey officers he had befriended, and they made conversation throughout the otherwise quiet meal.

Quiet, that is, until Gryffid stormed into the room, robes waving in the breeze of his passing, a staff of power in his hand, blazing hot with angry magic. The fair folk shot to their feet, alarm on their pale faces. Sensing the quick change in mood, Gowan and Seth also got to their feet, as did Captain O'Dare.

"Someone made it past all my protections during the battle," Gryffid said without preamble, looking at the assembled warriors. "They have made off with something that could ruin us all!"

"Fisk," Captain O'Dare swore, crumpling his napkin in one hand, his face a mask of anger. "I knew he ran away too easily." O'Dare sought the wizard's attention. "What did he steal?"

"A book. A very precious book containing—among other things—the spell that could release my misguided brethren from their icy prison at the Citadel."

Now, Hrardorr was on his feet, Seth noticed, his body trembling in alarm.

That cannot be allowed," Hrardorr said, his voice strong in everyone's mind. The wizard looked at him, as if noticing him for the first time.

"You are quite right, Sir Hrardorr," Gryffid agreed. "Someone must go after him. And someone must get word to King Roland of Draconia."

Gowan immediately stepped forward. "Genlitha and I will seek the king, if you will entrust us with the mission."

"I will, and gladly, Sir Gowan. Has your dragon friend reported anything about the ships that left here yesterday?" Gryffid asked, his eyes narrowing. Genlitha had been on high guard all day yesterday and had tried to follow the ships that had managed to escape the battle.

"It was strange, Sir. She was able to follow them quite a distance from your island, but at one point, a cloud bank moved in, and she lost sight of them. When it cleared again, they were nowhere to be seen. She should have been able to pick them up easily enough. Clouds are an obstacle we see all the time. But they just disappeared. She elected to return as it was nearing dark, and her natural camouflage works best in daylight hours."

"A wise move. I cannot fault her for that at all. Please express my thanks to her for trying. I fear the book may be affording them access to certain magics that have not been seen in this world for centuries. Hiding a fleet of ships would be an easy trick with that book in their possession. Which is why someone must follow in their wake." Gryffid turned to look directly at Captain O'Dare. "They can avoid being seen from above, but as you know, Captain, ships leave a trace of their passage. If you can get close enough to their trail, you'll be able to see them, no matter the magic they have in their possession."

"Sir, you speak of the book as if it is more than just a listing of spells. Is it magical, in itself?" Livia asked quietly, from her father's side. She looked worried, and Seth longed to comfort her, but now was not the time.

"Yes, my dear. A book such as the one that was stolen from my library yesterday is magical in and of itself. It has endured many centuries, and each being who handled it in all those years—especially during the ages when magic was more abundant in this world than it is today—have left traces of their personal magic within its pages. With such a book, a person wouldn't even have to be a very strong mage to make many of the spells work. The book itself is a dangerous object, which is why it was kept under lock and key—and many magical protections—in my private library."

"It has been said for a long time that Fisk was dabbling in the dark arts," O'Dare growled.

"To get through my protections, there had to be magic involved. No common sneak thief would have been able to free it from the bonds I had placed on my entire library," Gryffid confirmed, frowning. "I have made a thorough search, and they only took that one book. Whoever it was knew exactly what they were looking for. The most damaging spell in that book is the one that would free the prisoners from the Citadel, which is why it must never make it that far North. The book, and its inherent magic, must be there for the spell to work, which is one thing going in our favor." Gryffid paused. "The warnings must go out today. It will take some time for the book to go North, but they must prepare. I have no doubt this Fisk has allies we have not considered. In fact, I would go so far as to say that the entire attack was aimed at distracting us enough to pull off this heinous crime. Even the attacks along the coast and the attempt at taking Dragonscove were probably just a feint to draw our attention away from their true objective."

"You think the book was the object of this entire exercise?" O'Dare asked, his brows drawn together in concern. "I would not put it past Fisk, sadly. He cares nothing for the lives of his men. He would send all those to their deaths in order to accomplish his goals. He is a terrible man." O'Dare threw his wrinkled napkin to the table. "I will go after him and get your book back. This, I vow. And I will end Fisk, once and for all."

Said in that tone of voice, Seth truly believed the captain would do so...or die trying. Seth saw the worry on Livia's face, but he knew—as they all did—that of the assembled warriors, only O'Dare had the wherewithal to follow the fleeing pirates effectively.

"I thank you for your willingness to take on this grave task, Captain. If there's room on your vessels, I would ask only that you take some of my fey warriors with you. They have certain immunity to magic that humans do not and could come in handy in other ways, as well."

"I gladly accept your offer, as long as your warriors understand that, at sea, the captain is in command of every soul on his ship. I expect them to obey the orders of my officers and myself without question." O'Dare's expression was part challenge, part strength. If Seth wasn't so angry at the man for keeping Livia away, he would definitely admire him.

Gryffid looked at the fey officers who had gathered together on hearing the news. They looked grim, but nodded readily.

"You are the master of your ship, Captain, that is well understood. Many of my people have sailed before. I leave it to the Captains of my Guard, Lillith and Gerrow..." he gestured to the couple who were standing in the hall and had come in behind Gryffid, "...to settle who will go and have them on the beach within the hour. Sooner, if possible." The two officers took off, a few of the other fair folk in the room leaving with quick bows, following behind them.

"I will await them on the beach," Captain O'Dare said, looking like he was already making plans. "I must send word to my ships that we sail within the hour."

"Go then, Captain, with my compliments," Gryffid said, moving closer to the sea captain. "And take these with you as well." Gryffid handed over a purse that O'Dare took hesitantly. "They are cut gems and gold coins," Gryffid told O'Dare. "In case you need to grease any palms along the way or resupply somewhere. There is little else I can tell you except that you will recognize the book when you see it. Goddess go with you."

O'Dare bowed formally to the wizard and offered his thanks before leaving. Livia followed him out, her expression full of worry.

Livia followed her father right up to his room, helping him pack.

"You will be careful, Father, won't you? If this Fisk is using magic..." Livia was packing his bag, unable to look at him while her mind raced.

Her father stopped in front of her, putting his hands on her shoulders and making her meet his gaze. "I will do what must be done, sweetheart. No more, no less. But I will do all in my power to succeed and return to you. We have many years to make up for, daughter." He leaned down and kissed her forehead, tugging her close for a quick hug.

He released her with seeming reluctance, then looked down at her again.

"Now, I want you to stay here, if Gryffid will allow it. I think it's the safest place right now."

"But what about the business?" Livia asked.

"Stuart can run things for now," O'Dare said offhandedly. "I want you to be safe."

"If I can go back to Dragonscove safely, I will, and I'll continue as before, running the business. There's the little matter of the new stock of diamond blades to cut up. I'm going to have more dragon healing kits made and send them to the palace. If it comes to war, they will be needed."

O'Dare sighed. "Very well. But only if it is safe to return. You could stay here for a few days and learn all you can from Gryffid's people. It can't hurt to have solid contacts here, now that the island is open for business again."

Livia smiled at that. "My thoughts exactly. I'm glad to see you're still thinking like a trader. For a moment there, I thought you'd become a pirate yourself, with the way you waded into battle yesterday."

Her father's eyes shuttered, and she didn't understand what put that cagey look on his face, but he hugged her again, and she didn't think any more of it. He was learning, she thought. Maybe...just maybe...he was beginning to understand that she was an adult and capable of helping— and of running the business and making decisions in his absence.

"Don't worry about anything on this end. I'll keep the funds flowing to our fleet as needed, and I'll make the best deal for the new supply of diamonds as I can. I believe we are owed at least a portion of them for your actions yesterday— and your willingness to take on this new mission."

"I almost pity the fey you will be bargaining with," he said, shaking his head with a grin. "When did you grow up, Livia? And how did I miss it?"

His tone had gone wistful, and his gaze on her was troubled, even as he smiled. She felt tears gather in her eyes.

"You were grieving, Father," she said in a small voice. "As was I." She swallowed, trying to let go of some of her bitterness. "I only wish you would have turned to me. It was very lonely at home without you, but I learned how to depend on myself. In the end, it made me stronger, but I always missed your presence." She thought hard about what she wanted to say. She might never get another chance to clear the air with him like this. She had to say a few things while she could. "I'm grown up now, Father. I still need you, but not like a child needs a disciplinarian. I need you as a friend. As a mentor. Someone who has my back but doesn't try to tell me what to do."

"I've failed you so many times, my Livia." His gaze seemed bright, but he didn't allow any tears to fall. "I can only beg your forgiveness and tell you that I'm going to try to get it right when I return. I want to be those things for you. And I especially want to be your friend."

She embraced him, throwing her arms around his waist and hugging him tight. It felt so good to be in his protective arms. She'd missed this, growing up without him at home.

"I love you, Papa," she whispered.

"I love you too, sweet pea."

CHAPTER FOURTEEN

Gowan talked with his dragon partner, relaying the information that had just been revealed. Genlitha had gone out at first light to see if she could pick up the trail of any fleeing pirates, but the waters around Gryphon Isle were clear of seaworthy craft as far as she could see. She was on her way back now, so they could leave at the earliest opportunity to take word of the theft to Castleton and the king.

Livia had left the great hall with her father, and Seth was standing next to Hrardorr, with his hand on the dragon's neck. It looked as if Seth was trying to calm the dragon, and Gowan understood the need, listening to Genlitha's increasingly frantic words. Then, a thought occurred to Gowan, and he turned his attention to the wizard.

"Sir, were you doing anything to disrupt communication with our dragons yesterday while we were in this room together?" Gowan interjected into a lull in the conversation.

Gryffid looked at him strangely. "No, I was not. Why do you ask?"

"Genlitha was trying to speak to me yesterday and only when you left the room was she able to get through. Whereas, right now, we're able to communicate easily. We thought maybe it was you doing something deliberate yesterday, but now, I'm wondering—"

"If maybe it was some kind of enemy action. The magic that allowed them to enter my domain without my knowledge would probably have that kind of effect on silent communications. A dampening effect that would dissipate when the spell itself dissipated. It could be that when I left, the spell ceased at that moment by coincidence. Or, it could be that the spell was attached to me, personally. In which case…" Gryffid turned to the remaining fey in the room. "We may have a traitor in the keep."

The fey looked aghast, as if something like that was unthinkable. Gowan didn't understand why they were so surprised. There was usually always at least one bad apple in a barrel, after all.

Gryffid swept out of the room, the remaining fair folk close on his heels. That left Gowan, Seth and Hrardorr as the great hall's only occupants.

"What do you make of all this?" Seth asked Gowan, frowning.

"I think we've all been playing a part in something we didn't even understand. If, indeed, the pirate fleet was created with this one goal in mind, the situation is much more serious than we all thought," Gowan answered, still on his feet. Genlitha was on her way back. He would need to gather his packs and a few supplies before they took off again for the mainland.

"You'll have to go straight to the king with this," Seth said contemplatively. "I mean, you should stop at the Lair to resupply, but don't let them keep you there."

"If they try, then I'll have to suspect they are part of this conspiracy." Even as he said the words, Gowan felt the same stunned disbelief the fey had when the wizard suggested there was a traitor in their midst. It seemed inconceivable that knights and dragons would collude with the pirates, but Gowan again felt like they didn't know the whole story of what was going on. Perhaps the king had better intelligence from his spy network. Gowan hoped it was so.

Seth looked grim. "I must stay here to care for the sea

dragon, Lady Shara. Nobody here has treated dragons before, though if all goes well, I can leave the rest of her care to the healers here in a day or two, with a bit of instruction."

"*I will stay also,*" Hrardorr said, surprising Gowan. "*If the pirates come back for more, I can defend the island along with the sea dragons, if they will continue to help. Who knows what other dangerous things reside in the wizard's library?*"

"An excellent point," Gowan admitted with a respectful nod. "We can't assume they won't try again, now that they've succeeded once."

"*Plus, there is a massive trove of diamond blades in the wreckage that still needs harvesting. I plan to bring a substantial number of them back to Draconia for processing as part payment for our services. Livia wants to have a lot more dragon surgical kits made up, which is a noble endeavor—especially if we're going into all out war.*"

"Then, you and Seth will stay here with Livia for now. I assume Xanderanth and Leo will stay with you?" Gowan asked.

"It would be best for now," Seth agreed. "I'd hate to send them back to the Southern Lair to face the music all alone."

"*And it would take a herd of wild horses to drag Leo away from Lizbet right now,*" Hrardorr snorted, sending little circles of smoke rising toward the stone arches of the hall, high above.

"Really?" Gowan couldn't imagine sensible Leo becoming that attached to a female so quickly—even one of the beautiful fair folk.

"*There is something odd about the attraction,*" Hrardorr went on. "*There is a sound when they interact. Something above your hearing, and almost outside of mine too, but there is a vibration of...something. Some sort of connection there. I hear it between Xander and Shara too. It makes me wonder if...*" He trailed off, but Gowan thought he knew what the dragon was driving at.

"If maybe the Mother of All has taken an interest in creating a few more dragons with your special abilities, Sir Hrardorr?" Gowan challenged.

Hrardorr's head jerked upward in surprise, and then, his mouth dropped open. He closed it again in short order, but

179

his expression still seemed a bit stunned.

"It is something to consider, to be sure," Hrardorr said at length.

"For now, let me help you prepare for your journey," Seth said, gathering up some fruit, bread and cheese from the buffet table into a bundle. "Go get your packs from your room. I'll make up a satchel of provisions."

"And this…" came a new voice from the massive doorway. Lilith, one of the dual Captains of Gryffid's Guard, entered, carrying a sealed scroll. "Gryffid wants you to deliver this into the hands of the king. It is his assessment of everything we know so far. He also asked if your king would station a dragon on the island in a permanent post. I believe he requested young Xanderanth." Lillith smiled slyly when she said it, which meant she was probably speculating about Xander and Leo as much as they had been.

"I will deliver it gladly, Captain," Gowan said formally, accepting the scroll and placing it carefully in the inner pocket of his jerkin. He would not lose it easily from that most secure spot.

The next hour was filled with comings and goings. Livia had gone to the beach to see her father off. She came back to the keep in a solemn mood, tears gathered in her eyes, but she didn't let them fall. Seth wanted to comfort her, but he was kept busy helping prepare Gowan for departure.

He didn't begrudge Gowan the five minutes he spent holding Livia close. She needed comforting, and Gowan was leaving. He wouldn't be able to cuddle her for a while—and with the uncertainty surrounding them, maybe not ever again. They had to grab what moments they could, while they could.

Genlitha arrived back at the keep and spoke with Gryffid directly about what she had observed that morning and the day before. The wizard asked pointed questions but seemed to acknowledge her responses with increasing grimness. Finally, he stood back and spoke to the small assembly. His captains were there, along with several of the fey officers and a few of the gryphons, including General Falthith. They were all gathered in the courtyard.

"I blame myself for thinking my magic inviolable. It has been so long since I've been threatened by someone, or something, that was even close to my magical equal that I became over-confident in my protections."

Captain Lilith stepped forward. "Sir, we were sequestered in the fog for so long, we did not realize all the potential threats either. This is not all on you, Master. I'm sorry to say, we have failed you."

Gryffid put one hand on her shoulder in a fatherly gesture. "No, my dear, you cannot take the blame for this. Magic was the weapon used, and I am the one who should have answered it." He moved back, took a deep breath and seemed to shake himself. "What's done is done, and I have learned a hard lesson. Now, we must move forward with renewed intensity. I will be reinforcing the spells on our island for the next week, at least. I will also be scrying to see if I can locate our enemy and my stolen property."

"We will send out spies into every land," one of the fey officers said, stepping forward. He had to be the spymaster, though Seth had not realized it until now. "We will find the lost book and bring it back home."

"Before it is used, hopefully," Gryffid put in, his expression dark.

Seth saw Gowan off, then returned to the great hall, where a large group was gathering. It was made up of leaders from every part of Gryffid's island. Fey warriors were there in force, but also leaders from other disciplines. Bards, troubadours, smiths and innkeepers, which surprised Seth until he realized that all contributed something to the war effort. The bards, most interestingly, were revealed to be working close with—or in many cases, actually were—spies.

Seth spent the rest of the day in the great hall, meeting with those very interesting fair folk. Gryffid left shortly after the meeting got underway to search his library again and reinforce the spells that protected it. He was the one who wanted Seth and Hrardorr to contribute what they knew about the pirate fleet from the battle of Dragonscove and the interrogation of the prisoners taken during that action. Gryffid thought perhaps that they could draw parallels and contrasts between the two battles, since they had been present for both.

Seth realized the value of Gryffid's suggestion not long into the discussion. The prisoners from Dragonscove told a far different story than those from the more recent battle. The men aboard the ships that had attacked Dragonscove all said their captains were after plunder. A few even admitted to seeking slaves and pretty girls to kidnap.

But the prisoners being interrogated even now from the latest conflict told a different tale. Their captains had been hinting at greater rewards to come in the future, if they managed to pull off this mission. There was no promise of easy money and pillaging. This battle had been about some other objective that only the captains of some of the ships seemed to know. And they weren't talking.

The fey warriors who were in charge of those who were doing the many interrogations reported that the captains of the sunken ships—those who had survived to be taken prisoner—were somehow immune to the fair folk's normal methods of eliciting information. Whatever they were. Seth didn't know, and he knew better than to ask. The fey had many secrets. They lived apart from humans and didn't often show themselves. Seth felt privileged to be part of this discussion at all. He wouldn't jeopardize his position by asking a question that was really none of his business.

After the meeting adjourned, a young healer approached Seth, introducing himself as Lothar, brother of Captain Lilith and the healer, Lizbet, as well. He explained that he was interested in the medical instruments Lizbet had seen Seth use to treat the sea dragon, and Seth was happy to spend a few minutes showing Lothar his set of diamond-tipped instruments, explaining the use of each and why each instrument had been designed the way it was.

They stayed behind in the great hall, commandeering a

table off to one side. Lothar called over another man, who he introduced as Jarel. This man, it turned out, was the craftsman who would try to replicate the tools. He brought paper and stylus to make detailed sketches.

Seth let Jarel sit there, in the great hall, with Seth's most prized healing instruments, while he sought a more intimate supper with Livia, in an empty corner of the giant gathering place. Seth trusted in the integrity of the fair folk, and he knew Livia had to be craving some quiet time after everything that had happened. He sought her out, and they dined together, speaking softly, as if to speak too loud would shatter the momentary calm.

The others who came and went from the great hall left them in peace. Hrardorr was nearby, providing his natural warmth. Seth noticed that the servants left a few melons near his head, as if they were used to leaving treats for the gryphons who probably frequented the place. Hrardorr was able to sniff them out and nibble at his ease, which made Seth glad for his scaly friend.

"My father left a boat, in case I needed it. It's nothing big, and he couldn't leave a crew to man it since he's probably going into a fight, but he had a supply craft he could leave, and did so with the fey's agreement. The idea is to load it with some of the diamond blades to bring back to Dragonscove as payment for his intervention." Livia talked quietly as she ate. "I'm not sure how, or even if, we can do that, but it's available if we need it."

"So we could sail back to the mainland if we had to?" Seth asked, realizing that the captain had left his daughter a way off the island, if she needed it. Smart man.

"Yes, absolutely. The boat is even packed with some provisions already, so it's ready to sail whenever needed." Livia took a sip of her wine. "Of course, we can leave it here if we find another way back. It's just an option, Father said."

"It's a good option," Seth replied. "He's provided a way home for you, which was very thoughtful of him. He loves you in his way, Livia. Even though I could wish he hadn't come back to interfere with our...friendship..." He stumbled, not knowing the right word to use. Were they merely friends? Or did they truly have a relationship? And what about Gowan? Where did he fit in? What was the right word to use here? He watched Livia's face carefully, but she didn't seem to react to his hesitancy. "Well, even though I could wish he wasn't around sometimes, Captain O'Dare showed incredible loyalty to you in sailing here to make sure you were all right."

She seemed to ponder that for a moment, a wistful look entering her gaze. "Yeah, he did, didn't he?" She smiled, that soft look still on her face.

"He does love you, Livia," Seth said quietly, hoping to reassure her. "If he didn't, he wouldn't have come. And he wouldn't have tried to protect you from Gowan and me." Seth went one step further. "He must be a noble and brave man at heart to have gathered a fleet of ships and their captains and crews around himself. To even think to do so, to actively resist the threat Fisk and his band of pirates represented... That's quite an undertaking."

"You sound like you admire him," Livia observed.

"You know, I believe I do. I mean, he's always been known as one of the most successful men in town, but to find that he's created a defense force all by himself because he saw a threat and wanted to combat it—that takes a special kind of courage and gumption. I'll be interested to hear what the crown thinks of your father's initiative when word reaches the capital."

Livia frowned. "Do you think he's going to get in trouble?"

"On the contrary," Seth was quick to reassure her. "I think he's going to get a medal." Seth emptied the last of his tankard of ale and set it down again. "So many of us have been conditioned to always look to the Lairs when an enemy threat is detected—and rightly so. The dragons and knights exist to serve and protect the land. But this threat from the sea is something new. Something we're not equipped to combat. Or, at least, the present leadership of the Southern Lair has proven unwilling to even try to combat. But where everyone else looked to the dragons for rescue, your father went out and did something about it all on his own. That shows remarkable initiative and forward thinking. After all, the dragons don't seem well equipped to deal with a threat from the sea, but in this case, fighting fire with fire—or ships with other ships—seems to be a good solution."

"If not for Hrardorr and his abilities, Dragonscove would have been lost," Livia mused.

"So might this island," Seth agreed.

"But I thought Fisk only came for the spell book."

"Perhaps, but what about all those other ships? What were they going to do once they fought through and all those miscreants had made it onto shore?" Seth frowned, thinking of the reports from the interrogators. "They were promised plunder and pillaging. Rape and mayhem visited on any vulnerable fey they could find. Perhaps gryphons, as well. There were a lot of men on those ships, Livia. Only the fact that the gryphons are acting as guards to the prisoners on shore right now keeps them from running amok." Seth sat back, done with his meal. "Many were killed in the fighting. Some went down with their ships. But several hundred came onto shore, waterlogged and half-drowned by Hrardorr and the sea dragons' actions, even bedraggled as they were, ready to fight. The day could have ended very differently, and not in our favor."

Livia had a pensive look on her face as she, too, finished with her plate and pushed it away. She sat back in her chair, as well, staring for a moment as if thinking hard.

"Many things conspired to give us a good day," she finally said. "I'm glad my father was a part of the solution, as much as I'm happy that Hrardorr showed once again that he is well able to fight. I'm also glad he made some new friends. I had no idea there was a population of sea dragons here." She blinked and looked up at Seth. "It makes this island even more mysterious and magical, doesn't it?" There was a lovely twinkle in her eyes as she smiled at him.

"You mean, more than it was already?" he said, smiling back at her. "As if having an actual wizard in residence wasn't mysterious enough."

Livia shrugged playfully. "You may have noticed...I'm partial to dragons."

On their way out of the great hall, they stopped by the table Jarel had commandeered. Several other artisans were sitting with him as they went over the designs he had made from examining Seth's tools. The precious tools were returned to Seth with only a few more questions, and Livia was able to tell them what her gem cutters had told her when they were asked to create this set of instruments and several others like it.

Livia was glad to see that Jarel and his friends were eager to get started turning the weapons of war into something much more useful. The artisans didn't waylay Seth and Livia long, but their conversation left her with a good feeling about the people who would be working with the rescued diamonds. Jarel and his folk seemed to see the process of turning blades into surgical instruments as a challenge, just as her own people had done.

As Seth walked her to her room, Livia mused that artisans were the same regardless of age or race. They saw each new project as a puzzle just waiting to be solved. She liked that idea and wondered if there might be some way in the future of getting her people in contact with Jarel and his folk. They could compare notes and share ideas. She mentioned the thought to Seth as they walked quietly through the old stone keep.

"Of course," she added, "the fey probably know more about gem working than our people do. They live forever, don't they?"

"If not forever, then at least for many human lifetimes. I think they're more like our dragon friends than truly immortal, but our knowledge of them is limited because they don't often interact with humans anymore," Seth answered.

She hadn't thought of that, but it made sense. The only truly immortal beings she knew of were the great wizards of old, like Gryffid. But they could be killed. Many had been, of course, during the ancient wars. Only Gryffid remained, though he'd been hidden under a magical veil, now lifted, on this island for centuries.

Only since coming here had she learned that more of his brethren were imprisoned in ice in the far North of the world, in a place called the Citadel. A prison for evil wizards.

And her father's greatest enemy, Captain Fisk, had just stolen the key.

She hadn't even known her father *had* a greatest enemy, much less a pirate who would do something so audacious as raid the stronghold of the last of the great wizards with impunity. She wondered if she ever really knew her father at all. Her memories of him from her youth were of a much different man. He'd smiled more before her mother died. He'd been almost jolly.

But after her mother's death, he'd been…different. Cold. Quiet. And so, so sad.

As she'd been.

Only, he hadn't turned to her to share their grief. If anything, he'd turned his back on her. Or so she'd thought. Her father had said some things that made her question his motives. He'd told her a little bit more about Fisk and had made the startling statement that it had been Fisk who had murdered her mother.

If, all these years, her father had been actively hunting Fisk… It made a sad sort of sense that he'd left her alone, safe, in Dragonscove. If Fisk thought his daughter meant little to Captain O'Dare, she would be safer, so her father had all but ignored her. For her own safety.

It still hurt, but she thought she understood his neglect better now. He'd done it out of love, oddly enough.

They arrived at the door to her room, and Seth paused outside it. Livia shook herself out of her reverie and smiled at him.

"Father is gone," she whispered, moving closer to Seth and reaching out to finger one of the ties on his jerkin.

Seth smiled back at her. "Are you sure—"

She cut off his words by placing a finger over his lips. Opening the door behind her, she tugged him into her room.

"Never doubt that I want to be with you, Seth." She closed the door behind them and faced him, leaning back against the wood panel of the door.

She was feeling daring and free. The events of the past few days had liberated her in some indefinable way, and the newfound independence was coming out in all sorts of unexpected ways. Without Gowan and his dominant ways to subdue her, she was feeling friskier than usual at the idea that Seth was completely hers for the rest of the night.

Caressing his shoulders, she moved him toward the large bed. She freed him from his vest and began untying his jerkin even as his nimble fingers went to the closures on her bodice. They were undressing each other with smiles on their faces, each reveling in the idea that they would not be disturbed and could spend the rest of the night exploring each other.

"Do you miss Gowan?" Seth said, breaking her concentration for a moment. She looked up to meet his gaze.

"A little. But I had time alone with him last night. Tonight, it's only fair that I spend time with you, don't you think?" It shouldn't feel so natural to think of herself with both men, but somehow...

"You talk as if we're a bonded trio," Seth said, his gaze clouding over with regret. She hadn't meant to make him feel that way. She wanted tonight to only bring him pleasure.

Livia placed her finger over his lips once more. "Don't think about that now," she counseled. "I don't understand what's really going on here or how this is all going to work out in the end, but I feel drawn equally to both of you." She shook her head, unsure how to make him understand. "I don't understand it either, Seth. I just... It feels right. Can't we just enjoy our time together now and worry about tomorrow when it comes?"

Seth's frown was still firmly in place, but he nodded. "I guess that's really all we can do for now, but if I could commit to you, I would in a heartbeat. I hope you realize that, Livia. If I had a dragon partner, and he was Genlitha's mate, all would be perfect. As it is..."

"As it is, we're alone in my bedchamber, unlikely to be disturbed until morning, and we're wasting time talking about things we cannot change." She smiled to soften her words. "But that doesn't mean things won't change. I have faith that the Mother of All would not be so cruel to us. I have to believe that somehow things will work out, in time. We just have to be patient and have faith."

Seth shook his head again, but his expression had eased. "I'll try."

Livia smiled as she pushed him down onto the bed. "Don't worry. I'll make a believer out of you yet."

Those were the last words spoken for some time as Seth and Livia renewed their acquaintance on the most basic levels. She cried out his name in ecstasy more than once, as he did hers, and when morning came, they were wrapped in each other's arms, the bed sheets a tangle around them.

CHAPTER FIFTEEN

A little later that morning in the great hall, Hrardorr was in what looked like a serious conference with Gryffid when Seth and Livia made their way to the great hall. Gryffid had pulled up a chair near the dragon's head and waved them over when he noticed them walk in.

"What do you think that's about?" Livia whispered to Seth.

"I haven't the foggiest idea. Hrardorr and I haven't spoken since yesterday," he replied as they walked over to the wizard and the blind dragon.

If Seth was any judge, Hrardorr's expression seemed troubled. Not in an alarming way, but it definitely looked like the wizard had given the dragon something very important to think about. Seth couldn't begin to imagine what the two might have been talking about, and Hrardorr wasn't saying anything. He looked both distracted and perhaps a little miffed as they walked closer, and Seth wasn't going to be peppering him with questions when he had that sort of obstinate look on his scaly face.

"Good morrow, milord," Seth said to the wizard, pulling out a chair for Livia at the table just in front of Hrardorr when Gryffid indicated they should join him.

Livia also offered polite greetings of the day to the wizard.

Gryffid seemed in better spirits this morning, though the thought of his missing spell book cast a pall over everything and everyone within the keep. No doubt things would be subdued on the island until it was recovered.

As if by magic, two plates full of food arrived at the table, placed in front of Livia and Seth by pleasant-faced servants. It seemed, when dining with the wizard, you didn't have to go and fetch your own plates.

"I have had reports from the far cove about the sea dragons," Gryffid said as the three of them began to eat breakfast. "Lady Shara is healing nicely with Lizbet and your friends Leo and Xanderanth to look after her. I have also spoken to Lord Skelaroth, leader of the sea dragon community that claims this part of the sea for its own. He has agreed to ally his forces with us for now. Dragons were created with the sacred duty to protect the world from the use of rogue magic. Once Skelaroth heard what had happened, he was eager to be of service. He is also interested in learning more about Sir Hrardorr and his abilities." Gryffid nodded toward the dragon who sat just beyond the table. "I was asking Sir Hrardorr if he'd be willing to meet with Lord Skellaroth in the coming days and he agreed…with some reservations."

"Reservations?" Seth sent privately to Hrardorr, concerned for his friend. *"Are you all right with meeting this sea dragon lord? You don't have to do anything you don't want to do here, my friend. You've already saved this island once. They owe you, not the other way around."*

"Be at ease, Seth. My only reservations are that I am still blind, no matter what I may have been able to accomplish in battle. My…vanity…bothers me at times. I do not want to be seen as handicapped by these new dragons. It's bad enough suffering the pity of the dragons in our land."

Seth relaxed as Hrardorr's words sounded in his mind, ringing with truth. Seth was glad it was something as simple as Hrardorr's unwillingness to meet new dragons who might judge him because of his injury. The very fact that Hrardorr was willing to acknowledge the reasons behind his hesitancy was a big step forward, as far as Seth was concerned. He wondered if Hrardorr realized it, but Seth wasn't about to point it out. Especially not when the wizard was still talking.

"I want you both to stay as long as you wish," Gryffid was saying. "For your bravery in journeying here when the others in your land refused to come, you have earned an open invitation to travel between my land and yours whenever you wish and a guest room in the keep for as long as you want it."

"That is incredibly generous of you, milord," Livia answered politely as Seth nodded agreement with her words. "As you may know, my father left a small boat for my use. If it is all right, I'd like to stay on here for a while before returning home."

"As would I, milord," Seth put in. "Thank you for your kind and generous invitation. I would see Lady Shara healed more before I consider leaving. I might also be able to help with the other dragons if more will be joining her. I have been showing Lady Lizbet some of the techniques we use in the Lair and would be happy to train others while I'm here."

"Very kind of you," Gryffid said, nodding. "I have heard of the surgical instruments Jarel and his folk are working on. If they are successful—which they always are, eventually, I've found—I'd like to send you back with some of the sets of instruments as a gift to the dragons of your kingdom from us. And you are correct," Gryffid went on, not pausing for thanks. "There will soon be dragons patrolling in the skies as well as the oceans. You see, the sea dragons have kept themselves apart from the affairs of men for so long, they lack some of the necessary skills. Skellaroth and I have devised a plan in consultation with General Falthith. Sea dragons will learn how to patrol from the sky with gryphon partners, then take those skills into the depths with them. Skellaroth will set up regular patrols around the circumference of the island, but I have asked Hrardorr to organize the training and lend his considerable wisdom as the only dragon who knows air, land and sea tactics."

Gryffid nodded toward Hrardorr, and the dragon nodded just slightly as if he knew they were all looking at him. *"Although I fear I may not be up to the task, I am honored to try,"* Hrardorr finally spoke, including them all in his thoughts. *"Xanderanth will assist, of course. He will have to help do the things I cannot, and it will be good experience for him, young as he is. He needs more responsibility. I believe this is just the ticket."*

"It is good of you to consider your subordinate's needs," Gryffid said with approval. "Xanderanth may be young, but even I can see he will grow into a mighty dragon in the not-too-distant future. He has the makings of greatness in him, and his knight partner has a pure and true heart. They are a good pair and, like you, will always be welcome here."

"I may be crippled, but I will do what I can to uphold the ancient trust," Hrardorr went on, surprising Seth. *"We dragons were created to safeguard magic. We stand guard against infiltration of the Citadel, but we also have a duty to protect the knowledge from getting into the wrong hands. I failed here. The book that was taken is a great threat to our world and our way of life."* Hrardorr's voice had taken on a solemn tone. *"But there is more on this island, now that it is not hidden in the mists of time, that could be used against the forces of good. I will do all in my power to keep the rest of the magic on this island safe. If that means treating with sea dragons and training those who have not yet mastered the skills I once took for granted, then I will fulfill my duty."*

"And glad I am to hear it, too," Gryffid said, confirming to Seth that the wizard had been awaiting the dragon's decision. Perhaps that's what Hrardorr had been thinking about so hard when Seth and Livia had arrived. "But, my friend, you did not fail. The theft of the book was my failure and mine alone," Gryffid told the dragon, facing him, his expression one of compassion, fatigue and sadness.

"I don't think anyone could have expected a ragtag group like that of having such a lofty goal as sneaking into one of the most magically fortified places in the world," Livia said quietly, offering comfort.

"I should have been better prepared," Gryffid said, sighing

heavily. "In the old days, no one would have gotten past me, but I fear I've lived in peace for a little too long. When the island was hidden, I had little need for the strict vigilance I once took for granted. I must adjust to these new times and being out in the world again. I only pray it is not too late."

Seth had no idea what to say to that. How did one truly comfort one of the most powerful beings in the world? Gryffid might look, and even act, like some benevolent grandfather, but he was truly unlike any other creature Seth had ever met.

Unlike the fey and the dragons and gryphons, Gryffid didn't just seem immortal by human standards, he *was* immortal. He had lived longer than any of them had been alive. He had seen and done things in the faraway past that Seth only knew as ancient history.

Gryffid had participated in the wizard wars, for heaven's sake. He'd designed and created the gryphons. An entire race of mighty beings owed their existence to the wizard, which seemed almost unbelievable to Seth.

Gryffid wasn't a god. He didn't pretend to be all-powerful and omnipotent. But he certainly had abilities that put him up there, alongside any deity Seth had ever heard about.

Perhaps that's why so many of the wizards had turned bad. With such power, it wasn't too hard to imagine one being tempted to believe in his own magnificence. And from there, it was probably a slippery slope to thinking all other beings were beneath you. That Gryffid hadn't succumbed to that sort of thing spoke volumes for the man's character to Seth's way of thinking.

They continued their breakfast, talking about Lady Shara's progress, and Hrardorr even said a few things about his plans for teaching the sea dragons to do what land dragons did on land as far as security functions and training. Seth was pleased to hear that Hrardorr planned to take an active role in the work, using the much younger and less experienced Xanderanth as his assistant—his *eyes*, though Hrardorr never came out and said it that way.

When the wizard finished eating, Gryffid excused himself, saying he had more work to do in his library. Seth assumed the wizard was going to be casting protections around the remainder of his collection in hopes of preventing more theft. That left Livia and Seth with Hrardorr, finishing the last remnants of their meal.

"Has there been any more talk about a possible traitor in the keep?" Livia asked quietly.

"Not in so many words, but I did notice some new guards had been added to the corridors we passed on our way down this morning," Seth observed.

"I thought so," Livia said quickly. "And there are more armed soldiers at the entrances, as well. Both at the doors to this hall and at the entryway we passed on the way in."

"Indeed," Seth agreed, popping a last slice of fruit into his mouth.

He looked carefully around the great hall, noting the very obvious increase in the number of warriors standing watch over everyone within. He knew there were more stationed all over the keep now, after the vulnerability of Gryffid's protections had already been breached. Too late to stop the theft that had already occurred, but perhaps the visible increase in security would deter any further problems? Seth wasn't so sure.

If there really was a traitor among Gryffid's people, he or she wouldn't cease their clandestine acts so easily. Not when they'd already succeeded. They'd had plenty of time to lay their plans, while Gryffid had only had a day or two to realize his own protections hadn't been good enough. Seth thought privately that if the traitor was going to do further mischief, he or she would do it now, to prove the point that, no matter how many guards Gryffid put in place, he was still vulnerable.

The worst sort of punishment someone like Gryffid could have was knowing they were vulnerable, despite all their imagined power. Shaking Gryffid's confidence was the ultimate blow and could make the wizard doubt himself if and when he needed to act.

And if the worst should come to pass, and the Citadel was breached, there would be need for the good wizard's powers. If the Citadel released just one of its prisoners into the world, it could easily mean death or enslavement of thousands if not millions of souls…and war on a massive scale that had not been seen since ancient times.

Gryffid would be needed then, as he had been needed of old. But if he doubted himself, he would not be as useful as he had been a full strength. If there was a traitor in his court, then that traitor would be working to undermine the wizard at every turn—or so Seth believed.

He would make it his business over the next days, while he was in residence here, to keep a sharp eye out. Perhaps he, as a newcomer to the island, would see something others did not. Seth would tell the others to be equally as watchful.

The wizard had left Hrardorr with an impossible choice. Gryffid had come down to speak with Hrardorr that morning before breakfast, thanking him for defending the island and wanting to give him a reward for his bravery. Hrardorr didn't want a reward for doing his duty or being what he was. No, he wanted for little in life. There was only one thing he would wish for if wishes really did come true, and that was something even a great wizard could not restore.

Gryffid had told him as much, answering Hrardorr's unspoken wish as if he'd plucked it directly from Hrardorr's mind. Perhaps he had. The wizard had almost unbelievable abilities. Perhaps mind-reading was among his many talents. Then again, it didn't take a wizard to realize the one thing Hrardorr wanted most in the world was to see again.

"I can't give you your sight back," Gryffid had said quite plainly. "If the healers have not been able to make progress, then neither will I, but I can offer you something almost as good. It would require a sacrifice on your part, though," the wizard had warned as Hrardorr's emotions went flying skyward, then plummeting down again on a sickening ride. "If you were to bond with a new knight, I could probably devise a spell that would allow you to see through his eyes. At least when you are together, though the ability could be useful at other times, as well, if a bit disorienting." Gryffid shrugged. "Perhaps, over time, you'd learn how to manage the view from elsewhere—wherever your knight is—while your body remains in another place."

"I have vowed never to take another knight," Hrardorr told the wizard in a solemn voice.

"Yes. So I understand," the wizard said, not unkindly. "I know you have your reasons. For one thing, you have not been given adequate time and space to mourn the loss of your previous bonded knight. Your heart and soul must still be raw in the places where he was joined to you." Gryffid reached out and placed an open hand on Hrardorr's shoulder, in a gesture that was oddly comforting. "I know what it is to lose those we care for. I have lost more people to the next realm than you will ever know in all your years, my young friend."

Hrardorr thought about the wizard's words and, for a moment, sensed the eternity of his years. He understood, deep within, that the wizard had seen more—and lost more—than Hrardorr would ever know. It was a humbling thought.

"How do you go on, Master?" Hrardorr asked, unable to censor his words, even if he'd wanted to.

Gryffid sighed, breaking the quiet of the poignant moment. Hrardorr felt released, and as if he'd delved almost too far into the abyss.

"I will not say it is easy," Gryffid went on. "Losing those we love is never easy. Knowing in our minds that they continue on, in a new place, without us, in ways even I cannot fully comprehend is small comfort to those of us left here, alone, lonely, struggling without them." Gryffid patted Hrardorr's shoulder and stepped back. "In your case, you not only lost your bonded knight, but your eyesight, as well. Either one alone would have been cause for great sadness and retreat from the world, but to have both happen at the same time... Frankly, I'm amazed you have carried on as you have, Sir Hrardorr."

The fact that the wizard used Hrardorr's title indicated a level of respect that was not lost on the dragon. This mighty wizard respected him? How could it be? Hrardorr was dismayed, but the wizard kept talking.

"You have almost single-handedly saved not only the town of Dragonscove, but my island. Certainly, others helped, but only after they saw you doing what no creature of your kind has ever done before. You are unique in your heritage, to be sure, but there's more to what you did than just your ability to flame and swim. It is your courage, my friend. Your willingness to help, even when you are hampered by the sense you lost. Your willingness to lay everything on the line to protect others, to help those in need and save innocent lives. You are selfless almost to the point of folly, truly." Gryffid paused to huff out an amazed-sounding laugh. "You are a dragon among dragons, Sir Hrardorr. The lands have not seen your like in eons and perhaps never will again. Though I suspect there will be more matings among the sea dragons and your land-based brethren in future. The ability to flame is something the sea dragons have lost over the years, but I suppose, now that they've seen what you can do, they'll want that back. And the Mother of All plays a hand, of course."

"Of course," Hrardorr agreed by rote, his head still spinning. *"Master, I am not the hero you paint me."*

"Nonsense." Gryffid interrupted him. "You are all that and more. And you have a very big decision to make. My offer stands. If you choose a knight, I will work the spell that may allow you to see again...after a fashion. But I cannot and will not bind anyone to you in that way unless they are also bound to you with the knight's bond. It would not be fair to either of you, and could be dangerous. If you bond to a knight, I know you will both honor the bond until one of you dies. That is the only way this magic I propose will work."

Hrardorr wanted to shake his head, but didn't dare. He

might accidentally hit the wizard, which would be unforgivable. Despair filled him.

"I cannot take another knight, Master," Hrardorr whispered, his thoughts, his heart...broken. *"You ask too much."*

"Perhaps I do," Gryffid replied, his tone filled with understanding and tinged with sorrow. "I am only sorry I cannot do more for you, my friend. You have saved my people and my land. I owe you a king's ransom, yet I know that is not what you truly wish. I offer you a sad bargain instead, but it is the only thing I have to offer that can even come close to giving you what you most desire. For that, I am sorry." Gryffid patted Hrardorr's shoulder once more, proving that he had not moved too far away. "You are welcome here for the rest of your days, Sir Hrardorr. You are a hero among my people, and to me. For what you have done, you will always have my respect and thanks."

Gryffid moved off. Hrardorr could tell by the flow of air as the wizard walked away.

"But keep my offer in mind. It stands, if you ever can bring yourself to act on it," the wizard had told him silently.

That afternoon there was much activity on the beach near the dragon's cave. Leo and Lizbet sat on the beach with Lady Shara while the other dragons frolicked in the waves. Shara couldn't get her injury wet for a few more days yet, but she was healing well according to Seth and Lizbet.

Even Leo could see the wound was knitting as it should. With a bit more ointment and rest, they'd probably be able to take out the stitches soon. Maybe in a day or two. Then, it would be a few more days for the skin to knit more fully together. The scales would take a few weeks to grow back, though it might take more than one molt cycle for the scales to sit properly in the area of the cut again.

Sir Hrardorr had come back mid-morning and landed in the ocean, wading ashore with guidance from Xanderanth. Seth and Livia O'Dare showed up a short while later, riding on the back of a gryphon. A summit of sorts had taken place a short while later, involving the gryphon commander, General Falthith, Sir Hrardorr, Xanderanth and the leader of the sea dragons who had come ashore just after Hrardorr had arrived, a massive male dragon called Lord Skelaroth.

From what Xanderanth had passed along to Leo, Hrardorr was in charge of helping the sea dragons learn how to patrol and fight, should they be needed to defend the island again. Lord Skelaroth had agreed to help protect the island and the repository of magical objects and books in Gryffid's keep, but to do that, he acknowledged that his people needed to learn some basic guard skills. To that end, they'd asked Hrardorr to be the intermediary, since he understood the limitations of land, sky and sea equally.

General Falthith was there to coordinate training flights around the island with select gryphon teams, who would show the sea dragons how gryphons usually patrolled and how they spotted problems from the air. Xanderanth would fly those patrols with the sea dragons at first, as group by group, the gryphons and sea dragons learned how to work together. Xanderanth and Leo would share their knowledge of such things from their perspective, and Hrardorr would help them put it all together so they came up with a workable system that utilized everyone's greatest strengths at the end of the training period.

While the dragons and gryphon were ironing out details, Seth and Livia approached Leo and Lizbet, who were tidying up the cave and their campsite. Leo went to Seth at the other man's beckoning, concerned at the frown on Seth's normally jovial countenance.

"Is something wrong?" Leo asked, joining Seth by the fire that had all but died out.

"Could be," Seth said quietly, making room for Livia to sit on the log they'd used the night before as a bench. "We need you to keep your eyes open. There is a strong possibility that one or more of Gryffid's people is a traitor."

"Surely not!" Lizbet had joined them, objecting to the idea that one of her fey brethren could betray Gryffid.

"I'm afraid it's possible," Livia said quietly. "Even Gryffid has come to the same conclusion."

"I thought, being outsiders..." Seth went on, looking pointedly from Lizbet back to Leo, "...we might possibly be able to spot things the folk who live here could otherwise miss."

"Like what?" Lizbet asked, not really caring that Seth meant for the conversation to be between the folks from Draconia.

For his part, Leo wouldn't keep Lizbet out of any conversation he might have. This was her home. She was entitled to know what was going on as far as he was concerned.

"Could be anything. Someone walking where they shouldn't be. A sound out of place in the setting. A suspicious action that goes otherwise unnoticed," Seth said, clearly scrambling for examples. "Frankly, since you're spending most of your time down here on the beach, I don't expect that you'll see much, but you never know."

"I'll keep my eyes open," Leo agreed readily.

"Good. Now that's out of the way, I understand a memorial of sorts is being planned for three days hence, down here on the beach so as to include the sea dragons," Seth told them. "Lady Lizbet, can you tell us what we might expect?"

"Music," Lizbet replied at once, her expression somber. "And toasts to the departed. It is our tradition to sing them home. Such memorials have been going on all over the island since the battle. Many were lost, though not as many as would have been had Sir Hrardorr and the sea dragons not come to our rescue." Lizbet's beautiful blue eyes looked so sad Leo wanted to put his arm around her shoulders, but he dare not take such liberties, especially in front of others. "It is our way to share the celebration of the life that was lost with those around us. It is natural to my people to want to include the sea dragons in our ceremony. I should have realized..."

"You were busy with other thoughts," Leo told her

quietly, reaching out to touch her hand. Surely, that small touch wasn't overstepping the bounds of propriety.

Lizbet seemed to take comfort from his gesture. She smiled softly at him before squaring her shoulders and getting back to the topic at hand.

"There will be food and drink. A large crowd here on the beach. Music. Ceremonial dance. Offerings of flowers, grains and dried herbs. A ceremonial fire." She looked around at the beach. "We'll need to make preparations to host that large a group and provide the facilities they will need—the fire pits, the seating areas. The nests for gryphon families and comfortable spots for the dragons…" She trailed off, looking to Leo for guidance.

"Land dragons prefer heated sand pits for relaxation. I'll ask Xander what he thinks, but the dragons will probably be the easiest to accommodate since we're on a sandy beach already, and both Xander and Sir Hrardorr can supply any fire we need to get things heated up."

"I wonder what the sea dragons think of hot water?" Livia mused. "If we could create a shallow pool, one of our dragon friends could heat it with a quick burst of flame, right?" She looked to Seth, who nodded agreement. "I wonder if they'll think it odd, or if they might like it?"

"We'll have to ask," Lizbet said. "Shara and I have never talked about such things, since none of the sea dragons are able to flame like your land-based friends. I suspect they might like it, though. They enjoy basking in the noonday sun here on the beach. Shara told me they like the warm rays on their scales."

"Then, we should look into testing out this idea. Leo, can you and Xanderanth try digging out a shallow pool big enough for a dragon when you have a few free minutes?" Seth asked him.

Leo nodded readily. "We'll give it a try as soon as he's free."

CHAPTER SIXTEEN

As it turned out, the sea dragon lord himself was the first to try the heated pool Xanderanth and Leo had devised. All the sea dragons had watched with interest as they took a short break from the planning and training to enjoy the sunlight and a moment of peace together on the beach. Xanderanth and Leo, of course, did not rest, but set to work building a small pool down by the water. Sort of a manufactured tidal pool that would capture about a foot of water in a shallow depression big enough for Xander to sit in comfortably.

When Lord Skelaroth asked what they were doing, Xanderanth had explained the experiment, and the sea dragon leader volunteered to try it out first. He stood back, watching Xanderanth with what Leo read as respect, while the younger dragon blew fire onto the small pool of water, heating it to a steaming bath in just a few moments.

Lord Skelaroth dipped a toe into the water, and his head went up in surprise, then moved downward again in intrigue as he lowered his front foot into the warm water. A moment later, he was sitting in the pool, a dragonish sigh releasing from his nostrils. Leo had to grin. It was more than apparent that the sea dragon liked the hot water on his scales.

"This is divine," the dragon lord commented to all, his eyes closed in bliss as he settled deeper into the heated pit of sand

and water. *"Do land dragons do this all the time?"* he asked.

"We sleep in heated sand pits called wallows when we are not on duty elsewhere," Xanderanth told the sea dragon lord.

Leo added a little more to the story. "The Lairs are built into the sides of mountains and cliffs. There are platforms for flying and landing, and each dragon or dragon pair has a suite of rooms built around their wallow. The oval wallow is the heart of the suite, with a rim where people can walk and rooms arranged around the sides of the pit. Usually a small kitchen, bathing chamber, bedroom for the knight, or if it's a family's suite, rooms for children as well, supplies, equipment and other things. The key is, the dragons can see into every room arranged around their sand pit so they are part of the family, involved in every aspect of our lives," Leo told the sea dragon.

"Do you have to heat the sand yourselves?" Lord Skelaroth asked, tilting his head as he spoke to Leo directly for the first time.

"My understanding is that there was a bit of magic used in the construction of the Lairs," Leo told the dragon, scratching his head as he thought about it. "Science and magic both, actually. The wallows are heated automatically, but I don't know exactly how. There is also running water in the bathing chamber and the sink in the kitchen, but if I want a hot bath, I fill the tub and ask Xanderanth to heat it for me."

"It is a blessing to have fire in your belly," Lord Skelaroth said solemnly. *"That is something we have lost, but it is said of old, our forefathers could flame."*

Leo didn't know what to say to that, so he remained silent.

"Perhaps one day, you will flame again," Xanderanth said, with all the enthusiasm of youth. *"I, for one, would love to be able to swim like you or Sir Hrardorr, but I fear it is a skill beyond my abilities."*

Lord Skelaroth turned his head to really look at Xanderanth, giving him a critical eye. *"Maybe not,"* the sea dragon lord said, making Xander's head pop up in surprise.

"You have strong wings and a muscular build. You could be a very powerful swimmer, given a bit of instruction, I believe. Perhaps while you are here, we will get a chance to give it a try."

"Oh!" Xander seemed truly enthusiastic about the possibility. *"I would enjoy that greatly, milord. Thank you."*

"Don't thank me yet," the dragon lord chuckled, relaxing back into the water. *"Swimming lessons are hard work, even for our young. We will put you through your paces and see how you do."*

The older dragon seemed to doze off after that, and Xanderanth tiptoed away, loath to disturb the leader of all the sea dragons in the area. Leo followed suit, walking back to the main fire pit because Lizbet was sitting there, drinking a mug of tea.

He was drawn to her in a way he hadn't ever experienced. If she was near, he wanted to be with her. It was that simple. And that alarming. Leo knew his heart was in grave danger from the fey beauty, but he couldn't seem to stop himself from wanting to be near her. To just look at her. To talk with her. To bask in her gentle presence.

"I think Sir Xanderanth will be a better swimmer than you realize," Lizbet said as she offered Leo a fresh mug of tea. He took it and sat down on the log beside her, facing the rebuilt flames of the small cook fire.

"You heard all that?" he asked to make conversation. She nodded.

"I've known a few young sea dragons who were learning the ways of their water world over the years, including Shara. They are born on land, though I know not where. When they are little, their parents protect them and teach them swimming once they are big enough, but they have to come ashore to rest often, and many times, they come here, to this cove. Which is why I come here a lot, to see them and speak with them, if they will allow it."

"You have many friends among them?" Leo asked, intrigued.

"Some." Lizbet shrugged. "Shara is my best friend, really. She and I go way back, and we have earned each other's trust over the years."

"Xander's my best friend, though it was fast for us. He spoke the words of claim, and then, the bond formed between us and…it was like…" He searched for words to explain the sensational feeling, but couldn't describe it adequately. "It was like nothing I can explain in words. We were just instantly bonded. One, yet separate. He knew me to my soul, and I got a glimpse into something ancient and wonderful in his. I can't imagine my life without him."

"I feel a little like that about Shara sometimes," Lizbet admitted. "But of course, it's different. I'm not a knight, and she's at sea much of the time. But we talk every day, even when we are apart. We're more like sisters, I'd have to say. Sisters who are also best friends, no matter that she has wings and scales and I do not."

"I have a lot of siblings," Leo said, contemplating her words. "And yeah, Xander feels a lot like one of my brothers, but there's something more too. Something even deeper than the family bond. We are partners. And I know we will face whatever comes to us in this world together. That's something you can't say about just anyone. Even a sibling."

Lizbet leaned over and kissed his cheek, surprising him.

"What was that for?" he asked, wishing he'd known she was going to kiss him so he could have enjoyed it more.

"It's because you love him so completely. Because you're willing to give of yourself to him and expect nothing in return but his company. You're a noble being, Sir Leonhardt."

Were her eyes sparkling with tears? Was she nearly crying? Over him?

Leo couldn't help himself. He moved closer, putting one arm around her shoulders. He didn't care who might be looking. Lizbet was feeling deep emotions, and the least he could do was offer comfort. She'd been through a lot over the past few days. Perhaps she just needed a shoulder to cry on. His sisters were like that sometimes, and Leo had learned how to be there for them when they needed him.

"Hush now, Lizzie," he crooned as she buried her face in

his neck. Sure enough, she was crying. Just like his little sisters. "It'll be all right."

Of course, she was nothing like his sisters in any other way. For one thing, she was fey. For another, Leo was highly attracted to her. Holding Lizbet was not at all like holding his snotty little sisters when they cried.

"I'm sorry," Lizbet said, sniffling as she tried to move away. Leo held her gently, letting her go only so far, so he could look into her watery eyes.

"Don't be. You've been through a lot these past few days. We all have. It's only natural that your emotions are running high." He leaned in and kissed her softly, meaning it to be a quick peck, but it turned into something a little less tame.

Still, they were on the beach in full view of everyone, in the middle of the day. Leo had at least enough presence of mind to pull back before he ravished her right there under the sun in front of everyone.

Hrardorr was gladdened by how well the sea dragon training had gone that afternoon. He'd spent a lot of his time underwater, where he was able to "see" what was happening, and he was impressed by the way the sea dragons picked up new skills. They were fast studies, which would make this exercise work much better than he'd originally thought.

They could also teach him a thing or two about swimming, he realized. They were much more agile than he was, and Hrardorr intended to work on his skills now that he'd discovered what a dragon could truly do underwater.

The flying part of the program he'd have to leave up to young Xanderanth. Sea dragons could fly, but they didn't do much of it. Low-altitude hops around the island and the occasional leap from the surface of the water was about all they admitted to doing. That would have to change. Hrardorr thought it a crime that they didn't utilize all of their native abilities. Dragons who didn't do much flying was anathema to him, though he tried not to let it show.

They were making an effort, and he was glad of that. The

gryphons, too, would help with the flying part of the planned training. Gryphons had been flying organized patrols around Gryphon Isle for centuries. They would be teaching the sea dragons some of the skills the gryphons had perfected, using Xanderanth's guidance on any adaptations needed for scaled wings rather than feathered ones.

All in all, Hrardorr was well pleased with the results of the first day's work. He returned to the keep satisfied with the progress they had made. The sea dragons were already beginning to patrol the waters in a more organized fashion, and they would be learning more about patrolling patterns on the morrow from the gryphons.

He tried not to be concerned that young Xanderanth decided to stay down on the beach with the injured female sea dragon for another night. It was true that she needed protection while she was injured, and it was probably a nice gesture on his part to want to keep her company, but Hrardorr couldn't help but notice the attraction between them—and between their two-legged counterparts.

Lizbet and Leo showed every sign of being smitten with each other that Shara and Xander did. It was kind of poetic, but definitely different from what land dragons had long-ago accepted as the norm.

Hrardorr wondered how it would all work out as he took a place before the grand fireplace in the great hall. The fey servants had left a bushel of sweet melons for him to snack on, as well as a bucket of clear, fresh water. They were good to him, and he did his best to show his appreciation.

It wasn't quite as comfortable as his sandy wallow in the Lair, but it was definitely a snug place to sleep, warmed by the fire on one side, a soft rug beneath him, and snacks within easy reach. He dozed off, content.

After dinner in the keep, at which the wizard did not put in an appearance, Seth was summoned to Gryffid's tower. Apparently, the wizard wanted to quiz Seth about life, and politics, in the Southern Lair. Seth had seemed loath to betray anything that might injure the Lair in the wizard's eyes, but Livia knew he would tell Gryffid the truth when asked. She parted with him in the great hall, promising silently that they would meet again in her bedroom once the wizard was done with Seth.

With Hrardorr sleeping by the fire and the few gryphons she knew off doing whatever it was gryphons did, that left Livia with a bit of time on her hands. Knowing she would probably never get such an opportunity again, she went exploring in the massive keep, enjoying the carved stonework and delighting in each new surprise as she discovered it.

One room was devoted entirely to stringed instruments. It had tightly sealed doors and a water barometer inside, along with strategically placed braziers to keep the temperature and humidity just right. Livia crossed paths with a wizened old fey man in that room, who was checking the readings and lighting just every other brazier. He explained the workings of the room to her and how sensitive some of the instruments were to changes in environment.

That room, he told her, housed some of the greatest stringed instruments ever made. Each was a treasure, and Gryffid kept them safe and available for the master bards to play when they wished. They were also there for artisans to study and try to replicate the skills of the great masters of old. It was a treat, the old man had told her, to handle and play such finely crafted instruments, and his honor to be one of those who cared for them, making sure they would live on in perfect tune for the next generations.

She'd spent a good half hour with the friendly old man, and he suggested further rooms for her to explore. There were similar rooms devoted to woodwind instruments and one for metal horns. Another for drums. And each instrument held in these special rooms, he assured her, were the finest of their kind.

Livia spent an hour or more going from room to room in the musical section of the great house. She was enchanted with all she saw, but especially when she happened upon a room devoted to crystals and gems, uncut and cut. The walls sparkled with specimens in display cases.

That the wizard could leave such valuable things lying around, free for all to view and touch spoke volumes about the trust he had with his people. Again, she thought about the possibility that someone could have betrayed his trust, and the feeling just didn't sit right. Why would anyone turn traitor on a man who, from everything she'd seen, truly cared for and trusted his people?

She'd spoken to many of the fey in her days here, and from all accounts, there was no poverty on this island. Nobody was going without the basic needs of life. If someone had something bad happen in their family, the community came together to help—as happened in the best of the human towns in Draconia and elsewhere in the world.

Fair folk were even allowed to come and go from the island as they wished, though until recently, they'd had to disguise their origins. When Gryffid had reversed the spell that had hidden the island for so very long, the world again became aware of its existence, and the need for secrecy had diminished.

Until now, though, no human ships had been allowed to dock, and very few humans had been welcomed ashore. There was no trade between the island and the mainland, but Livia hoped to change all that. Once things settled down, she would broach the subject of opening a line of commerce between Gryphon Isle and Dragonscove, using her father's shipping company. Now was not the time to ask about it, of course, but when the time was right, she would propose the idea. She'd been planning how it would all work in her idle minutes, though there were precious few of those.

These stolen hours touring the magnificent house were a rarity in her life of late, and Livia enjoyed them for all they were worth. She went from room to room, working her way toward one end of the massive keep. She meandered more or less in a line heading due East, starting from the central great hall and working her way through the Eastern half of the house. Her guest room was on the Western side and up one floor, so she'd have to return to the great hall, and the many stairways that led into other parts of the structure.

On her way back toward the great hall, Livia stumbled upon a small gathering of fair folk in one of the drawing rooms. They were sitting around the fire, drinking dark wine when she unwittingly barged in on them.

"Oh, I'm so sorry!" Livia exclaimed when all eyes turned to her. "Please excuse me. I was trying to get back to the great hall."

A beautiful young woman stood and smiled as she came over to Livia. "You're the sea captain's daughter, aren't you? Mistress Livia O'Dare?"

"Yes," Livia replied, wondering where this might be leading, but the woman seemed friendly enough.

"I've been wanting to meet you, but I've had to lay low, lest I run into any of the human males now on the island. I'm Gwen. Gryffid's granddaughter." She held out her hand and pulled Livia into the room.

"Oh. I didn't know he had any family. I'm sorry. I should have realized. You are the lady of the keep." Livia's mind raced to keep up with this unexpected turn of events.

Gwen laughed, and it was the tinkling sound of magical bells, pleasant and musical. She really was the most attractive fey Livia had yet seen. That was really saying something, because they were all incredibly beautiful. They hadn't earned the name fair folk for nothing.

"Perhaps you've already met Lilith, co-Captain of the Guard," Gwen gestured toward the woman seated by the fire. Livia had seen her before, in the great hall, but never at her ease. "And this is her brother Liam." The younger of the two men nodded as he stood politely, both of them having gotten to their feet when Livia approached. "He's a diplomat, if you can believe it. And their brother, Lothar, who is one of our most skilled healers." The second man nodded this time, and Livia returned the courtesy. "They've been keeping me company on and off, since I can't really go outside with all the humans here now."

"Not without causing a riot, at least," Lothar joked. Livia didn't understand what they were talking about but hesitated to ask any questions. She had interrupted them, and they were being nice about it so far.

"Perhaps our guest does not realize what you are, Gwen," Lilith said, almost chidingly.

"Yes, of course. I'm sorry," Gwen said, turning to Livia again. "I...have an odd effect on men due to my heritage. One of my ancestors was what you might call a siren. Her magical allure bred true in me, and as a result, I have to be careful around human males. That's why I live here with Grandfather. The fey aren't quite as susceptible."

Livia felt compassion for the beautiful girl who couldn't venture out in the world. "That must be...difficult."

"At times," she agreed. "But, come, I've wanted so much to meet you. I watched your father sail away and thought you must be quite something to have stood up to such a formidable man."

Gwen's friendly manner invited confidences, but Livia wasn't sure. She didn't know much about the fey, but then again, she'd come here with the idea of learning more about them and forging alliances that might help in the future. Who better to start with than a member of the wizard's family?

"My father has been away for much of my life. I run the trading business when he is not in port, which means I run it most of the time." That was common enough knowledge to anyone in Dragonscove.

"So she is smart as well as lovely," Lothar said, raising his glass to Livia with a charming smile. Liam, not to be outdone, poured a small glass of the aperitif they were all enjoying and brought it to Livia.

"Our family distills this vintage from a secret combinations of fruits and flowers that grow in our vineyard. It is called Essence of Starlight, and you may well be the first human to sample it," Liam said as she accepted the small glass of pale amber liquid. It seemed to have a slight effervescence, but perhaps that was a trick of the light. She couldn't be sure.

She wasn't sure if she should trust these beings, but she also didn't have all that much to lose. She doubted very much that any of these folk would be the traitor they thought might be in the keep. Livia calculated the odds and decided to take the risk and try the drink.

Sipping cautiously, she discovered that there were, indeed, the tiniest of bubbles bursting against her tongue as the most delicious flavor she had ever sampled in a liquor enveloped her mouth and her senses. She smiled, unable to contain her reaction, and the others smiled back at her.

"This is…it's indescribably delicious." She felt a little flush of heat rise to her cheeks. "And, if I'm not mistaken, very, very alcoholic."

CHAPTER SEVENTEEN

The others chuckled. "That's why the glasses are so small," Lilith told her, laughing. "Two or three of these knock even large men out until sunrise."

"But one has merely a relaxing effect," Lothar assured her. "This drink, unlike most, has a sort of multiplying factor. The more you imbibe, the higher the level of the alcoholic effect. So a single small glass won't get you drunk, but ingest another, and the effect is increased about five fold."

"I've never heard of anything like that," Livia told them, intrigued. If this drink was something she could import, she knew she could find a market for it. Probably a very lucrative market at that.

"As far as we know, it is unique to the island," Liam confirmed.

"Now that the island has been revealed to the world at large again, have you given any thought to opening trade?" Nothing ventured, nothing gained, she thought. Might as well broach the subject now and study their reactions. "Something like this aperitif could command high prices on the mainland. And perhaps there are things you'd like to import from the mainland, as well?"

"Raw materials," Liam said at once. "I know the artisans are always complaining that they can only bring back small amounts of ores and gemstones when the travel abroad."

"Herbs and medicinal plants that only grow on the mainland," Lothar added.

Livia nodded, taking mental notes as they each added items to the list. "My father's company specializes in trade," Livia told them when the conversation went into a natural lull. "In fact, I had no idea he'd been building a military force until he showed up here. But be that as it may, our primary mission has always been trade and profit. If he decides to change that now that he's revealed his fleet of ships capable of fighting, that's his choice, but I believe he'll still have to run a trading fleet—even if just a small one—to help pay for the military arm." Perhaps the drink was making her say more than she would have normally, but these folk needed to know some of this, if they were going to consider trading with her company. "If you do decide to pursue trade with the mainland, I hope you would consider using us."

"But of course," Gwen replied with an ease that made Livia blink. "Grandfather trusts you, which is all the endorsement any of us need. When things settle down a bit, perhaps we can fill that little boat your father left for you with the first batch of trade goods for you to take back to Dragonscove whenever you decide to leave."

"That..." Livia was stunned. They had been thinking way ahead of her. "That would be fantastic!" She couldn't hide her enthusiasm. "And I can either sell the trade goods for cash or do exchanges for the items you want from the mainland and have them couriered back to you by one of our ships, or come back myself with a full ship, if I'm able."

"Either will work," Lilith said casually. "We'll have procedures set up for a working port by then. Between the sea dragons patrolling the waters and the gryphons in the air, we'll see any approaching ship long before it makes landfall in future."

Livia spent a pleasant half hour with the fair folk, planning for the opening of trade. She took note of the items they thought would be most wanted on the island and began thinking about places and merchants she could sell their goods to for the highest prices or exchange rates. This could be very profitable, as well as being a good route toward replenishing supplies on the island.

"Where are you?" came Seth's voice in her mind as she finished her aperitif. Talking with Seth or Gowan this way wasn't as easy as speaking with the dragons, but it was a skill she was learning.

"Just finishing up. I met Gryffid's granddaughter and some of her friends."

"I didn't know he even had a granddaughter," Seth replied, clearly surprised.

"There's a reason for that. I'll tell you when I get there. I'm leaving now and will be with you in a few minutes. I just have to find my way back to the great hall and go from there. I'm on the other side of the keep."

Even as she sent her thoughts to Seth, she began to take her leave of the fair folk. Within moments, Livia was back on the path that would lead her to the great hall. From there, she was well acquainted with the path to her guest suite, where Seth was waiting.

She hadn't meant to be gone so long, but she was glad she'd stumbled across Gwen and the others. Not only could it prove profitable, but Livia had genuinely enjoyed their company.

She was smiling as she made her way down the hall, a little tipsy from the beverage, but not drunk. She had her wits about her—and it was a good thing too, when she saw a furtive movement going up a hidden staircase farther down the hall. Something wasn't right there.

The woman had looked exactly like Lilith, but Livia knew for a fact, she'd left the Captain of the Guard back in Gwen's parlor. Livia didn't think Lilith had a twin. Surely, the three siblings she'd just met would have mentioned it when they'd laughingly told her about all the other members of the rather large family.

"Seth?" Livia concentrated on sending the message to the

only person she knew for certain wasn't a traitor in this keep, even as she followed the woman disguised as the captain up a staircase she'd never seen before.

"What's wrong?" Seth must've heard something in her tone.

"I'm not sure, but there's someone sneaking up a back staircase who I don't think is what they appear to be." Livia reached the landing and cautiously peeked out to see the woman moving to another set of stairs. All the stairs in this massive house were wide enough for a gryphon to climb and made of worn stone. Livia had marveled earlier at the many years talons and feet had tread these same paths to make them smooth.

"Where are you?"

Livia gave him exact directions as she flowed down the hall to the next staircase. She caught just a glimpse of the woman's sword as she left the second stairway. She was armed. Of course. The Captain of the Guard was seldom unarmed. But Livia had seen Lilith resting at ease—sans sword—in Gwen's parlor not five minutes ago. And she'd been wearing different clothing. Similar, but different.

"I'm on my way. Be careful. We know this traitor—if that's the person you're following—is dangerous." Seth sounded worried.

"She's armed, Seth. Bring your sword."

"I'll do better than that. I'll bring reinforcements."

The two women climbed ever higher on the wide stone staircases, one behind the other. Livia realized they must be in one of the many towers that made the keep look so formidable from outside. The towers, she'd been told when she was first admitted to her guest suite, were off limits to all but a trusted few. It seemed Gryffid liked to work at height, and he used each tower for a different secret purpose, known only to him and his select friends.

They were very high in the tower now. In fact, the next staircase was a spiral. Livia held back. There was no way she could follow unseen on a spiral staircase.

"Seth? Where are you?" she sent desperately. "She's on the last staircase that leads to the pinnacle of the tower."

"I'm right behind you. Stay out of sight. I'll be there in a few minutes."

His voice in her mind was reassuring, but there were too many doors leading from the spiral staircase into hidden rooms. Livia would have to try her best to see where the woman was headed. If Livia missed the correct room, she could blow right past the traitor and either lose her completely or be trapped at the top of the tower with her below.

And Livia was unarmed.

The first thing she'd do after this, she vowed, was to get a weapon that she could conceal on her person at all times. Gowan could teach her how to defend herself, surely. Livia shook her head at the distracting thought. None of that would help her now.

"Why are you following me?"

The demand was made in a strong voice, similar in tone to Lilith's, but not exactly the same. Still, the air of command about this woman was very similar, but she carried a disdain in her bearing that Livia knew, firsthand now, the captain did not.

Was the woman bluffing? Livia would bet the confrontation was all bravado, because clearly, this woman wasn't where she was supposed to be. Nobody was supposed to be up here in this deserted tower without the wizard. Not now. Not after everything that had happened in the past few days.

Livia decided to challenge. "Why are you skulking around in this tower, when the last I heard, Gryffid had sealed access to every tower in his keep until further notice?"

"I'm the Captain of the Guard. I go where I will, when I will. Who are you to question me, human?" Livia heard the fear and falsehood ringing in the woman's voice.

"Oh, so you're Captain Lilith?" Livia couldn't help the cunning smile that crept over her face. "Lilith Eliadnae?"

"Of course. Who else?" The impostor's tone rang with affront, but it wasn't convincing to Livia's ears.

"Funny thing, I just left Lilith and two of her brothers

sipping wine with Gwen. If you truly were her, you would remember meeting me not an hour ago. So, tell me, impostor, who are you, really?" Livia tried to be nonchalant, leaning against the stone wall, but inside, she was quaking.

Especially when the woman cursed and drew her blade.

"None of your damn business, human. I didn't want to kill you, but you've left me no choice."

The traitor started walking toward Livia, menace in every step. The wide hallway behind Livia was empty. She knew help was on the way, but would it get there in time? Livia began praying, even as she backed up, keeping pace with the swordswoman in a dance as they moved back down the arched hallway that was the top level of the keep proper before the circular stair to the tower.

They were almost to the stairway Livia had climbed to get to this hall when the swordswoman stopped in her tracks. Livia didn't dare look behind her, but she felt the heat of a dragon's presence on her back.

"Hrardorr? Is that you?"

"I am here, Livia. Seth is on my back. He guided me to you. Come to me and touch my neck so I know where you are. If I must flame, I want you under my wing, protected."

"Thanks be to the Mother of All. I really think this woman was going to try to kill me!"

"Not on my watch. Seth is keeping me informed of her movements, but I need to know you're safe if I let loose with my fire."

Livia didn't need to be told again. She backed up until she was standing with her back against the dragon's chest, her hand on his shoulder. She could duck under his wing if he flamed, just as he'd told her to do. She cast a quick look around and saw Seth on Hrardorr's other side, his sword drawn.

"You draw steel in the wizard's house?" Seth challenged the woman, who now looked as if she was calculating her chances of getting past the blind dragon.

"You're the trespasser here, human. You and your scaly friends. This is *Gryphon* Isle. It is not meant for the likes of that." She cast a disgusted glare in Hrardorr's direction.

"Tell me," Seth said, almost conversationally. "How is it that you can wear another woman's face? Are you bespelled?"

"I need not answer your questions!"

The woman darted forward as if to speed past Hrardorr, but Seth must've given Hrardorr the word, and the dragon let off just a lick of flame that stopped the woman in her tracks. She backpedaled away from the line of fire, her gaze furious…and scared.

"Try that again, and he won't just fire a warning shot," Seth drawled, seemingly unfazed by the dragon's flame.

The hallway was made of stone, with only the occasional tapestry hung here and there along the walls. Vaulted stone ceilings supported delicate arches that let in light during the day, but were shuttered up tight at night against the chill. Between each arched window burned a wall sconce, lighting the scene in a flickering golden glow.

"You can't hold me!" the woman screamed at them.

"I certainly can," boomed a new voice as the wizard himself made the scene.

Gryffid arrived, moving forward to stand next to Seth. He was waving his hands around in front of him, making arcane gestures that Livia didn't recognize. Perhaps it was some sort of prelude to magic? She wasn't sure.

And then, all doubt was removed as a beam of white light shot out from the wizard's hands to envelop the woman. She writhed and screamed as the appearance of Lillith melted away to be replaced by another face…and then another. And another.

Sweet Mother of All. The woman hadn't just assumed one false identity, but at least a half dozen. But how?

The obvious answer came to her even as Gryffid's spell faded. Magic.

The face that was finally revealed was one Livia hadn't seen since coming to Gryphon Isle, but it was a familiar face nonetheless.

"I've seen her before," Livia whispered. "The fisherfolk

call her Mad Meg. She comes into port every few months to sell her wares, most of which are of questionable origin. She runs a small sailboat and goes from port to port peddling her wares." And probably her body, though Livia wasn't going to mention that unless asked because it was only a rumor as far a Livia knew.

"Are you certain?" Gryffid asked quietly.

Livia nodded. "She came into my office on her last trip, trying to sell me stolen property. I reported her to the Harbormaster, and she disappeared."

"What was her cargo?" Seth probed further.

Livia thought back. "Well, she claimed to have rare spices and wines from the East, and come to think of it...she boasted of having a selection of gryphon feathers for sale. But the deal breaker for me was when she showed me a sample of what she claimed was skith leather, but was really the treated leather old William Tanner sends up to the Lair. It had his stamp on it and everything. And the whole town knew he'd been robbed the week before."

"That was your test," the woman known as Mad Meg sneered at Livia. "You failed."

The pieces fell into place in Livia's mind. "If you were testing me to see if I was crooked, I'm glad I failed."

More people arrived in the hallway, moving out from behind Hrardorr. The real Captain Lilith, looking all business now as she approached Meg, who still brandished the sword, disarmed the imposter with a quick sweep of her blade. More guards bound Meg's hands as she started screaming epithets at them.

At Gryffid's nod, they gagged her. If she knew magical spells, it was probably a wise precaution, making her unable to form the words that might unleash who-knew-what.

As the warriors dragged her away, Gryffid turned to Livia, Hrardorr and Seth.

"Again, you do me a great service. Thank you."

"You're very welcome, milord, but...can you tell me...is she human?" Livia asked hesitantly.

Gryffid shook his head. "Sadly, she is one of ours. A journeyman bard of good family. Her name is, actually, Meg, but she has been out in the world for a while now, and I had no idea she'd returned to the island. I'll be following up with her family, of course. I don't know every coming and going from here anymore. Not since I dropped the veil."

"Is she a mage?" Seth asked, sheathing his sword, now that the danger had passed.

"I thought not. Oh, the gift crops up now and again among the islanders, and I take an interest in their training and character, but as far as I knew, Meg had only a slight bardic gift. Not true magic like that which she used to disguise herself. That had to have been learned elsewhere."

"She regularly traded in goods from Skithdron," Livia put in. "King Lucan is said to have been dabbling in sorcery. Perhaps she learned it there?"

"It is a distinct possibility," Gryffid agreed. "I will be looking into it. For now, can you tell me where she was heading when you spotted her?"

Livia went through, step by step, the path that had taken her to this point. Gryffid asked her to walk with him to the circular stair and describe exactly where Meg had been when she spotted Livia.

She answered all his questions—even the ones that didn't make a lot of sense to her. At length, he seemed to be satisfied and turned away, calling two guards to stand watch at the base of the circular stairway.

Livia realized then that Meg might not have been alone. There might yet be other traitors wandering the halls of the keep. Just because they'd caught one, didn't mean there weren't others.

After taking their leave of the wizard, Hrardorr walked with them back to their rooms. When they got there, Livia realized she didn't want the dragon to leave. She felt safer with him, and knowing he was safe too. The situation on the staircase had shaken her badly, and she wanted her friends around her, close, where she could be sure everyone was all right.

The entire keep was built on a grand scale, big enough for gryphons, so it was easy enough to guide Hrardorr through the big arched doorway and into the suite. Then, all it took was a few minutes of pushing chairs and a table out of the way to prepare a clear spot for Hrardorr directly in front of the big fireplace.

It wasn't the massive hearth of the great hall, but it would do. Livia and Seth sat with Hrardorr for an hour or more, just talking about the day's events and speculating on what might happen next. She needed that time with them both. Safe time to just be. Away from danger and people they didn't know and might not be able to trust.

She yearned for simpler times, but knew she had to find a way to play the hand she'd been dealt. Tomorrow. Tonight, she would lean against her dragon friend and hold hands with one of her lovers, basking in their warmth of spirit, friendship...and love.

CHAPTER EIGHTEEN

The following morning, Sir Gowan found himself in heady company. Not only was he arriving back at the Southern Lair in the company of two of the greatest knights in the land, but they were escorting Prince Nicolas and his wife, Princess Arikia. Gowan had only met them in passing when he first became a knight. To be traveling with them was something else, indeed.

For both Nico and Riki, as they called each other, were royal black dragons. They didn't ride dragons, they *were* dragons. They could shapeshift in the twinkle of an eye between human and dragon form. Both of them fairly crackled with magic.

As did the two knights who accompanied Gowan and the royal pair on the return journey to the South. Sir Mace and Sir Drake. Two of the most revered knights of the current age, they were both said to have magical abilities far beyond that of normal men.

Sir Mace was a steady man. A fierce fighter. He was serious and somewhat forbidding, though when he spoke with Drake, he was much more carefree. And when he was with Krysta—their shared mate—he was downright jovial. Surprisingly, Krysta had come along with them on this journey.

Gowan knew the look of her when he met her. She was a fighter too. A warrior woman with grace and style. Gowan had heard about her, of course. She was rumored to have been a guardswoman before meeting her mates, and she still wore a sword that looked more than comfortable across her back.

Sir Drake was something else altogether. A fighter, sure, but also a charmer. Lair rumor had it that he had spent many years roaming the lands as a spy for the kingdom. Having met the man and conversed with him now, Gowan was inclined to believe it. Drake was usually smiling, spinning tales and talking non-stop, in general.

Such verbosity would have quickly gotten on Gowan's nerves if he'd been partnered with the knight, but Sir Mace seemed to take it all in stride. Drake had surprised Gowan during their travel by asking very pointed questions about Gryphon Isle and the people there. Apparently, the two knights had been to the island before, though information on the place and the wizard who lived there wasn't freely disseminated in the kingdom. All anyone knew was that the island had reappeared after centuries of hiding behind a magical veil, and it was best to stay clear of the place, unless specifically invited by the wizard.

Gryffid, to Gowan's knowledge, had issued no invitations.

Gowan had expected some sort of rebuke for taking things into his own hands and all but invading Gryphon Isle without invitation, but the king was surprisingly forthright. He'd thanked Gowan and Genlitha for doing the right thing and reserved his anger for the rest of the Southern Lair.

With the continued hostilities in the North and on the border with Skithdron, King Roland himself could not leave the capital, but Prince Nico had volunteered to check things out. A few hours later, they'd been on their way back, with Drake, Mace and Krysta riding on the backs of Lady Jenet and Sir Nellin. Krysta was riding double with Mace and the two royal black dragons were flying between Jenet and Nellin. Genlitha and Gowan were acting as rear guard.

They flew through the night to arrive on the outskirts of the Lair's watch at dawn. Genlitha scouted ahead, her natural camouflage in the light of day allowing her to make certain the way was clear for the rest of their party. With all the strange goings on in the Lair of late, they couldn't be too cautious with members of the royal family's safety. Dragon shifters were too precious to both races, for they bound the dragons to the men and vice versa. The shapeshifters were the only ones who were deemed worthy to rule over both dragons and knights.

When Genlitha gave the *all clear* signal, it was only after a meticulous inspection on her part. They also didn't announce themselves. The posted sentries would see them soon enough, and when they did, the dragons would trumpet a welcome to the royal blacks in their midst. All dragons revered the royal family, as did their knights.

Lady Jenet was also famous among her brethren for her amazing coloring. Pale peach and gold, she was a stunner among dragons and as recognizable as the golden-haired man on her back. Drake and Jenet together just…sparkled. All that golden beauty in one place was a little overwhelming, even to Gowan's jaded senses.

By contrast, Sir Nellin's bronze wasn't nearly as flashy, but he was a fierce dragon just the same. As was Sir Mace. They were as well matched as their counterparts. They were around the same age as Gowan, but their dragons were of a younger generation than Genlitha. Both Sir Nellin and Lady Jenet had only ever partnered with one knight—their current partners. Apparently, Jenet and Drake had been raised together, more or less as siblings, since Jenet's parents were partnered with Drake's fathers.

Gowan could see from the way they worked together that theirs was a long-standing relationship. They seemed to anticipate each other's moves and would, no doubt, be wicked in battle.

When the Lair's sentries spotted their group, it was as Gowan had imagined. One by one, every dragon in the Lair began to trumpet a welcome. A cacophony of sound greeted them in the early morning light as the group made for the landing platform, high atop the Lair.

Mace and Nellin, along with Drake and Jenet landed first, followed by the two royal dragons, with Gowan and Genlitha bringing up the rear. Gowan appreciated the placement. He feared he'd be *persona non grata* in the Lair after disobeying orders and going to Gryphon Isle's defense. This way, the presence of the royal dragons took the spotlight off him a bit.

Still, the knights just stared at him as they made their way down into the hall. The leadership would be at breakfast at this time of day, and Prince Nico and Princess Riki were bound and determined to catch them off guard.

The two black dragons shifted into their human forms as they strode through the halls, flanked by Drake, Krysta and Mace, with Jenet and Nellin right behind. Gowan was in front this time, with Genlitha, leading the way.

When they entered the dining hall, which was almost as large as Gryffid's great hall, though it was contained inside a mountain, several knights jumped to their feet. Apparently, there were standing orders to stop Gowan on sight, which he'd expected.

But what the knights in the dining hall hadn't counted on was the presence of the royals or the famous knights from Castleton. The moment they caught sight of Riki and Nico, they were forced to step back and bow to the prince and princess in their midst. The few dragons in the hall did the same until the entire place was so quiet Gowan could hear only the slight click of dragon claws on the stone floors as their party moved forward toward the high table.

Sir Jiffrey and Sir Benrik were seated there, with their dragon partners, Sir Tiluk and Lady Anira behind them.

"This place reeks of magic," Riki said to Nico in a quiet whisper that Gowan could hear. "It stinks of Loralie."

A shiver went down Gowan's spine at that name. He'd heard it before in Castleton. Rumor had it she was a witch who had done nefarious deeds on behalf of the former ruler of the Northlands. She was the one, it was said, who had caused the queen's Ice Dragon ward, Sir Tor, to be orphaned. The woman was evil and had the ability to command dark magic.

Gowan moved aside to make room for Nico and Riki to see the leaders of this Lair face to face. He went to Nico's side with Sir Mace, while Lady Krysta and Sir Drake stayed on Riki's side. The dragons flanked them, with Genlitha moving around to the rear of the head table to cover the leaders' dragon partners. Gowan saw Nico nod to his wife in agreement before he spoke to Sirs Jiffrey and Benrik.

"Greetings of the day to you all," Prince Nico began in a pleasant tone that rang through the quiet hall. "I have come from Castleton to find out why you refused to help allies of our kingdom who were in distress. I'll hear your explanations now."

All eyes turned to the head table and the sputtering leadership. Benrik got red in the face, but said nothing, while Jiffrey began to mumble excuses. Their dragon partners rose up on their hind legs, and things took on the slow motion quality of fast action, happening in a blur.

Gowan heard the telltale click of the dragons' preparation to flame, but when the fire came, it came not from the two dragons standing behind their hapless partners, but from the hands of three humans—well, two humans and one royal black dragon. And the flames were not the normal red, orange and yellow of fire, but an eerie blue-green and purple mixture that put it in a category all its own.

Gowan looked again. The fire leaping from Princess Riki's hands was the blue-green-purple, while the flames issuing from Sir Mace and Sir Drake's hands was closer to the expected colors of fire, though meshing with Riki's overpowering influence.

Riki's fire was aimed at Jiffrey and Benrik while Drake and Mace took on their dragons, somehow stopping the flame in the dragons' throats before it could issue out to fry the hall and all those in it. Something...melted away, was the only way Gowan could describe it…in front of his eyes as the magical flames worked on the quartet behind the high table.

It took long moments. Again, it felt like time slowed to a crawl while the magical fire filled the hall. When it was done with the leaders, leaving them limp and staggering, it wound its way around the hall, stopping here and there among the older knights. Not all were touched by it, but it seemed to consider each and every being in the Lair as it made its way around.

"What, by the stars, was that?" Gowan heard Jiffrey whisper as he leaned heavily against the high table. Benrik had collapsed into his chair, panting.

"It was evil, Sir Jiffrey," Drake answered in a voice that carried. Gowan began to believe the stories about this handsome knight having the gifts of a bard. "The four of you were heavily bespelled. Tell me what you remember of the past weeks."

"I—I…" Jiffrey stuttered, falling into the chair next to his fighting partner, rubbing his head. "Can it be that we…?" He turned to look at Benrik, his face growing even paler. "Sweet Mother of All. What have we done?"

"It's more what you failed to do," Prince Nico said.

The princess was still engaged in coiling the magical fire around the room, though both Mace and Drake had pulled their fire back. Riki, it seemed, was doing a more thorough examination of everyone present, sending her blue-green flames out into the crowd, and even out the door, into other parts of the Lair. Gowan realized she must be quite the mage to be able to power her spells all around the Lair.

"Gowan, the dragons," Genlitha warned him a moment before both Tiluk and Anira collapsed, their long necks twitching as they seemed to lose consciousness in some sort of fit.

Drake and Mace raced around the high table, one on each side, moving swiftly to the fallen dragons' sides. Drake took the female, Anira, while Mace concentrated his mage fire on Tiluk. Krysta stood watch over Drake's shoulder and motioned for Gowan to do the same for Mace.

"What's happening to them?" Gowan sent to Genlita.

"The mage fire is holding them here. The spells it dissolved were deep-seated and connected to their own magical core. How else could they be so corrupted? That's all I can think of, and frankly, it scares me, Gowan. It scares me to my bones that a dragon could be so overcome by an evil spell. We have built-in protections against such things. That someone, somewhere, has found a way to override our basic natures... It doesn't bear thinking about."

Gowan had never heard that note of sheer shocked terror in his partner's words before. If whatever this was had Genlitha this upset, it was something really awful.

"When you say, holding them here... *Do you mean to say they are dying?"*

"The evil spells that wrapped them in confusion and treachery must have drained them. When they were broken by the firedrakes, it left them open. Magically bleeding. Drained of magic, which to a dragon, means drained of life. The firedrakes are working now to help restore some of the balance, but it will be a long road to recovery...if they make it."

Gowan was stunned. This was much worse than they'd thought. It wasn't just laziness or old age that had made the leadership of the Lair shirk their duty. It was evil. Something outside had taken control of them all and made them do things they otherwise would not have done.

If such was the case, they were to be pitied, now that they were free of the taint.

Jiffrey was weeping, his hand clinging to his fighting partner's arm. Benrik had struggled back to consciousness, but was staring at his dragon partner, the most heartbroken expression on his face that Gowan had ever seen.

Gowan took stock of the hall, evaluating possible threats. Several of the older knights were sitting hard in their chairs, looking as stunned as those at the high table. They would have to be examined once the immediate crisis had passed. But what about their dragons?

"Gen, can you tell if any other dragons have been struck down like these two?" Gowan asked her quickly.

"A few, but none as bad as these. The princess moderated her magic when she saw what was happening here. Her mage fire is holding them in place, not stripping them all at once of the evil taint. There will be much work to do here for her and the firedrakes, and it will take a long time for this Lair to heal. If it can heal at all. This is terrible, Gowan. Truly terrible."

The next hours were spent going from chamber to chamber within the Lair in the company of the two firedrakes. Gowan hadn't known what a firedrake was before today, but it seemed to have something to do with the ability to handle magical flame and root out evil spells. Both Drake and Mace were human firedrakes, apparently, and their dragon partners were able to help stabilize some of the bespelled dragons around the Lair.

One by one, they cleared the evil from each of the residents of the Lair that were affected. As they worked, Gowan tried to piece together a pattern in his mind based on who was affected. Most of the older knights were tainted, except for Seth's parents, thank the stars. Once Gerard and Paton had been cleared by the firedrake magic, they and their dragon partners, Randor and Alirya, were put to work helping their comrades who were weakened by the loss of the evil magic that had surrounded them for who knows how long.

It was a long, long day. The affected were moved to the dining hall, which had been set up as a makeshift hospital. The Lair's elderly healer, Bronwyn, had taken over the kitchen and was helping brew restorative broths for everyone and ordering special meals for the dragons who'd been afflicted. Seth could have been of great help here, but of course, he was still on Gryphon Isle. Paton pulled Gowan aside for a quick word, asking him to tell Seth that all was well with his family and they were very proud of him. Gowan was only too happy to agree to deliver the message.

Gowan realized, about that time, that he actually missed Seth. He'd become so used to working with him as his partner. They fit together comfortably, their skills complementing each other's perfectly. Seth would have been a huge help here, both to Bronwyn and those she'd drafted to help her with basic healing and to shore up the fighting reserves. With so many senior knights down, the Lair was incredibly vulnerable.

Of course, there were two royal black dragons in residence, and it didn't look like either Nico or Riki were going to be leaving anytime soon. Riki was doing her best to help heal those who had been laid low while Nico took on the running of the Lair, handling the administrative details that had fallen by the wayside under the previous leaders. He sent dispatches back to his brother, the king, in the capital and had pulled Gowan aside to ask about going back to Gryphon Isle as soon as Genlitha was rested enough to make the flight.

Gowan knew Nico would have gone himself to speak with Gryffid, but the situation at the Lair was dire. Instead, Nico prepared a series of messages for the wizard, which he entrusted to Gowan.

"I'm sorry to send you and Genlitha out right away like this, but it's imperative we open lines of communication with Gryffid as quickly as possible," a harried Nico told Gowan after summoning him to the messy office the previous leaders had used. "Thank the stars you and your friends took it upon yourselves to do the right thing. The problem here is much worse than any of us could have expected." Nico looked grim as he sorted through scrolls, looking for another blank one. When he found it, he began to write rapidly.

Gowan felt relief, on one hand, that he and his small group of mutineers wouldn't be in trouble with the crown for taking the actions they had. On the other, he lamented the seriously bad things that had happened to the leadership and key knights and dragons here that had required Gowan and company to mutiny in the first place. But at least things were being fixed now.

Genlitha wasn't optimistic about a quick reversal of the damage here, but at least she believed it could be fixed. In time.

"You can tell Gryffid that I'm going to install Drake, Mace, Jenet and Nellin as the leaders here for the time being. We need a strong Lair here, and I believe they are the least susceptible to the kind of magic that was used to corrupt the previous leadership. I expect they'll fly over when time allows, but it won't be right away. If Gryffid is willing to show them more of his magic tricks, that would be very welcome." Nico talked even as he wrote the latest missive, signing his name with a flourish before he put the scroll aside to be sealed later.

Gowan realized he could help. "Sire, I'm not much of a clerk, but I'd be happy to help seal those for you, if you're in a hurry."

Nico looked up at him, gratitude in his eyes. "Dig in, Gowan. I can use all the help I can get right now."

Nico made room behind the standing table, leaving space for Gowan to do the final touches on the scrolls he'd written and signed. The prince gave Gowan his signet ring as soon as he'd lit the special opaque red candle that would provide the official wax to seal the scrolls. The signet was heavy and carried the prince's personal sigil that would indicate to any who saw the seal that it had come directly from the hand of the prince himself.

It was only a few hours later when Genlitha took to the sky, Gowan on her back, his satchel filled with sealed scrolls, his head still reeling from the unexpected problems of the day. Working side by side with the Prince of Spies all afternoon had taught him a thing or two about the state of the kingdom. Not only was the fighting in the North intensifying, but Nico had already sent word through his spy network to seek Fisk and any who might deal with the pirate.

In addition, Prince Nico granted Gryffid's request to assign Xanderanth and Leo as ambassadors, messengers or in whatever other capacity Gryffid needed them. In fact, Nico offered the wizard any knights or dragons he wanted. All he had to do was say the word. In essence, Nico was giving Gryffid *carte blanche* with the personnel of the Lair. The trust the Prince of Spies—and therefore the crown—had in the wizard was greater than Gowan had believed.

Nico was also requesting a gryphon representative, or pair of representatives, to act in the same capacity at the Lair. Nico left it up to Gryffid and his folk as to who they sent and in what numbers, but he'd given a more or less open invitation to gryphons and their fey fighting partners to join the ranks of the Southern Lair.

Gowan was grateful to be away from the chaos, but worried about how things would settle out in the Lair. Still, he would rather be heading for the people he'd left behind on Gryphon Isle. He wanted to be certain Livia, Seth and Hrardorr were safe and well. Only then would Gowan's heart be content.

*

Seth had spent part of the day down at the beach with the sea dragons. Livia had accompanied him, but she'd gone off with Flurrthith, who had flown down to the beach with his mother to say hello. It was good to see the young gryphon safe and happy with his family. He'd taken a moment to speak with Seth, as well, thanking him for coming back to the island to help. Seth had spent a few minutes assuring the young gryphon that he'd done a heroic deed in flying to the mainland all alone to seek aid from the dragons and knights, giving the gryphon full credit for his actions.

Seeing the half-sized gryphon flying alongside his mother, though, really brought home how young Flurrthith still was. He would grow into an amazing being, Seth knew, and he hoped their paths would cross again in the future, on much more pleasant terms. Seth rather liked the idea of having a gryphon as a friend.

Hrardorr was truly in his element underwater with the sea dragons. He'd confided to Seth that the sea dragons were teaching him quite a bit about swimming while he tried to share his knowledge of patrol formations and strategies. It was an equal exchange, Hrardorr insisted, and it made the blind dragon's emotional state almost buoyant. Unlike the Hrardorr Seth had come to know at the Lair.

The thought cheered Seth, but also worried him. Would Hrardorr want to stay with the sea dragons when this was all over? Would he go back to the Lair? And if he didn't, how would Seth survive losing his friendship?

Seth realized he was deeply attached to the dragon. Way more than he should be. But there'd been no way to stop the bond forming between Seth's heart and the dragon who had needed someone in his corner so badly. Seth admitted—if only to himself—that he loved Hrardorr like a brother, and his life would be incomplete without Hrardorr in it.

He inwardly cursed himself for allowing it to happen, but he really couldn't see how he could have avoided it. Hrardorr was such a great dragon. So full of contradictions and so in need of friendship, even though he claimed to not need anyone or anything.

While Seth was happy Hrardorr had found some friends among the sea dragons, Seth couldn't help but hope that the blind dragon wouldn't want to stay. Seth wanted him to come back to the Lair. Seth knew he was being selfish to think it, but he couldn't help himself.

After a full day on the beach, they made their way back to the Lair to consult with Gryffid. A thorough search had been made of the keep, turning out each and every person in the massive structure, room by room, until it was completely empty of life except for the lone wizard. Gryffid had then done some kind of magical spell that put a sort of glowing barrier around every entrance and exit, every window and chimney. Nothing could enter the keep again without first passing through the barrier.

Seth and Livia had to pass through it on their return, and Seth felt firsthand what it did.

It was hard to describe the feeling exactly, but it was as if, for that split second that it took to cross the glowing threshold, Seth was being examined by whatever magical intelligence ran the spell. He was being weighed and measured, considered and judged.

Having apparently passed muster, he was allowed into the keep. Seth supposed that if someone tried to pass through who was not what they pretended to be, the barrier would react quite differently, but nobody was saying exactly what would happen. He supposed they'd find out if and when it happened.

So far, though, only the one traitor had been unmasked.

Captain Lilith came into the great hall as Seth and Livia said down to dinner. The Captain of the Guard joined them and, surprisingly, filled them in on what she'd so far learned about the traitor who had been impersonating her.

Captain Gerrow, Lilith's mate and co-captain, was continuing the interrogation, she told them, but they had already learned a great deal from the prisoner. Meg, it turned out, had been Captain's Fisk's lover. She had roamed the lands after leaving on her journeyman trip to the mainland, in disguise, hiding her fey nature. But about a year ago, she had run into Captain Fisk and become enamored of the man.

Gryffid suspected—or so Lilith told them—that Meg had been struck down by a simple love potion. Magical charms to coax one to love another were commonplace, and some were more powerful than anyone of Seth's acquaintance realized. Gryffid had examined the prisoner thoroughly, checking for further signs of magical tampering. He'd found traces of a simple love charm that had run amok, as Lilith put it, and a dreadful compulsion that had made Meg act out of character and do things she otherwise never would have.

Meg was full of contrition at the moment, her moods swinging between sobbing and begging forgiveness, and anger and shame. The anger was directed at Fisk, which was a healthy reaction as far as Seth was concerned, but the shame could become a problem for the woman, if handled incorrectly.

If Meg had been an unwilling pawn in Captain Fisk's game, then Seth wished her well in recovering. If, however, she proved to have been willing, then she deserved whatever was coming to her. So far, though, it looked like she had been completely duped and was genuinely contrite.

It was sad, really. All that evil perpetrated by someone who'd had no real desire to do any of it. She'd hurt her homeland, her family, herself and, potentially, the entire world, just by being in the wrong place at the wrong time and coming under the influence of someone truly evil.

The more Seth learned of Captain Fisk, the more he realized the man must be motivated by something very strong, indeed. The rumors about him being in cahoots with a demon might not be too far off the mark, after all.

"Apparently, Fisk promised to take Meg with him, but instead, he kept leaving her behind. That's when she started trading to make her way. Her bardic gift was blocked, somehow, by the binding magic Fisk used on her, and she had been given instructions under compulsion to become a recluse trader of oddities. In this way," Captain Lilith told them, "Meg passed information and gathered intelligence vital to Fisk's plans."

"That's incredibly devious," Livia said as they all shared a glass of wine after dinner, still seated around their table in the great hall.

"Incredibly clever, as well," Lilith said, surprising him. "She was able to gain access to places and people that Fisk never would have been able to compromise otherwise. He had her whore for him, when there was no other way to get the information he wanted." Lilith sighed and cursed under her breath. "It's going to be hard for her to recover from this, if she even can."

"I hope for her sake, she does," Livia said quietly.

That was his Livia, with her heart as big as the world.

"Once Fisk has magicked her into loving him, she would do anything he asked. Thankfully, Gryffid has released her from the compulsion, and she is filled with remorse."

"What about the way she was able to impersonate you?" Livia asked. "And those other faces we saw when Gryffid did that spell reversal thing on her in the upstairs hallway? That had to be some other kind of magic, right?"

"Oh, to be sure," Lilith agreed. "Gryffid isn't saying too much about it, which worries me in some respects. He's often very straightforward with us, since he's always told us he believes we need to know as much about what we're dealing with as we can, in order to protect the island and its inhabitants to the best of our ability. This time, though, he's playing his cards very close to his vest. To me, that indicates something deeper—something more than a simple love spell turned ugly. That kind of chameleon magic hasn't been seen in these lands for centuries. I've only heard stories about such things, from the oldest legends. Frankly, I didn't really believe it was true that someone could take on the appearance of another person entirely, but now, we have seen it for ourselves."

The silence that followed Lilith's troubling words was tinged with weary worry. They'd all been through a lot the past few days, and things still hadn't settled down. Every time Seth thought they were due for some peace and quiet, something else popped up.

Speaking of which, Seth had to blink a few times upon seeing a light blue dragon and a weary looking warrior enter the great hall.

Seth shot to his feet. Genlitha and Gowan had returned.

CHAPTER NINETEEN

Seth's greeting on Gowan's return was everything he could have hoped for. Seth pulled him into a back-pounding hug that made Gowan feel as if he'd genuinely been missed. This was the kind of caring relationship he should've had with his older brother, but had never developed.

Gowan had come to realize over the past few days that Seth was the kind of brother Gowan had never had and always wanted. Gowan was touched by his reception, and when Seth let him go and Livia flew into his arms, he knew he was truly home.

Genlitha was over with Hrardorr by the fire, their necks twining in dragonish welcome. It seemed Genlitha had been missed too.

"Where is Gryffid?" Gowan asked when he finally could pry himself away from Livia's embrace. He didn't want to, but he knew he had to deliver his messages post-haste. Things on the mainland were happening fast, and Gryffid needed to know what had happened.

Captain Gerrow, Lilith's co-captain and mate, appeared at Gowan's side. Gowan met the other warrior's gaze and saw the grim determination on his face. Things must've been happening here while Gowan had been on the mainland. But Livia, Seth and Hrardorr appeared in good health, so Gowan was at ease. Still, he was intrigued to learn what had happened here while he'd been away.

"Come this way. The wizard awaits," Gerrow said formally. When Gowan made to follow the captain alone, Gerrow looked back and motioned for Livia and Seth to come along, as well. He glanced at the dragons, then shrugged. "I assume your scaled friends can listen in through you?"

Gowan nodded. "What I hear, Gen hears. If she wants to."

"Good. That'll work. We've had to make our conferences private since the unmasking of our traitor. No more open talk in the great hall." Gerrow grimaced, clearly unhappy with the need for such restrictions. "Not until we're sure she was the only one."

"You caught a traitor?" Gowan asked as they walked briskly along the hallways and up staircases.

"Your Lady Livia, Goddess bless her, noticed the woman—posing as my mate, no less!" Gerrow seemed truly angry by that, but he nodded thanks at Livia, who tagged along with the group, just behind him. Gowan couldn't wait to get the whole story out of her later. "There was a confrontation, and the master was able to counteract the spells that had been put on the woman, both to betray her people and to take on the guise of others. If there is one good aspect to this, it is that, after questioning her thoroughly, I now believe she did not willingly betray us. She was trapped by Captain Fisk, months ago, and put under magical compulsion to do all she did. Still, such a troubling event has shaken us all to our core. We believed ourselves impervious to such magical attacks and have been proven totally wrong, if not shamefully prideful and believing ourselves superior to the enemy. A lesson hard learned—and hopefully, not too late."

They kept climbing upward in the keep until they arrived at the foot of one of the many towers, if Gowan was any judge of architecture. Gerrow didn't stop there, but led them up a winding spiral staircase to one of many doors dotted along the wall of the stairwell.

Knocking just once, Gerrow opened the door to reveal an office of sorts, in the shape of a crescent moon. The tips of the moon-shape held storage racks with everything from office supplies to potion bottles on them. At the largest width of the oddly-shaped room sat Gryffid, behind an ornately carved wooden desk made to fit the shape of the room.

There were several others already there, including two fey men who greeted Livia with smiles and familiar nods. They were introduced to Gowan as Captain Lilith's brothers, the healer Lothar and a diplomat named Liam. Livia seemed to know them already, and Gowan was curious as to how she'd met the handsome fair folk.

He wasn't jealous—or so he tried to convince himself. Surely, Livia was too level-headed to be swayed by a pretty face. He hoped.

"Glad I am that you have returned to us, Sir Gowan," Gryffid greeted him, taking Gowan's thoughts away from Livia's possible attraction to the strange fey. "What news do you bring?"

Gowan heard his cue and began to pull the scrolls from his satchel, placing them in order of importance in front of the wizard. "A great deal of news, as it turns out, milord. Prince Nico and Princess Arikia are now in residence at the Southern Lair. The former leadership has been removed and are recovering from dark magic worked upon them—knights and dragons alike. They almost lost the dragons before they realized what was happening."

Gryffid held up a hand to halt Gowan's words. "Who, exactly? Who broke the spells?"

"Sorry, milord. The firedrakes. Sir Drake and Sir Mace, along with their dragon partners, Lady Jenet and Sir Nellin. They are also at the Southern Lair helping to sort things out. It wasn't just the leadership that was affected. Many of the senior knights and dragons were ensorcelled. Princess Riki claims she felt the taint of someone named Loralie."

Gryffid frowned deeply. "Grave news, indeed. I knew Loralie's people of old. She is the hereditary caretaker of the Citadel, but she is rumored to have done...terrible things. If she had a hand in this, then the level and complexity of the magic involved is somewhat understandable. I just never thought..." Gryffid broke off, his face showing his age for a moment.

"The good news is," Gowan went on, hoping to give the wizard some comfort, "that they were able to put a stop to it. Prince Nico is setting things to rights from an administrative standpoint while his princess is working with the firedrakes to go over every person and dragon in the Lair with a fine-toothed comb. I expect, once they're done there, they might venture into the town, as well, to see what's what. I have reports from Prince Nico, for your eyes only, milord." Gowan laid the last of the scrolls onto the table. "And his profound apologies that Draconia let you down when you needed her most."

Gowan bowed his head, showing contrition as the appointed representative of his land.

"Draconia did not let me down. On the contrary, the best of your land came to help, Sir Gowan. You and your friends did what was right, no matter the potential cost to yourselves or your careers. I am not disappointed in Draconia's response, and you can tell the Prince of Spies that when you see him next."

Gowan felt a wave of relief come over him. Prince Nico had been concerned that this slipup would cause major problems in the relationship between Draconia and Gryphon Isle. Probably, that's what Fisk had wanted—to drive a rift between the allies. But it sure sounded like that wasn't going to happen, and for that, Gowan was grateful.

"Who will lead that Lair after Nico leaves? Has he said?" Gryffid asked as he perused the scrolls the prince had sent.

"He's appointing Sir Drake, Sir Mace, Sir Nellin and Lady Jenet as leaders for the Southern Lair when he and Princess Arikia are done purging the place and are satisfied that Drake and Mace can carry on. The Prince said he believed the firedrakes were likely less susceptible to the kind of magic wrought on the previous leaders and several other key knights and dragons."

Gryffid nodded slowly. "That is a wise choice, though I suspect the firedrakes will be needed elsewhere when the real battle begins. But perhaps we have enough time before that befalls us. Perhaps we can still prevent it, if someone can stop Fisk and get my book back."

"To that end, Prince Nico has already alerted his network throughout the land and in several others. If he gets word, he'll act on it, and let you know, of course. He also said, that if you would be willing to teach the firedrakes more about their magic, if there's time, the kingdom would be grateful. The prince said that the firedrakes would probably like to visit with you themselves, but it will have to wait until after things settle down a bit at the Lair. In the meantime, he grants you leave to request any knight or dragon you wish to act as go-between, or in any other capacity. He also gladly assigns Sir Leonhardt and Sir Xanderanth to be at your disposal as ambassadors, messengers, or for whatever else you might require of them. He also suggested you might want to have some of your gryphons on the mainland to act in the same capacity, so information can flow more smoothly. He has made the Lair available to any gryphons and their fey partners who wish to make use of it. It is an open invitation." Gowan gestured toward the scroll containing the details on that offer, and Gryffid picked it up and scanned it.

"Excellent," Gryffid said a minute later. "We will station two pairs of gryphons and their fey counterparts. Gerrow, see who wants to go, will you?" The Captain of the Guard nodded solemnly, accepting the mission. "And I'm very glad to keep young Leonhardt and his friend, Xanderanth. They might even end up living here permanently, if things work out as I suspect they will." Gryffid's eyes twinkled as he looked up from the scroll. "Are there any other knights and dragon pairs you would recommend? I don't want to deplete your

Lair in time of need, but by the same token, we are in need of more senior and skilled dragons and knights to show the sea dragons the way of things."

"Milord," Seth piped up. "I believe my family would be suitable for the task. As far as I know, they did not come under influence of the evil magic and are all highly ranked teachers of young—knights and dragons alike."

"Seth's family was not under magical influence," Gowan confirmed. "They were all checked first, since it was one of Seth's fathers who flew to the capital—against orders—and got the crown's attention. They have been consulting with the royals and the firedrakes since their arrival at the Southern Lair."

Gryffid smiled at Seth. "It's an excellent suggestion. If they can be spared, I will request them in the next dispatch."

When Gryffid had finished with the scrolls, he began to ask detailed questions of Gowan about what had happened in the Lair. He wanted minute descriptions of everything from the color of the flame the firedrakes and the princess had used to the way the afflicted reacted, and the timing of the entire ordeal. He wanted to know how the dragons had fared and required specific numbers of casualties and the severity of each case.

He took notes and began to create a sort of chart that correlated the severity of the enchantment with the position of the person or dragon in the Lair hierarchy. When Gryffid was done with his analysis, it became pretty apparent that very specific positions and people had been targeted. Gryffid directed an aid to make a copy of his analysis to send back to the Lair, with his compliments, when the first gryphon pair was ready to leave for the mainland.

After that, Gryffid dismissed them all, saying that he had much to write for Prince Nico's eyes and would be working through the night to send as much as he could with the gryphons who would leave at first light. Gerrow escorted Seth, Livia and Gowan back down to the great hall and then left them, racing off to make arrangements for the gryphons who would be flying out the next morning.

Gowan checked on Genlitha and Hrardorr, but they were both fast asleep already, necks entwined by the fire. He didn't have the heart to wake her, so he tiptoed out, leaving the dragons to their rest. Stars knew, Genlitha had earned it that day. They'd been flying pretty much all day, which had to have been hard on her.

The trio of humans worked their way from the great hall to the guest quarters, deciding without words to congregate in Livia's room. There was a set of chairs by her fireplace, and some kind soul had already lit the fire and left a bottle of wine and some snacks for them. Settling in front of the fire, Gowan asked Livia to tell him about how she'd uncovered the traitor in Gryffid's house.

He was alternately appalled at the risk Livia had taken and filled with pride at her courage. Livia had stared a dangerous operative in the face and had stood firm in the face of deadly threat. He couldn't help himself—he had to put his arm around her shoulders, drawing her close to his side on the couch on which they both sat. Seth was in a wingchair, just a few feet away, and he smiled benevolently at them as he sipped his wine.

The mood was both mellow and filled with gladness at being together again. Gowan basked in the feeling, recognizing at last what it truly felt like...home. Wherever Livia was, and astoundingly, wherever Seth was, that was beginning to feel like home to Gowan. More than the place he'd called home and been forced to leave by a brother who had never acted as a true brother should.

Here, with these people, was the closest Gowan had ever come to having a real family. A brother. A lover. And two four-footed siblings with wings who could breathe fire and would stand by them all through thick and thin.

Yes, that was home. And Gowan felt the warmth in his heart that made him want to stay like this...with them all...forever.

"You're awfully quiet," Livia said, turning in Gowan's loose embrace to look up at his handsome face. His mood was introspective, and she wondered about the shocks he'd been through at the Lair earlier that day.

Gowan sighed and stroked her shoulder gently. "I'm just glad we're not going to be facing an angry monarch when we get back. Prince Nico was grateful we'd taken it upon ourselves to come here."

She relaxed and snuggled into his embrace. "Honestly, I was more worried about my father than the king." She chuckled and stroked one hand over his hard chest. "Although I'm sure he'd still rather have me back at home playing with dolls, I think the worst of the confrontation with him is behind me now, and he's off on another adventure anyway...chasing Captain Fisk."

"Does it help to know he stayed away all these years to protect you?" Gowan asked quietly.

"I guess, in a way, it does. Though I wish he could've just been honest with me from the beginning."

"You were only a child, grieving the loss of her mother when this all started," Seth put in. "He probably did what he thought was best at the time."

Livia sat up and looked over at Seth. "I can't believe you're taking his side."

Seth shook his head. "I'm not saying it was right or wrong, but merely that he was doing the best he could at the time. The man was probably out of his mind with grief himself. I doubt either of you got over the loss of your mother easily."

Livia had to admit Seth had a point. "You respect him, don't you?"

"Your father?" Seth asked rhetorically. "Well, of course, I always respected the name. Captain O'Dare was legendary in Dragonscove. But I'd never really dealt with him before now. I have to admit..." Seth shifted in his chair. "His actions in this situation have both surprised and impressed me. He certainly proved he loves you, Livia. He amassed a fleet of ships to fight Fisk and turned them for Gryphon Isle, not even knowing Fisk was here. He did that for you." Seth met her gaze, his own filled with a sort of solemn respect.

She thought about his words. "Yeah. I guess he did, didn't he?"

"For an older man, he certainly didn't hesitate to put himself in the thick of battle. If he were an army man, he'd be a general, well-loved by his troops, I think," Gowan put in, surprising her. "Or perhaps an admiral, if we had a naval fleet. He's certainly commodore of his own force at this point, though Prince Nico had some thoughts about making your father a more formal offer, if he could catch up with the good captain."

"Really?" Livia felt her pulse quicken. The Prince of Spies was interested in her father and his fleet of merchant-fighters?

Gowan nodded. "He mentioned it in passing. I believe riders were dispatched to all the seaports with instructions to make contact with your father or members of his fleet if they were found in port. I don't know the exact message they carry, but I have to assume it's an offer of mutual support. The Prince of Spies knows the value of traveling networks. After all, he has long been rumored to be affiliated with the Jinn brotherhood. A fleet of sea-going vessels would be a handy asset, especially since your father is going after something the crown has a great interest in right now—the book and the pirate captain. Both are wanted quite desperately by more than just Gryffid and his folk. King Roland and Prince Nico both know the importance of the book and preventing the fall of the Citadel. I heard them discussing it when I was in Castleton. The war is not going well. Hostilities are increasing in the North and along the border. We are spread thin already, and now, this… They see this as a very grave threat."

"So it's not just Gryffid overreacting to the loss of one of his prized possessions," Livia stated. She'd already known in her heart that was the case, but she'd sort of hoped maybe it wasn't as dire as everyone here on Gryphon Isle thought. But if the king...

"No, my dear," Gowan said quietly. He was clearly exhausted from his long day of traveling. "They are treating this just as seriously as Gryffid himself."

Livia couldn't handle any more fear and worry right now. There was nothing she could do about it, after all. Not tonight. She'd done her part when called upon, but she wasn't a fighter. She wasn't a mage.

She was a woman. In love with two men. One of whom had flown the length of the lands to be here with her tonight. Gowan was clearly fatigued, but she wanted...no, she *needed* to be with him. And with Seth. The three of them, together, affirming their mutual passion and caring.

Livia got to her feet and held out her hands. One to each of her men.

"Come to bed. The day has been long, and it's time for us to take our rest...and our reward." She smiled gently at them, and suddenly, they weren't too tired to follow her to the giant bed at the other end of the suite of rooms.

Gowan even let her direct him for once. He must be very weary, indeed, to allow her to make love to him instead of the other way around. She wasn't asking questions, though. This was what she needed tonight. She wanted to lavish her attentions on her men and show them how much they were appreciated...and loved.

She stripped them both—one on her right and one on her left. Sinking to her knees, she did something she hadn't done with them before. Going from one to the other, she fondled one while tasting the other, taking them all the way into her eager mouth, telling them without words how happy they made her. The three of them together felt right. The way it was supposed to be.

Seth moaned as she took him deep into her mouth. His hand sank into her hair, guiding her movements, but she wanted to be in charge tonight. This night was for her to show them how much she...loved them. Though she found it hard to speak the words aloud, she felt the truth of them in her heart.

"Ease off, sweet," Seth grit out through clenched teeth as she sucked him down. "If you don't, I won't last."

She decided she wasn't done playing with him just yet, so she moved back, directing him toward the bed with a little shove and a nod. Seth didn't argue.

Turning her attention to Gowan, she licked him from bottom to top, laving her tongue around his tip until she felt a little tremor run through his body. Good. She was more than ready to get down to business.

Livia rose to her feet and took Gowan with her as she moved the few paces to the bed where Seth sat, watching them. Livia climbed onto the bed, claiming the middle spot, then patted the empty side as she looked at Gowan.

He joined her on the high, thick mattress, allowing her to push him down so that he lay on his back. Climbing over him, she kissed him deeply, taking his lips with the hunger that had risen within her just thinking about this moment. She had missed him so much while he'd been away. She had missed this...the three of them, together.

She couldn't wait, and from the feel of him against her thigh, he was more than ready. Sliding into position, she moved downward onto him, taking his hardness fully inside her body in one long slick slide. Hard and soft met and became one. Yearning spiked, and she began to move, even though there was still an element missing.

She couldn't seem to make herself stop kissing Gowan, but she needed to tell Seth...

And then, she realized, she could. She didn't often use the silent communication Hrardorr had taught her with the men, except during the times of crisis they'd shared, but it was there. Waiting. Available. And useful in the extreme.

"Seth, I need you too. I need to feel you both," she sent to him, knowing her tone was almost pleading.

A moment later, without words, Seth began to caress his way down her spine, touching, soothing, exciting. That was just about all it took before she shattered into a million pieces, taking Gowan with her. He groaned, stiffening beneath her as he came, and she cried out, loving the way Seth squeezed her ass with his calloused hand.

She rolled off of Gowan and found herself being taken into Seth's arms. They were both on their sides, facing each other, limbs tangled when he raised her top leg to drape over his hips, finding her slippery core and sliding home within her. Her breath caught at the feel of him inside her, and she found her passion rising again as Gowan trailed little biting kisses on her shoulder, while his hands caressed her spine and lower.

She gasped when he reached between her and Seth to run his finger over her clit. Seth stilled, too, for just a moment, then redoubled his efforts as Gowan's dominance reasserted itself, just a little.

It wasn't long before she came apart in Seth's arms, crying out as she climaxed again. Four strong arms held her while her body shook with exquisite pleasure. And two warm bodies bracketed her as she slipped into a deep and satisfied sleep.

CHAPTER TWENTY

A flight of gryphons left at dawn the next morning, leaping from the ramparts of the keep and into the air. They'd received last-minute scrolls and instructions from Gryffid before departure, which was why they left from the keep rather than the cliffs where they nested.

Livia, standing at the window of her bedroom in the faint light before full dawn, saw them leave. She knew they were heading for the Southern Lair, and for a moment, she longed for home. Then, Seth walked up behind her and spooned her, looking out at the small specks that were the gryphons fading into the distance.

"Come back to bed," Seth whispered in her ear, nibbling on her earlobe.

"In a minute. I just want to see the dawn," she whispered back, and he settled down, holding her as they faced the window.

"Is everything all right?" he asked quietly.

She'd woken from a bad dream and hadn't been able to go back to sleep. That happened to her sometimes, and at such times, when she was home, she usually got up and went down to the waterfront, where the fishing fleet was already hard at work at this hour. She would talk to her friends there and sometimes even take out her own little boat, sailing out of the

251

cove with the others as the first rays of the sun hit the water.

Being out on the water calmed her restless soul. She finally made the connection that it must do the same for her father. Perhaps they had more in common than she'd thought.

But this morning, Seth's arms were having the desired effect. His caring embrace calmed her restless thoughts and allowed her to relax. It also made her brave enough to tell him the truth about her occasional restless sleep.

"I...had a bad dream. I have them a lot, sometimes," she told him. "And sometimes...the events I see actually do come to pass, though not always in the way I interpreted them from the dreams."

Seth turned her in his arms, looking deep into her eyes. "Do you have the gift?" he asked, serious suddenly. Thank the stars he wasn't laughing at her.

She began to shake her head, but then thought about everything she'd heard about her mother...and her mother's family. "I don't know. It's said...my great-great-granny did, though of course, I never knew her. I'm not even sure that it's not just a tall tale. But I get these dreams..." She shook her head in full this time. "They've been getting worse as I get older."

"What did you see this morning?" Seth asked in a concerned tone, his hands on her shoulders, rubbing light circles, trying to comfort her.

She scrunched her eyes shut, seeing the bizarre images that had disturbed her sleep so greatly.

"Feathers and fire," she whispered. "Fire and feathers. Not a good combination."

"Would it ease your mind to talk with the wizard about this?" Seth asked.

"He's so busy with everything that's happened. I hate to bother him with something this silly." She really didn't want to bother Gryffid with something that could just be her imagination run amok.

"It's precisely because of everything that's been going on that we should ask him about this," Seth said reasonably.

"He's up. I have no doubt he was talking with the gryphons until the moment they set flight. Maybe we could catch him at breakfast and just ask a leisurely question. Perhaps it will put your mind at ease."

She couldn't argue with that. But... "What about Gowan?" She looked over to the bed where Gowan still slept peacefully.

"Let him rest. He traveled more in one day, yesterday, than most dragon knights cover in a week. He deserves to sleep in."

Seth had a point. "All right." Livia stepped away from Seth and quickly got ready. There was a bathing chamber in the suite of rooms she'd been given, and she took her clothing in there, so as not to wake Gowan.

A few minutes later and they were on their way down to the great hall. Sure enough, Gryffid was sitting with Gerrow and some of his other trusted advisors, breaking his fast. When the wizard saw them, he waved them over, indicating Livia should sit next to him, in the spot just cleared by a departing warrior who had finished eating and was off to fulfill some task Gryffid or Gerrow had given him.

Seth sat across from her, where she could see him, and she was glad for the unspoken support. She felt foolish, intending to bring up such a personal, and probably foolish, subject with the last of the great wizards.

"You want to ask me something," Gryffid said after wishing her a good morning. His ancient eyes twinkled, and she could almost swear he knew what she was thinking.

She hesitated, knowing the entire table full of fey folk were listening, though they were polite about it. But Gryffid's gaze was encouraging.

"I've been having dreams..." she began, not really knowing how to go on.

"For how long?" Rather than laughing at her, Gryffid's eyes were now serious, his tone intrigued.

"All my life, that I can remember," she admitted. "But they're getting stronger the older I get. And this morning was the strongest yet."

"What did you see?"

She had tried to come up with a better description since Seth had asked her the very same question, but was unable to articulate it better. "Feathers and fire."

"Gryphons and dragons?" one of the fey put in, seeming so sincere in his suggestion that Livia couldn't take offense.

"Possibly, but this had a desperate feeling to it, and it was set in Dragonscove. I fear the pirates—or some other evil—is not done with the town yet. Your gryphons need to know they are possibly flying into danger. There could be more violence."

"The gryphons who flew to the mainland are all warriors. We will be certain to send only those who are prepared to face battle," Gryffid said quietly, putting her mind a little more at ease. But his gaze bored into hers, as if seeking something. "Your family has history of the sight, does it not?"

"My great-great-gran, or so I've been told. I didn't really believe it until recently," she admitted.

"This could explain a great deal," Gryffid said, surprising her as he sat back in his chair as if contemplating the solution to a great puzzle. "Why, for instance, you could see through the spells of deception layered over Meg. That is not something everyone would have noticed. I know you had just seen Lilith in another part of the keep, but the kind of spells that afflicted Meg would have compensated. It would have shown her as someone else to you. Such considerations are made in spells of that complexity. Yet, you saw Lilith. A clear dissonance that bothered you enough to investigate. If your line was even slightly Goddess touched, that would explain why."

"Goddess touched?" Livia repeated, unfamiliar with the term.

"There is an innate goodness about you, Livia. All my people have remarked upon it—fey and gryphon alike. Young Flurrthith is one of your biggest admirers and would have been at your side like a hound if his mother had not kept him busy and under her wing. Sending him off like that at such a tender age distressed her greatly."

Livia nodded. She understood and was glad the young gryphon had such a loving family. She'd missed him too, though. She'd come to enjoy traveling with the youngster.

"Gryphons know instinctively when they meet good people. They have a built-in deception detector, I always thought, which is why the imposter stayed far away from any gryphon who might've crossed her path while she was doing her foul deeds under the evil compulsion." Gryffid's expression grew hard. "Furthermore, you can bespeak dragons and people. That is not a skill afforded to many females of your species. Some bespeak dragons, but will never be able to hear the thoughts of their husbands or gifted children. Yet you are not even mated to a knight pair and you can speak with either dragon or knight. I suspect you have the same reach as many knights and will be able to speak silently with any resident of the Lair, in time."

He was speaking as if it was inevitable that she was going to become a Lair wife, mated to two knights, but that seemed so impossible right now. So many obstacles had to be overcome for that to happen, but she wasn't about to argue with the wizard. This table full of fair folk didn't need to know every facet of her existence.

She merely shook her head, unable to hide her disbelief. "If you say so, milord."

Gryffid laughed outright at her response, but it wasn't unkind. "Mark my words for now, young Livia. In time, you'll see I was right. In the meantime, you must pay attention to these dreams of yours. They come for a reason. Portents of things to be—and you can help steer events in the right direction. Such is the gift the Mother of All bestowed on certain special women in your land. I believe you are descended from such a woman, though we would have to do some investigating to know for certain. Still, all the signs are there." He shrugged. "Speak your dreams to your friends,

Seth and Gowan especially. Let them help you decipher the meanings and spread any warnings that need to be known. It is a gift of your line and should not be squandered in self-doubt."

Livia wasn't sure what to make of the wizard's advice, but she nodded, thanking him, and letting the matter rest. She'd talk it over with Seth later.

"Don't be troubled, Livia," came Hrardorr's unexpected comment in her mind. She thought he'd still been asleep next to Genlitha, behind them by the fireplace, but apparently, he was awake and had heard the whole exchange. *"It does make a logical sort of sense. You are so easy with us—with dragons, in general. I can assure you, such is not the case with most humans. Yet you befriended me as if it was the most normal thing in the world. You are comfortable with magic in ways the other residents of Dragonscove are not. It is something I've noticed from the beginning, and it marked you as exceptional. If you ever have need to discuss images you see in your dreams, please know that I am always here for you. I will help you decipher them, if you need help."*

"Hrardorr, I..." She was touched so deeply by his words and the solemn tone in which they were delivered, she had to express it. *"Can I hug you?"* she asked, surprising herself with the request. She hadn't touched the dragon often. It was presumptuous at the best of times, but with Hrardorr being blind, he could not see her coming and might move unexpectedly. Getting too close to him could be dangerous at times, so she had always kept a distance unless specifically invited.

"Come here, Livia. You know I would come to you, if I could." Hrardorr's words and the emotion behind them found an answering note inside her troubled soul. The dream that morning had shaken her badly. It had been so vivid.

Livia stood from the table and went over to Hrardorr. She knew the others were surprised by her movement. Even Seth seemed a little taken aback as he watched her walk right up to Hrardorr and throw her arms around his neck, but he smiled. Livia caught his eye as she hugged her best friend in all the world, glad of the dragon's support.

The folk in the great hall were staring, but she didn't care. She needed Hrardorr's warmth and support right now. Her world had been turned upside down, and there was no end in sight to the upheaval, merely moments of respite like this one. She would take what she could get.

Hrardorr needed to know how much he meant to her. She needed to tell him so much about how profoundly he'd affected her life, but she could only think of one way to express the complicated thoughts filling her mind, distilled down to a simple emotion.

"I love you, Hrardorr."

"I...love you too, Livia. You're the sister I never had."

"It is good to see such a deep bond between humans and dragons," Gryffid said quietly to those remaining at the table, but looking straight at Seth.

"Hrardorr is a special dragon, but I have seen the same between my fathers and their dragon partners," Seth told the wizard and his folk around the emotion clogging his throat. "And between my mother and my dragon sibs. It is a beautiful way to grow up, surrounded by all that strength and love." Seth knew he'd thrown away his chance at that kind of family for himself when he'd chosen to forego knight training, but he still counted himself blessed to have grown up in that environment.

"The bond is still as strong as Draneth always hoped. It has not faded over the years," Gryffid pronounced, his gaze on Livia and Hrardorr, still locked in an emotional embrace that spoke of deep trust and love.

It hit Seth then that Gryffid had actually *known* Draneth the Wise, the ancient wizard who had created the first dragons. Seth realized that was why the dragons had all been so keen to meet Gryffid. He was a link to their Maker, just as Gryffid himself, was the Maker of the gryphons.

"I know it has been that way for centuries in your land, but I believe the concept of Lair marriage is about to be shaken up on a grand scale," Gryffid announced, seeming almost gleeful.

Seth didn't pretend not to know what the wizard was driving at. "You mean Leo and Lady Lizbet? And Xanderanth and Lady Shara?" Seth frowned. "Are you sure that can actually work? I'd hate to lose Leo to madness if it doesn't. He's a good lad."

"I would not countenance it if I feared for any of them. I believe you have to trust more in the Mother of All, my young friend. "Gryffid's eyes twinkled as he smiled. "Besides, I have given my blessing. Lizbet and Leo came to me to ask my advice, and I gave them permission to marry. We are to have a celebration," Gryffid announced, seeming to take the fey at the table by surprise as well. "Spread the word to those who want to witness the first union between fey and dragon knight, as well as the first mating between a land dragon and a sea dragon in centuries. There's going to be a double wedding on the beach where the sea dragons gather this very evening."

The fair folk at the table recovered quickly, asking a few questions in concern for Lizbet—particularly the problem of age. Fey were long-lived by human standards, but Gryffid assured his fey friends that knights bonded to dragons took on several lifetimes worth of magic from their partners. He turned to Seth to add further reassurance to his words.

"I'm the youngest in my family," Seth told the gathered folk. "My mother is over three hundred years old. My brother Gerry is a knight in the Northern Lair, partnered with my younger dragon sib, Mowbry. He's mated and has children of his own now, some of whom are older than me. My brother Pat has been a knight for more than a century now, though unmated as yet. And my other dragon sib, Llallor, is partnered with a knight named Karlac and is stationed at the Border Lair. When a dragon chooses to join his or her life to yours, they give you some of their magic, which extends to the whole family—especially the knights' spouse. I suppose that I will have the shortest life of my family unit because I am not a knight. I will age as a regular person, but they will go on, and I hope my dragon parents are blessed with another egg at some point. They are just the best."

"So you see, it's possible that young Leo will outlive Lizbet, all things considered," Gryffid told them. "But with the way things are now, and the dangerous times ahead, I cannot abide keeping young people in love apart. Having talked to them at length and observed them together, I believe this is no rash decision on their parts. I believe the hand of the divine had something to do with this arrangement. I mean, it's too perfect. We meet the first dragon in centuries who can both flame and swim beneath the waves, and now, we have a new pairing between a land and sea dragon that might produce another magnificent dragon such as Hrardorr? I can't believe the Mother of All didn't have something to do with that."

That seemed to convince the fair folk as nothing else, and skepticism soon evaporated into a healthy eagerness for the celebration to come that evening. But if Leo was getting married, then that meant Seth was going to have to make some preparations. There were gifts to be acquired, if at all possible, at the very least.

Seth asked a few pointed questions about local marketplaces where he might be able to find suitable gifts and was rewarded with a wealth of information he would put to good use later that day. He finished breakfast and was ready to go when Livia finished talking with Hrardorr. She had gone from hugging the dragon to sitting beside him, curled against his side and almost tucked under his wing.

They made a touching tableau, Hrardorr on one side with Livia, Genlitha still sleeping on his other side, closer to the fire and away from the bustle of the great hall. Livia stroked Hrardorr's scales as she and the dragon communed silently. The image brought a pang of emotion to Seth's tender heart. It was clear the woman had gotten to the dragon's bruised and battered heart and found a way in to soothe Hrardorr's damaged soul.

Likewise, the blind dragon had become a source of

comfort and strength to Livia, whose very foundations had been shaken by all that had occurred. Hrardorr was her safe port in the storm that had become her life of late, and Seth was pleased down to his toes to see it. They'd let each other in, and Seth knew that meant a great deal toward Hrardorr's continued improvement.

Training for the day was abbreviated, but still commenced that afternoon for the dragons. Seth, Gowan and Livia took an hour to visit the local marketplace and shop for gifts for the happy couples. Livia, of course, was quietly taking stock of the local wares with an eye toward later commerce, but for now, there were presents to be found, and Livia had brought a purse of gold and silver with her, just in case.

She was glad that she had come prepared. The wares available for sale were simply lovely. Exotic to her eyes, but of the highest quality and craftsmanship. Of course, fey craftsmen had centuries to learn and perfect their skills, unlike the shorter-lived humans. Here, even the journeyman's wares were equal in quality to a master's at home.

Livia bought practical gifts for both the dragons and their two-legged companions—colorful fabrics to feather their nests, so to speak. The dragons were going to select a suitable cave near the beach where the sea dragons liked to gather and use that as their home until a better structure could be built. The tall cliffs surrounding that beach would be perfect, Livia had thought, for a Lair, but it would do as well for one dragon pair, especially since one of the pair was a sea dragon. Easy access to the water was important for Lady Shara, though she hadn't been allowed to dive too deeply just yet with her healing injury.

Seth had supervised her flying for the past day or two and pronounced her to be coming along fine. In fact, he had cleared her flying, just not deep swimming yet, since he wasn't sure what the pressure at depth would do to her newly forming scales. She'd been flying more and more each day, though, making a fine sight in the skies over the water, with some of her friends.

Sea dragons didn't often flex their wings in the air—especially during the day when their dark coloration made them stand out against the blue sky—but they'd been making more of an effort while they trained. Some flew patrol with the gryphons over the island now, learning the way of things. And even Genlitha had been asked to help with the afternoon's flying lessons, since the sea dragons were much more used to water currents than air currents beneath their wings.

Gowan had bought gifts of wine and delicacies to be delivered to the happy couple tomorrow. He'd also ordered bushels of fruit and melons for the dragons. Thoughtful, useful gifts from a practical fighting man, Livia had thought. Seth, on the other hand, had gotten them jars of balms and ointments for various uses. A first-aid collection any home would be proud to have—for both the human-fey home and the dragon Lair. He'd also selected finely scented soaps and cleansing products for the home and those who lived in it. Livia noticed he added some of the dragon-specific items he'd brought with him to the basket of jars and bottles, each labeled with its uses and ingredients.

In fact, Seth had spent some time talking with the best of the apothecaries they had visited, discussing blends and recipes that were especially useful for dragon hide. He'd made some contacts and promised to show a few of the fey how to make some of the items they discussed if there was time before Seth left the island. Livia knew Seth wanted to pass on his knowledge so that the dragons wouldn't have to do without simple things that could make their lives more comfortable.

That night, just at sunset, the two couples—dragon and fey-human—were joined in a beautiful ceremony on the beach. As the last rays of the sun kissed the sky, a happy cheer went up from those gathered to celebrate the new unions.

The fair folk were there in force, much to Livia's delight and surprise. Fine bards played lively tunes, and laden tables of food and drink were shared by all. Sea dragons frolicked on the beach and in the surf, having stood solemn witness to the union of Lady Shara with Sir Xanderanth.

The dragon leader had come to speak words of approval and blessing over them before letting loose with a trumpeting cry echoed by every dragon present. The gryphons had sent representatives, too, clacking their beaks with approval before they took flight in joyous celebration.

Many mated pairs were flying already, enjoying the celebration as only two mated behemoths could. In a Lair celebration, every mated dragon pair's passion would be sending their bonded knights into a mating frenzy of their own, shared with their mates. Here, the gryphons and sea dragons were free to share passion among themselves without worrying about how their actions might affect any two-legged beings they were bonded to—except for Xanderanth and the other land dragons…and now, Lady Shara, as well, since she was part of a Lair family now, even if it wasn't the typical five-personed structure.

No, in their case, they would only have four beings in the family structure, but the wizard had assured them all it would work. He'd told them that, in private, and he reiterated it before starting the ceremony over which he'd presided that bonded them forever as mates.

That Gryffid had come all the way down to the beach for the ceremony meant something very special to Livia. It meant that he had welcomed Xander and Leo to his island and into the flock of beings that gathered around him. Gryffid was both grandfather, elder statesman, benevolent protector and respected teacher to every soul on his island, and he had just publicly acknowledged the addition of two more. That meant a lot to Leo and Xander, Livia knew. It touched her heart, as well.

With the music came lively dancing. Livia was partnered first by Seth, then later by Gowan, and even later, as the party wore on and alcohol was consumed in abundance, both men in dance patterns designed for trios in the Lair. They weren't very good at it, but they did a creditable job of showing the fair folk how it was done, much to the delighted whoops and hollers of the fey dancers and musicians.

When Xander and Shara finally jumped into the sky for their very first mating flight, the human-fey couple had already been shown to the bower created by the fey woman for just that purpose. Atop the cliffs, there had been built a shelter that would protect the young couple for the next few days. It featured a large bed, covered in the finest satin sheets, and enough food, water and wine to last them a week at least.

Lizbet had wept when she'd seen the place, hugging those who had built it and thanking them profusely. Gryffid had announced just before the ceremony that he'd approved the building of a permanent home on the site, to house the newlyweds. He had already set his finest builders to work on the plans and would give it to the new couple as his wedding gift.

To the dragons, Gryffid had promised to build a sand pit like those in the Draconian Lairs, using his magical skills to assure it was always heated, like the Lair wallows. All they had to do, he told them, was select the spot where they wanted to nest and he, and a team of the finest stonemasons on the island, would do the rest.

Handsome gifts, to be sure. And many others followed. In addition to the items Livia and the men had arranged earlier that day, the fair folk had brought a bevy of beautiful gifts for the new couple. Livia knew more presents would come to them once word went back to Dragonscove and Leo's family, but for now, she was happy that the newlyweds were receiving such a warm welcome from the fair folk.

Livia had enjoyed shopping for them and had even started filling the boat her father had left behind with a few purchases she'd made both for herself and for the company. When she finally set sail for home, she'd have some tangible goods to show for her sojourn on Gryphon Isle. She wasn't a merchant captain's daughter for nothing.

The music was the finest Livia had ever heard, and it went on long into the night. Even after the happy couples left to start their honeymoon, the fey remained on the beach with several gryphons and sea dragons, who seemed to be enjoying the two-legged creatures' antics and especially the music.

Livia was surprised to recognize many of the tunes the musicians played. Had they come from the mainland or been imported there by fey who traveled in disguise among humans?

"That song," Gowan had told her at one point when they were talking on the topic, "was written by Sir Drake when he was a traveling bard. It was the talk of Castleton when he was chosen by Lady Jenet as a knight."

"Then, Sir Drake really is Drake of the Five Lands?" Livia had asked. "And he'll be running the Lair once Prince Nico and Princess Riki leave?" She admitted to feeling a little excited by the prospect of seeing the famous bard in Dragonscove, should he venture down from the Lair.

"He and the rest of his family unit. Sir Mace is a steady fighting man and their mate, Lady Krysta, was a guard. I know they'll be of great help fortifying the town against further attacks from the sea. But yes, Drake is *that* Drake. The famous bard." Gowan rolled his eyes in a comical way, but humored her. "And if at all possible, I'll see that you get to meet him. Even if it is against my better judgment."

"Why?" She loved it when Gowan unbent enough to tease her, and she could see the merriment in his dark eyes now.

"Because Drake is a charmer. As handsome as he is talented, and before meeting Lady Krysta, he was a terrible womanizer. I wouldn't introduce any female I cared about to him back then. Now, though, Krysta has made an honest man of him, and though silly females might still throw themselves at him occasionally, he is devoted to his mate."

Livia didn't take offense at Gowan's words. Instead, she thought about how nice it must be for Lady Krysta to know that her mates were hers and hers alone. Committed, acknowledged and part of the fabric of Lair society, their relationship was something Livia wanted…but would probably never have. At least not with Seth and Gowan. The thought made her sad, but she resolved not to ruin the happy occasion with unhappy thoughts. There was too much to celebrate tonight.

As the dragons trumpeted high in the sky, consummating their new union in the darkness of the heavens, the rest of them partied below on the beach. Livia had her two favorite men with her and her two favorite dragons were nearby, chatting with sea dragons and gryphons alike. Everybody was having a great time, and the sorrows and fears of the past few days were pushed to the side for a few hours to celebrate the new life their four friends would have with each other.

It was the start of something new. Something precious. Something worth celebrating.

While Captain Fisk was still out there with Gryffid's dangerous book, Livia's father was hot on his trail, and the Prince of Spies himself had everyone in his network looking for news of both the book and the pirates, there was time yet to step back and be glad for Leo and Lizbet, Xander and Shara.

Livia was content in the company of her men and her friends, new and old.

Hrardorr was happy enough to sit on the beach, talking with Genlitha and the sea dragons, plus the occasional gryphon. They were good creatures, all of them. Particularly Genlitha.

The mating of young Xanderanth had been a bittersweet thing for Hrardorr. It had reminded him of what he had vowed never to seek when he'd been blinded. He'd sworn to never choose another knight or seek a mate, but then, he'd been reunited with Genlitha, and the old attraction had come back to him.

She was the only female he'd ever felt this way about. And yet, how could he sentence her to sharing her life with a blind mate? That wouldn't be fair to her. And how could he choose a knight when he couldn't even see?

The past two battles had proven to him that he could still fight, at least. That was something. Something momentous, in fact. But it wasn't enough. His only ability to fight now was from underwater, where no knight could join him. And he didn't dare join his life to another human. He'd barely survived the loss of his last knight. It had broken him. Inside.

He couldn't open himself to that kind of pain again.

Then, there was Gryffid and his offer. He'd given Hrardorr a temptation unlike any other. The promise of even a partial restoration of his sight was better than never seeing at all, but the price was too high.

Hrardorr was too afraid to join himself to another knight, even if it meant being able to see through that man's eyes...wasn't he?

If that man was Seth... Hrardorr tried to stop the thought before it could form, but it would not be denied. If Seth bonded to Hrardorr and Genlitha could be convinced to mate with a blind dragon—which Hrardorr doubted she would ever do—then the five of them could form a family.

The scenario teased him. It could be so good for all of them. Or it could be a total disaster.

What if Hrardorr took the chance and bonded to Seth, but the wizard's magic was unsuccessful? Or what if, after all that, Genlitha spurned him? There were too many variables in this situation and absolutely no guarantees.

If Hrardorr took the wizard up on his offer, it would be the biggest leap of faith he had ever taken—probably would ever take—in his entire life. And it might all come crashing down and leave them all worse off than they'd been before.

Or, it could really work. If Hrardorr could just get over his heartache. He just didn't know if he could manage it, or if it would be fair to Seth and the rest of them.

The wizard had left Hrardorr in turmoil that wouldn't right itself anytime soon. So the dragon brooded, and spoke quietly with those who sought him out at the party. He tried to forget the terrible decision facing him for a few hours to celebrate the unions of four beings he had come to call friends.

Mostly, he succeeded, but when Genlitha settled next to him in the warm sand, he couldn't help but wonder what it would be like to feel her warm body next to him always...

# # #

ABOUT THE AUTHOR

Bianca D'Arc has run a laboratory, climbed the corporate ladder in the shark-infested streets of lower Manhattan, studied and taught martial arts, and earned the right to put a whole bunch of letters after her name, but she's always enjoyed writing more than any of her other pursuits. She grew up and still lives on Long Island, where she keeps busy with an extensive garden, several aquariums full of very demanding fish, and writing her favorite genres of paranormal, fantasy and sci-fi romance.

Bianca loves to hear from readers and can be reached through Twitter (@BiancaDArc), Facebook (BiancaDArcAuthor) or through the various links on her website.

WELCOME TO THE D'ARC SIDE...
WWW.BIANCADARC.COM

OTHER BOOKS BY BIANCA D'ARC

Brotherhood of Blood
One & Only
Rare Vintage
Phantom Desires
Sweeter Than Wine
Forever Valentine
Wolf Hills
Wolf Quest

Tales of the Were
Lords of the Were
Inferno

Tales of the Were – The Others
Rocky
Slade

Tales of the Were – Redstone Clan
The Purrfect Stranger
Grif
Red
Magnus
Bobcat
Matt

String of Fate
Cat's Cradle
King's Throne
Jacob's Ladder
Her Warriors

Grizzly Cove
All About the Bear
Mating Dance
Night Shift
Alpha Bear
Saving Grace
Bearliest Catch

Guardians of the Dark
Half Past Dead
Once Bitten, Twice Dead
A Darker Shade of Dead
The Beast Within
Dead Alert

Dragon Knights
Maiden Flight
The Dragon Healer
Border Lair
Master at Arms
The Ice Dragon
Prince of Spies
Wings of Change
FireDrake
Dragon Storm
Keeper of the Flame
Hidden Dragons

The Sea Captain's Daughter Trilogy
Book 1: Sea Dragon
Book 2: Dragon Fire
Book 3: Dragon Mates

Resonance Mates
Hara's Legacy
Davin's Quest
Jaci's Experiment
Grady's Awakening
Harry's Sacrifice

Jit'Suku Chronicles ~ Arcana
King of Swords
King of Cups
King of Clubs
King of Stars
End of the Line
Diva

Jit'Suku Chronicles ~ Sons of Amber
Angel in the Badlands
Master of Her Heart

StarLords
Hidden Talent
Talent For Trouble
Shy Talent

Gifts of the Ancients
Warrior's Heart

THE SEA CAPTAIN'S DAUGHTER TRILOGY
BOOK 3
DRAGON MATES

The pirate Fisk is on the loose with a dangerous artifact and Seth, Livia, Gowan and their dragon friends must get it back. The very future of not just their land, but all people everywhere, is at stake.

They'll dodge pirates, bar fights, and undue interest from unsavory characters to fulfill their mission. And the dragons will risk everything to help.

But at the end of the day, will the blind dragon be able to come to terms with his disability enough to embrace the future—and the love—that is waiting for him? Can he take Seth as his knight partner and Genlitha as his mate, solidifying the union between humans and dragons?

Or will it all fall apart, and evil prevail? Only the dragon knows...

The third and final installment in The Sea Captain's Daughter Trilogy will be available in January 2017.

JIT'SUKU CHRONICLES ~ ARCANA
DIVA

She needs only one name...Diva. Galactic superstar. Brilliant musician. Chanteuse extraordinaire. But she has a number of deep, dark secrets. For a woman who lives her life in the spotlight of a billion lenses, she managed to lead a double life, full of intrigue.

When her path crosses that of Captain John Starbridge everything changes. Here is a man who sees beneath the mask she wears for the public. Here is a man in love with the woman behind the music into which she pours her soul. Here is a man who could be hers...if they didn't both have duties that must be fulfilled.

John's allegiance has always been to the human race and his band of Spec Ops brothers, but the music of the woman known only as Diva has accompanied him on every deep space mission he's ever undertaken. Her voice croons him to sleep in his lonely bunk each night and her intense lyrics haunt him throughout his days. When he finally meets the object of his fascination, he realizes there is even more depth to the woman than he expected. He gives her his heart, though he knows it's likely a futile gesture. What would a superstar like her want with a plain old soldier like him?

Circumstances throw them together and tear them apart, while enemy forces gather to invade the galaxy they both try—in their own ways—to protect. She will have to walk into the lion's den in order to save the galaxy...and perhaps, the man she loves. If there's a way, she'll find it, but it might just be the mission that finally breaks them both once and for all.

Or not...

WWW.BIANCADARC.COM

CPSIA information can be obtained
at www.ICGtesting.com
Printed in the USA
LVOW10s1615261016
510385LV00010B/894/P